MOLLY K

was born in Co. Kildare, Ireland, in 1904 into "a rather serious Hunting and Fishing and Church-going family" who gave her little education at the hands of governesses. Her father originally came from a Somerset family and her mother, a poetess, was the author of "The Songs of the Glens of Antrim". Molly Keane's interests when young were "hunting and horses and having a good time"; she began writing only as a means of supplementing her dress allowance, and chose the pseudonym M. J. Farrell "to hide my literary side from my sporting friends". She wrote her first novel, *The Knight of Cheerful Countenance*, at the age of seventeen.

As M. J. Farrell, Molly Keane published ten further novels between 1928 and 1952: *Young Entry* (1928), *Taking Chances* (1929), *Mad Puppetstown* (1931), *Conversation Piece* (1932), *Devoted Ladies* (1934), *Full House* (1935), *The Rising Tide* (1937), *Two Days in Aragon* (1941), *Loving Without Tears* (1951), and *Treasure Hunt* (1952). All of Molly Keane's M. J. Farrell novels are now published by Virago. She was also a successful playwright, of whom James Agate said "I would back this impish writer to hold her own against Noel Coward himself." Her plays, with John Perry, always directed by John Gielgud, include *Spring Meeting* (1938), *Ducks and Drakes* (1942), *Treasure Hunt* (1949) and *Dazzling Prospect* (1961).

The tragic death of her husband at the age of thirty-six stopped her writing for many years. It was not until 1981 that another novel – *Good Behaviour* – was published, this time under her real name. *Time after Time* appeared in 1983, *Loving and Giving* was published in 1988. Her cookery book, *Nursery Cooking*, was published in 1985. Molly Keane has two daughters and lives in Co. Waterford.

VIRAGO
MODERN
CLASSIC

NUMBER

389

Molly Keane
(M. J. Farrell)

THE KNIGHT
OF CHEERFUL
COUNTENANCE

With a New Introduction by
Molly Keane

Published by VIRAGO PRESS Limited 1993
20–23 Mandela Street, Camden Town, London NW1 0HQ

Copyright © M. J. Farrell 1926
First published by Mills and Boon, 1926

Introduction Copyright © Molly Keane 1993

*A CIP catalogue record for this book is available from
the British Library*

Printed in Great Britain by
Cox & Wyman Ltd, Reading

Introduction

The Knight of Cheerful Countenance was my first novel. I was seventeen years old when I wrote it. Re-reading it now, some seventy years later, I am forced to accept that the world of my youth has vanished and that, for the modern reader, there may be some explaining to do.

During the days of my childhood and girlhood, in the earlier years of the twentieth century, the title "daughter-at-home" carried no stigma as it did later. Daughters were not educated to fit them for any job, and life in the family had many advantages and pleasures. One was sure of a horse and two or three days' hunting in the week. A dress allowance, if meagre, was a certainty. Travel expenses were paid. With a full staff of servants, there was nothing in the way of housework to be done. A girl with a talent for music or painting had leisure to practise her art.

Maiden or widowed aunts were an accepted part of any ascendancy family. Sitting in their long, elegant skirts, they seemed as stable a part of the house as the lean, grey chimney stacks built by their forebears. There was a certain glory in their ignorant defiance of bad times to come. They spent their eyesight and skill on the restoration of tapestries and were knowledgeable and tender gardeners. Even my Aunt Bijou, a tough lady in all things, grew the poppy *Mecanopsis Baileyii* where its blue flowers might float in the shelter of a hazelnut walk, and would go out on the coldest night to put a stable lantern near some delicate darling, while the woman in the gate lodge might die in childbirth for all she knew or cared.

Servants were numerous, even in the smaller houses of the landed gentry. In the more important houses, they were so numerous that only the butler was known personally to his employer. He was always called by his surname, while the first and second footmen, no matter how often they changed, were always "John" and "George" in order to save their employer from having to tax his memory with new names. The cook was always "Mrs", no matter how youthful or unmarried she might be—a custom maintained to emphasize the authority of her position in the household. The kitchen maid was nameless.

Our mothers never went into the kitchen if they could help it. I knew one kitchen that had a gallery round it so that the mistress of the house might call a chosen menu from it or, if necessary, let a written order float its way down to the recipient.

Food and its cooking was not discussed and appraised as it is today. Mrs Beeton was the bible of the kitchen and, when religiously and extravagantly followed, the food was excellent. But there were kitchens and cooks who had never heard of her, and few mistresses of the house showed any proper interest in the subject. However, the ingredients of the day were often so ambrosial as to demand only the plainest cooking. Wine was an accepted necessity for sauces. Without frigidaires, everything from spring lamb to green peas was eaten in its season. Game was well-preserved and plentiful. Grouse-shooting began, as always, on the Holy Twelfth of August, when we walked the mountain with the "guns", perhaps leading the pony that carried a vast luncheon picnic. A little later, snipe came in their hundreds to the vast stretches of undrained bogland. In the hardest winter, woodcock found shelter in the deep glens. Even the plainest cook knew enough to undercook such game, and the memory of its flavour and tenderness stays with those who expected and appreciated perfection in their eating.

Puddings played a more important part than now. Fruit from the kitchen garden was there in season and, out of season, well-preserved in the skilful bottling that took the place of freezing. Queen of Puddings or chocolate soufflé were abiding favourites for party lunches. For everyday eating, no one despised a steamed marmalade or lemon sponge. Custard was made as an accompaniment to most desserts and rich cream in a squat silver jug was always on the table.

Breakfasts were really memorable. Porridge and cream were usual as a first course. A grill of bacon and tomatoes and scraps of game hovered on the sideboard, together with a kedgeree, a vast ham and boiled eggs, preferably brown. Coffee, always in a silver coffee-pot, waited on the spirit-heated hot-plate with hot milk and cream at hand. Scones, toast and marmalade concluded the meal, which was eaten by even the stoutest.

Morning prayers were a daily ceremony, performed after breakfast. I remember the butler quietly shrouding the parrot's cage. Before removing it, he walked very softly so as not to disturb the bird into a screaming fit. After that, he rearranged the chairs—a carving chair placed separately from them, like a pulpit. He returned later, leading the procession of capped and aproned domestic servants, headed by the cook. The family came in later. The prayer reader was the head of the family, unless a cleric happened to be a house guest.

In the 'twenties and earlier, families of the ascendancy

divided themselves sharply from the "proles" (the word deriving from "proletariat" and comprising those in business, the law and even, sometimes, the Church). Marriage beneath one's social status was looked on as a disaster and almost never occurred, no matter how scarce the contemporary and social equals of the young ladies of the time. I once asked why we knew nobody who lived in the neighbouring river valley and was told: "Because all their grandfathers married the dairy maid." Seduction was understandable; marriage not.

The sons of the ascendancy invariably went to English public schools, and afterwards into the Army, the Navy, or perhaps the Diplomatic Service, if their languages were good. As a matter of course, the eldest son was heir to the estate, large or small, and to any money that went with it. The younger sons might starve out the middle and end years of their lives on whatever pensions they had attained in the forces. These younger sons often had graceful names, probably from their mothers' side of the family. I had an Uncle Vivian and an Uncle Sholto, and I had a friend with an Uncle Hyacinth. He is still Major Hyacinth Devereaux on his memorial tablet in the Parish Church. Daughters had to make do with Alice or Edith or Harriet. Eldest sons and heirs could remain Henry down the generations.

The prolonged celibacy of a gentleman went unquestioned in those days. Lack of finance to set up a matrimonial establishment was a readily accepted reason for a long bachelor life in which a man, unencumbered by family, could enjoy, for free, all the outdoor sports at which he managed to excel. The very few with a literary turn were shunned as penniless "creeps" and were a source

of embarrassment in conversation where horses, hunting
and racing were the accepted topics. Another admissible
reason for a single life was that given by a bachelor
brother: "Of course I do mean to marry her, but she *must*
realize that horses come first."

The title "ascendancy" was invented to describe the
class of English settler who had obtained grants to land
from the English conquerors of the Irish Celtic kings.
Queen Elizabeth I, with Essex as Governor, was the first
English monarch who decided to settle Ireland as a colony
rather than a battlefield. Her example was followed by
James I and Charles I. Cromwell was a reliable grantor of
lands to officers whom he was unable to pay—and the
same applies to Dutch William. Most of those who
benefited were Protestants, as Catholics were suspected of
French sympathies and loyalty to James II.

Over the years, the language difference widened
between the landowners and the native Irish, but with this
widening grew a deep appreciation of the felicity and
acumen of the Irish-into-English speech. It was the
"refined" speech of the "proles" that brought out the
unborn Nancy Mitford in everyone, and John Betjemen
in a few. I remember being told: "Never say 'material'.
Say 'stuff'. Even if the person doesn't understand you,
keep saying 'stuff'."

Memories and impressions come back to me as clear
and searching as the bell in a Chekhov play. I can still
hear the sound of carriage wheels on gravel or macadam
and the slam of the silver-crested door on the dark blue
brougham that took us to dancing class and tea-parties.
And in the hall I can see the silver hand-candlesticks with
their saucer-shaped bases, and a tiny glass globe over the

candle flame. They were set out early in the evening on an oak chest, one candle for each member of the family and one for each guest staying in the house.

At bedtime, it was customary for a gentleman to hand a lady her candlestick as they said "goodnight". All down-stairs rooms were lighted by oil lamps, the globes of their oil containers sitting high on silver standards. In the dining-room, there was a great branched candlestick on the table—sufficient light for the butler or parlourmaid to serve by.

With hot water dependent on the mood of the Eagle range in the kitchen, the hip bath before the bedroom fire was a luxury enjoyed by the older ladies. The bedroom fire was lighted about eight o'clock, when tea was brought to the bedside, the china invariably patterned with tiny violets. Ladies could lie back and relax, listening to the busy crackle of sticks and wood while they waited for the warmth to grow. The younger members of the family walked the cold mile of corridor to the still colder bathroom and bathed in vast baths made of some stuff that was nearly marble. Only after a cold day's hunting were we allowed the luscious comfort of a hip bath set to wait before the bedroom fire; great cans of hot water sitting on a thick batmath (always with the word BATHMAT printed in large letters on it) and a large bath-towel baking on the ex-nursery wire fender with its brass rail.

To excel as a horsewoman was the ambition of most of us. Even without achieving that object, our horses were a source of unparalleled interest and enjoyment. But dress had to be our first consideration in life. With Dublin a distant shopping place seldom attained, catalogues from such shops as Debenham and Freebody, illustrating the

INTRODUCTION

discreet fashions of the day, were of great value and use. The village dress-maker made or altered all our clothes, following Debenham's inspirations as closely as she was able. Dance dresses, usually of brocade, had boat-shaped necklines and puff sleeves and dripped and drooped almost to the floor behind, rising to a naughtier knee-length in front. An artificial rose or gardenia was the usual shoulder-piece. Louis heels and ankle straps were invariable evening wear. For outdoors it was always laced leather or suede and very flat heels. Outdoor clothes, and those worn for race meetings, were always of the "coat-and-skirt" style. Only for the Dublin Horse Show did we wear a flowered number with an almost-Ascot hat. I can recall my real sense of shock when I saw two English debutantes leaning on shooting sticks at a ring-side, wearing navy blue sweaters and no hats. Such simplicity was not our aim. Hats were important and our felt "Henry Heaths" stayed on our heads, even at lunch parties.

Dress catalogues were not the only ones to reach Ireland. Every quarter, the handlebars of the postman's bicycle bent beneath the load of the giant catalogues from the Army & Navy Stores, Victoria Street. They advertised pictorially, as well as descriptively, the probable tastes and needs of their distant customers. In consideration for the possible embarrassment of gentlemen with lubricious tastes, the page opposite the one which illustrated corsetry, the brassiere or split knickers was devoted to hardware, from Purdie guns to hedging tools and lawnmowers. Huge parcels of tins of coffee and China tea, as well as the more exotic groceries such as Carlsbad plums and other specialities unobtainable in Ireland, followed the perusal of the catalogues.

The warm intimacy we had with established shops has sadly lapsed. Even as a young member of an established family, one met recognition across the glove counter at Switzers—Ireland's Harrods. There will never be another Mr Tyson, white-bearded proprietor of the gentlemen's shirt shop, a rival to any in Jermyn Street. Hunting stocks and polo-necked sweaters were always in stock, racing colours a speciality. "Going to Leopardstown Races today? You'll need a little change for small bets. Would you care to add £5 to your account?" Notes and cash came crisply across the counter in exchange for a possibly doubtful cheque.

Another Sacred Monster was George, Hall Porter of the Shelbourne Hotel, who knew everybody and everything. "You're a friend of Major Watts," he greeted me. "You should hurry to Tyson's. He's in there buying presents for all his lady friends."

Country houses were often many miles distant from each other and, without telephones, friends and neighbours visited unannounced. Television and radio were undreamed of, so they, young and old, depended on each other for entertainment. Dinner dances were regular events. We danced happily to the piano and to records on the horned gramophone. Even as a child, I was popular as a good mimic. To reproduce the voice of stable-boy or cook was to be an entertainer. Perhaps the wonderful transference of Irish to English speech which I heard and mimicked taught me to listen to dialogue and, together with my small talent to amuse, fostered early, resulted in the plays written thirty years later in my life. From the age of six I was educated by governesses, with the help of Gills' *Geography* (a strict torture), Henri Bue's *French*

Grammar and Mrs Markham's *History of England*. My mother was a poet and a recluse and, with her, I read the shorter poems of Tennyson: "Beat, beat, beat, on thy cold grey shores, oh, sea . . ." and I learned to recite French verse, from *Fables de la Fontaine*, of course, and, later, with appropriate emotion: "Quand je revois ma Normandie".

Apart from three hours of lessons in the day, life was free for us. Cars, lorries, child-stealing and abuse were as far away as television. Without question, we rode our ponies whenever and wherever we pleased. But, at four-teen, I was sent to a prim, suburban school. After my free childhood, rules and disciplines irked me unbearably. Having to ask, before a full classroom: "May I have permission to leave the room?" when I needed to go to a lavatory which I had to learn to call the "toilet", struck me as an invasion of both liberty and good manners.

When we were told by the headmistress that a cloud hovered over the school until the girl who had thrown her orange down number eight toilet confessed, and confessed in French, nobody stifled a giggle. The situation was too serious—until the confession was made, there was to be no hockey practice. What did I, with fox-hunting behind me, care about hockey, the hockey captain or the games mistress?

It was the custom for friends to link arms on their way to a distant classroom, playing field or church. I would deliberately lag behind the clatter of twin footsteps, using the gap to mask my loneliness. Unliked and unlinked, my place was always at the back of the crocodile. I might never have become a writer had it not been for the isolation in which I suffered as an unpopular schoolgirl.

My unpopularity, that went to the edge of dislike, drove me into myself. I was walking among stars that had a different birth and I certainly learned the meaning of the black word "Alone".

The thought of home tore strips from my heart. Letters from my mother brought on such spasms of emotion as to make them almost unwelcome. I found my escape in English composition. Exaggerated essays on "home" put me back where carriage wheels still turned, and herons (birds as lonely as myself) flew over silently before dropping to a fishing ground.

At home, on holiday from the open prison of the boarding school, I read my sister's books with ecstasy. Kipling's *Brushwood Boy* set me dreaming of the purest love. Kipling was followed by a blind sailor author called Bartemeus. His Naval Officer heroes were called "Flags", "Guns" or "Sparks". They were not given wives or sweethearts; they belonged to us. They were ours. A little later Dornford Yates fed our romantic yearnings. His characters had real glamour. Rich and aristocratic, they travelled from one luxurious scene to the next in silver Rolls Royces. Love-making was so discreet as to be nearly unwritten: "I kiss your little hand, madame," was as far as a yearning gentleman was allowed by Mr Yates to go. It was far enough to set our hearts beating. Undeterred by my unpopularity at school, this was the life I hoped to share.

The sparks of invention were probably ignited when I discovered my elder sister on the edge of something rather more than friendship with an attractive young man—of course, a brilliant horseman—who had been employed to make and break my father's young horses. Of course, his social status was slightly beneath our own and, for this reason alone, he would never have been countenanced as a suitor. Before long, I was in love with him, and felt more distress than my sister when my father, perhaps sniffing the situation, dismissed him.

This first awareness of the Real Life ardour and anguish of romantic love was stopped in its tracks when I was struck down by a mysterious fever and confined to the sick-room for several long weeks. In this predicament I had to rely on my imagination and writing became my escape. *The Knight of Cheerful Countenance* began to take shape in my mind as I decided to write about the girl I most wished to be myself.

Molly Keane, 1993

CHAPTER I

An Arrival

THE local train from Scaralin clattered haltingly into its terminus, Bungarvin—which, like most Irish towns, was mainly notable for its dirt, its idlers, and perhaps for the number of RIC who had met their deaths in its licensed premises and neighbourhood.

Visitors seldom came to Bungarvin, save only those of the commerical ilk—"travelling gentlemen," with cheap suit-cases full of still less valuable goods, to be foisted upon the small shopkeepers of the town.

It was, therefore, with some surprise that John Galvin, who successfully combined the duties of station-master and porter at Bungarvin station, saw—emerging from the door of a first-class compartment—a young, and to him an unknown man; a man moreover who, while he could by no stretching of possibilities be considered a traveller, did not sufficiently resemble any of the local gentry to be identified—with that familiarity which is so striking a feature of the modern Irish workman's attitude towards his superiors—as "young Dennys St Lawrence," or "One o' thim brats o' lads out of Trinity."

He was a tall and slow-moving youth, with a charming smile and an admirably waisted overcoat. Clearly a Saxon, to whom it was honest John's duty to show that such a smile, together with the wearing of spats, was not to be tolerated in an Irish Free State. Therefore did he turn his back, whistling abstractedly through his teeth, as the Saxon advanced upon him with inquiries respecting his luggage. . . . "Trunks, you know; should have come on an earlier train. And a bulldog in the offing somewhere. Well?"

The station-master jerked his head sideways to summons a small and dirty youth, who wore, as insignia of office, the uniform cap of his predecessor—the size of which clearly showed that the former porters of Bungarvin had been heftier men than the present representative of the race.

"Hey, Jimmie," said the station-master, completely ignoring the tall young man, "did any trunks come in on the mail?"

"Or a bulldog? A nice beast," interpolated Allan.

"Is it a dog?" said Jimmie mournfully. "It's not one dog, but six o' Misther St Lawrence's hounds is above in the van. And as for getting them out of it, 'twould be as good for me to be ate altogether."

"Ah, go on!" exclaimed the station-master encouragingly. "They'll not bite you. Don't be one bit afraid o' them. I have more to do than to be running after young St Lawrence's dogs, or I'd go clear the whole lot out of it meself."

Allan, at the outset of the discussion, had hastened towards the van, and now emerged from it, without his dog, and in a distinctly dishevelled condition.

In the meantime the more practical Jimmie sped away to seek further assistance. Once outside the station, he came upon the head and fount of all the trouble, in the person of Captain Dennys St Lawrence, who was discoursing to Miss Ann Hillingdon on an evidently engrossing subject, with some earnestess. Ann was giving him a fair half of her attention; the remainder she bestowed on the good-looking chestnut mare, which backed and sidled between the shafts of the rather battered dog-cart in which she was sitting.

"Yes, Dennys," she said, in answer to some question, "but—stand, mare!—of course, as you say, he may be very nice. On the other hand I shouldn't wonder if he was an awful fool. Oh, look! there's Jimmie trying to talk to you—Jim, did a gentleman come in on the train?"

"There did so, miss," replied that loquacious infant, "he's below in the van this minute tryin' could he get his dog out of it. But sure you wouldn't wonder if Mr St Lawrence's dogs is in it would have ate him altogether—they're fighting mad, surely." After which information Jimmie looked appealingly in the direction of the owner of the mad dogs. Dennys turned to Ann to make his adieux—pensively, as was his wont.

"Well, if the hounds are there, I must be off. It wouldn't do to let them eat your English cousin before you'd set eyes on him, even. Good-bye—mind that mare, she's indecently fresh."

He sauntered off—a tall, broad-shouldered figure; graceful, with the grace a life in the saddle alone gives, despite the fact that the same life had slightly bowed his long legs, encased in ancient but well-cut riding breeches, and long mahogany-coloured field boots.

Ann looked after the retreating figure a little wistfully; then straightening her slim shoulders, she sat upright in the driving seat. "I'd love to go in and see the fun," she murmured, "but I suppose I'd better not. Specially if Allan isn't shining—it'd be hardly fair. Bad for Dennys too," was her mental postscript, as she thoughtfully and firmly put a stop to the efforts of "Pet Girl"—the chestnut

18

mare—to back the trap into a not inconsiderable ditch on the far side of the road.

The appearance of Allan and Benbow, the bulldog—both in a dishevelled condition—lulled Pet Girl into a momentary calm. She gazed at them, round her blinkers, with truly feminine curiosity, thus giving Ann and Allan leisure to exchange cousinly greetings. Allan oozed apology.

"I'm positively distraught, old thing. So's Benny. He's really the cause of all this culpable delay. Jimmie swore the hounds had him ate, and I was positively beginning to think something unpleasant of that sort had happened, when a friend-in-need turned up. Your MFH, is he? No? Well, anyway he seems to have a way with hounds. He unearthed Ben here, who was taking cover behind the mail bags with two ladies. He'd got himself mixed up with their couples—he's a tough laddie, takes a lot of turning down. Shall I shove him in the back of the cart?"

"No, don't," said his cousin, coming out of the dazed stupor in which she had listened to the above remarks. "Put him up in front. There's meat for a week in the back! And hurry up, for the mare won't stand much longer."

"All right," Allan made answer patiently, "but he wouldn't hurt the meat. He's muzzled. However, I dare say he'd rather see a new country then lie down in the dark with a lot of meat."

"If," said Ann, as she turned the mare's head towards home, "you really would enjoy eating meat that's gone to bed with Benbow, of course I've nothing to say against it. I'd hate for him to feel out of it in a strange country and all; if it'd make him feel more at home to lie down with the lamb, shove him under the flap by all means."

"Ben my lad," observed his master feelingly, "I fear Cousin Ann is trifling with us . . . you know what I mean, just trifling . . . so make yourself at home where you are, sonny."

Benbow slobbered enthusiastically, while Allan turning to Ann, with his charming smile, made dutiful inquiries respecting the health of his elderly cousin, her father, and that of all his little second cousins, her brothers and sisters.

"Father's quite well, thanks," Ann assured him, adding, "D'you know him, by the way?"

There was just a shade of anxiety in her expression as she awaited his reply. When it came, it was not very reassuring.

"Well—er—slightly, don't you know. He stayed at Willingdon once, for the pheasants, when I was quite a kid. But—er—did you want to tell me something? Warn me off the grass, so to speak, or anything? It'd be awfully nice of you if you would."

He spoke with some embarrassment, but deep intuition. He had already received sundry warnings anent Cousin Ronnie's peculiarities. It would, however, be as well to obtain direct information, if he was going to make a lengthy stay beneath that gentleman's roof, as he contemplated.

Ann gazed abstractedly between the mare's ears, thus giving her companion the opportunity of studying unobserved her remarkably attractive profile, while he awaited a reply. She wasn't quite pretty, he decided, but immensely taking, with that decided little chin of hers and those gorgeous eyelashes. He wondered why more girls didn't allow their felt hats to grow old so gracefully . . .

hers had blown up in front, as she was driving against the wind. A brown ribbon stock, too, gives just the right touch of subdued smartness, albeit the wearer's tweeds have seen better days—a long time ago. Allan, an unconscious artist, continued to study his companion. Was her hair brown or red or gold? And *was* it short, or had she only cut off the side pieces in that hideous way girls had? He could bear the suspense no longer.

"Excuse my interrupting your reverie, cousin, but is your hair short or not?" he inquired, gently yet firmly.

"What? Oh, yes it is. Life was too brief to do it up in, and any way I got five guineas for it from Jules. Father was furious. Oh, about father. Well, there are some things it's better not to mention to him—you'll find them out by degrees—one of them is the St Lawrences."

"Oh, why?" Allan became distinctly interested. "The friend in need struck me as a decent sort of cove and all that, don't you know?"

Ann flicked Pet Girl approvingly. Allan even thought she looked a trifle pleased.

"Father loathes them," was all she said, however, and then concentrated her undivided attention on the mare, who, having shied violently at a harmless and necessary pig seeking pasturage by the wayside, was now doing her utmost to break into a gallop.

Allan, having replaced beneath the seat several loaves of bread, a pale piece of meat (which he suspected to be the lamb that was to have made Benbow feel at home) and some stray pots of marmalade, all of which Pet Girl's activities had loosened from their moorings, sat upright and proceeded to study the landscape. It was worthy of some consideration. They were driving along a narrow winding road, bordered by stretches of purple bog, or by good grass land, fenced with firm banks, broad enough to fill the heart of a fox-hunter with prayerful joy. Allan made some remarks about them to his hostess.

"Oh, yes," she conceded. "But this is the only good bit in the country. The rest is all stone-faced banks, and slate walls, and little fields not the size of a handkerchief. Wait till you get a hunt along the mountains——" She pointed with her whip to the distant line of hills. Softly, deeply blue they were, with the great cloud shadows of an Irish September changing and reforming upon them. "*Then* you'll know what Irish hunting can be like." She laughed, a quick musical laugh with a funny little quiver in it.

"Here we are now," she observed, some minutes later. A turning in the road had seemingly changed the face of the country. Instead of the low thorn hedges and sparse Scotch firs—the only trees they had passed since leaving the station—they now drove beneath tall beeches, growing behind high old demesne walls. Ann turned in at an immensely imposing, but intensely ugly, entrance gate, and the dog-cart wheels scrunched in the gravel of the dark evergreen-shaded drive.

"I suppose I should take you up to the front door," said Miss Hillingdon, as they neared the big, ugly grey block that was Ballinrath House. "But I'm just going straight to the yard." With which she turned down a rutty side lane, that finally ended its half-hearted career in a large and untidy stable yard. Ann descended lightly, and, after calling vainly upon an invisible host of retainers, proceeded to unbuckle the harness herself. Later, as she fastened the mare's halter to a ring in her hay-rack, some sound from a neighbouring loose-box caused her to swing on her heel and leave the stable so precipitantly as to upset more than half the bucket of water, which Allan, according to her behest, and at great risk to the skirts of his immaculate overcoat, was carrying across the yard.

"I say, old friend, why all this unnecessary haste?" he expostulated gently; then, noting the light of battle in her eyes, he said no more, but depositing the bucket, followed her, as she herself would have said, "to see the fun."

Ann opened the door of the box, disclosing to view—

(a) A youthful bay filly in a thoroughly overheated and muddied condition:

(b) A stable satellite, also youthful and also in an extremely heated condition. He was rubbing down the bay filly under the directions, and with the capable assistance of—

(c) A long-legged hoyden of some seventeen summers of evil doing. She was clad in a scanty riding-habit and also wore a disarming smile.

"Hello, Ann!" she chirped. "So you've got back all right. How d'ye do, Allan? I'm one of your wild Irish cousins. It's great, seeing you here!"

Allan saluted her gravely, noting the while that her black eyelashes seemed to possess all the tricks of coquetry so noticeably absent from Ann's. Her eldest sister, however, was not thus lightly to be turned from the path of righteous wrath and just vengeance. She ran a hand over the mare's hot shoulder, then turned stonily to her erring junior.

"Sybil! what *have* you been doing with the mare to get her into such a condition? You know father'd jolly well slay you for taking her out at all, much less——"

The sisterly and well-merited rebuke might have

continued indefinitely, but for the heated arrival of a small and dirty boy.

"Sybil!" he breathed, "here's Daddy coming. He'll be in any minute now. You'd better bunk, quick!"

"Oh, God help us!" murmured Aiden, the accomplice. "The master's very passionate. Will I throw the sheet on her, Miss Ann, and chance him not coming in?"

"Yes," said Ann. "Quick, Sybil! Get into the loft. If he sees your habit, he'll twig at once. Allan, go out and meet him. Here, Aiden; can't you give Miss Sybil a leg up? I'll fix the sheet."

Thus, under the able management of the elder Miss Hillingdon, matters began to take some sort of shape. Before Major Hillingdon, in his Ford car, arrived upon the scene, Sybil was safely ensconced behind a pile of hay—using some surprisingly bad language over a bruised knee; Allan was standing carelessly in the yard, while Rickard (the youngest and most wily of the Irish Hillingdons) had gone to open the yard gate for the motor; one of the few actions known to his family which called forth their parent's approval.

Ann and Aiden, meanwhile, worked away upon the mare's toilet; their difficulties augmented by the fact that the recent nerve-shattering events had reduced her to a state bordering on hysteria.

"Ah, she'll have to do now," Ann decided, as a well-aimed kick wafted Aiden towards the stable door. "Here's the master, anyway." Ann carefully closed the door of the loose-box, breathing, as she did so, an ardent prayer that Allan might not greet his cousin as "companion of my youth," or even "old friend."

Her fears on that score were, however, quite groundless.

Allan's bearing was perfect—respectful, yet without any sign of adolescent coyness or gaucherie. His greeting, also, was singularly devoid of those flowers of speech so dear to his tongue.

The Major, for his part, was quite charmed with his young cousin, and considered the interest displayed in the latest development of Henry Ford's genius intelligent and sympathetic, although perhaps a trifle sustained. He was not sorry to be interrupted by the arrival of Fox, the coachman, looking even more like a sour crab-apple than usual.

"I beg your pardon, sir," Fox began acrimoniously, and not at all as if he felt inclined to beg any man's pardon, "I'd like for ye to throw an eye on the bay filly till ye'll see the state she's in. She cot great hardship some way. I'd say 'twas Miss Sybil had her out, by the look of her now."

"And who the devil's business was it to see she didn't go out?" stormed the Major, suddenly transformed from a mild exponent of the works of Henry Ford to the snarling personification of rage. "What good are you if you can't keep my horses in their stables—tell me that, eh? Is the mare lamed? No? I tell you, Fox——"

As they crossed the yard to the mare's box, he did tell him several things—and would doubtless have told him several more but for an interruption from above, in the shape of two long gaitered legs, which made their appearance through the trap-door of the loft. Sybil's honeyed tones also made themselves heard above the stimulated snortings of the little mare. No myrmidon should bear the blame which was her own due portion—pride demanded that.

"Father dear, it's all my fault. Fox didn't know a thing

about it, he was away getting in the young ones. I took her myself, and—" there was a melting sob in her voice— "nothing I do ever turns out right," she finished pathetically.

"Get down at once, Sybil," the Major ordered sternly.

Sybil got down, neatly enough, and stood—the image of repentance—before her accuser (on whose head she had so adroitly heaped coals of fire) and her judge. The eyes which she raised to the judge would have melted the heart of a stone. Even Fox, her inveterate enemy, felt some compunction.

"Well," Sybil's overwrought parent regarded his erring offspring with a cold eye, "I'd like to know the meaning of all this."

Sybil was quite ready to enlighten him. There was more than one excellent reason why it was quite impossible for her to have taken out, on this particular day, any of the five other horses; all of which were "standing idle, eating their heads off," according to Fox. She summed up her arguments with, "You —*do* see it wasn't my fault, Father dear?"

"I see nothing of the sort. But you'll find your hunting this season will be considerably curtailed owing to to-day's disobedience. As for you, Fox——" The storm continued, and Sybil, having done all that honour demanded, withered tactfully away. She and Fox were very old enemies.

During the later family differences, Allan had drifted out of the stable yard and, joined by Ben, made his way round to the front of the house. There he found Rickard, taking shots at jackdaws with a catapult. He was a shy child, with polite though distant manners. Gravely ignoring their late hurried meeting, he greeted Allan politely; then, having no gift for small talk, he lavished his attentions on Benbow. Allan opened the conversation.

"Good catapult, that," he observed. "What shot does she take?"

"Stones mostly," was the answer. "I pipped a blackbird with her last week. Like to see it?" Allan, shuddering inwardly, signified his readiness to view the corpse.

The inspection over, they made tracks for the house. In the large and hall-like hall—so different in its trim conventionality from the sporting confusion which Allan, by his reading of Irish sporting novels, had been led to expect—they met Sybil. She stuck her crop in the rack and came forward jauntily.

"We-el," she greeted them, "that little family breeze is safely over." She sat on the corner of an oak chest, swinging one of her long gaitered legs, and glanced at Allan through her eyelashes. Rickard looked at her with brotherly disapproval.

"I suppose that means that Fox or Aiden's getting the row," he observed.

"Fox is—dashed good for him too. Beastly old cat! You bet it was him gave me away," she answered vengefully. "Come on up to your room, Allan; if you're late for dinner there'll be the devil to pay."

Allan followed her, wondering inwardly what his position would be in the midst of these manifold family rows. Had he known his cousins better, he would have realized that their capacity for fighting without drawing blood was almost incalculable. To quarrel *en famille* was the salt of their lives. Feuds bitter and devastating were kept up for weeks, only to crumble and fall as soon as

27

some crisis occurred in which it was necessary to play the game, the family versus the world. When such was the case, the family closed ranks and presented an unbroken front to all outsiders.

CHAPTER II
Tells Why

A FULL week had passed since Allan's arrival at Ballinrath House. He had filled in the time very profitably in reviewing carefully his first impressions of Ireland; in learning the language (from Sybil) and endeavouring to steep himself in the atmosphere—the Celtic atmosphere, be it understood—by holding daily conversations with the postman, though why his greeting of "Thirrum Pogue"—or words to that effect—should cause the worthy to smile dourly (he was a man with a large family) Allan never could understand. Sybil had told him that it meant "Good morning," and surely there was nothing in that to excite any man's risible faculties.

The atmosphere of battle, horror, and murder by night, in which he had naturally expected to find himself on his arrival in Ireland, was strangely non-apparent. Deeds of unbelievable foulness and treachery were still—judging by the newspapers—of almost daily occurrence in the land, but they seemed to leave untouched the district round Bungarvin. Yet wrecked police-barracks and courthouses, country houses standing empty, and the charred walls of what had once been country houses, all went to show how little of a myth was the state of civil war in Ireland.

Now Allan, being something of an enthusiast, was mildly surprised at the lack of interest displayed by his relations and their friends in the country and her present rulers. Why, he asked himself, did they not learn the language, or some little thing like that, to bring them nearer to the people? A link of sympathy between the landlord and romantic peasantry. He mentioned something of the sort to Cousin Ronnie, whose answer—that any sympathy between landlord and tenant had long since been crushed by English Land Acts—seemed to Allan the height of reactionary unreasonableness. By the end of a week, however, his interest in Eire had somewhat elapsed; he had found out the meaning of "Thirrum Pogue," and had written to his aunt that he found Ireland and his Irish cousins very jolly.

This aunt, Lady Mary Semple-Maughan, his mother's only sister, was also one of the few relations who took a decided interest in the boy. True, she had a daughter, and Allan was far from being an impecunious youth, despite several years of untrammelled extravagance as a subaltern in a cavalry regiment, at present stationed in India.

But though Allan was not poor, his relations were rich, and Lady Semple-Maughan, while "only too glad" to give her nephew a *pied-à-terre* during his nine months' leave, in her beautiful Surrey home, flew at higher game for her only daughter, Dillys—a maiden brought up from her earliest youth to be a social success. It was, therefore, with some anxiety that she observed her exemplary and eminently hard-headed little daughter preparing—as she told herself aggrievedly—"to make herself thoroughly idiotic" over her good-looking cousin. The fact that the cousin, while always "ready to do things" and evidently appreciative of his cousin's unquestionable prowess (all that she did, she did well), yet scarcely seemed to appreciate her delicately patent advances, weighed with his aunt not at all. She knew her Dillys, and kept for reference a small suède-bound book entitled "D's scalps."

Lady Semple-Maughan's broad *bonhomie* concealed a will of steel, an unalterable purpose and a mind of some originality. Still, even to her fertile brain, her nephew presented something of a problem. She was his nearest living relative, and, as such, had naturally invited him to spend the greater part of his leave in her house. She could not, therefore, very well turn him out on the score that she did not wish him to stand in any closer relationship to her; especially as she knew there was no other household so congenial to him as her own. It was unfortunate that he should have paid all his duty and other visits, on his first arrival in England, before coming to spend the remainder of his leave at Semple Holt.

To those who seek diligently, however, many things are revealed. To Lady Semple-Maughan, who diligently sought relations for her nephew to visit, was discovered the memory that Allan's father had had a cousin, one Ronnie Hillingdon. That Ronnie Hillingdon had married an Irish lady of some property, and subsequently left the army to bury himself inaccessibly on his wife's estate, somewhere in the fastnesses of Leinster. The wife had died, a good many years ago now, leaving a family. . . daughters, Lady Semple-Maughan vaguely understood. Really it was an inspiration! She would write to Ronnie Hillingdon at once. Dillys was getting quite too infatuated for safety . . . the very thing for Allan . . . Irish hospitality was notorious . . . splendid chance for one of those Irish girls . . .

Lady Semple-Maughan, to whom the inspiration had come in the blue watches of the night, turned heavily on her yielding mattress, and fell into the self-satisfied peaceful sleep of those whose habit it is to solve the vexing problems of their lives.

Thus it happened that Allan, he scarcely knew why or how, except that Aunt Mary had seemed to think he ought to do so, found himself and Benbow making two of one of the most attractive family parties in which they had ever had the luck to find themselves.

CHAPTER III

The Minx and the Maid

SYBIL sank down in the middle of the tennis court, still graceful though exhausted.

"Victory, comrade!" she breathed. "Was't well done?"

Her cousin lowered his frame beside her, joint by joint. "Very nice indeed," he admitted. "If I could improve your outlook on life, as I have your game of tennis, in two short weeks, I'd——"

The interruption came from their erstwhile opponents. "When you two are quite ready," said Ann, "I'd like to get another four going."

"Righto, Ducky!" Sybil put her aggravating chin in the air and held out square brown hands to Allan, with a mute request to be helped to her feet. "Only let's have a rabbit game"—thus did Miss Hillingdon junior unkindly designate the futile efforts of her elders, and the strained gyrations of her inferiors, on her own pet stamping ground—a tennis court. "Mr Jarrot, I *think*, Ann."

She indicated a young and lusty parson, whose untiring exertions during tea-time had left him limper than the many sets of tennis which he had not played. Sybil's calculating eye wandered over the groups reclining in various attitudes of midge-bitten discomfort beneath the trees. It would be well to weed out any conies that Ann might possibly see fit to include in her long-suffering young sister's next set.

"Mr Jarrot," she continued dreamily, "Lady Muriel, Tessie and Daddy. I think that will do nicely. We might have given them you, Dennys," she regarded her sister's

33

late partner thoughtfully, "for a bit of stiffening; but I don't think we will. In gratitude for such an act of clemency on our part, you might be a lamb and look for the ball that went into that monkey puzzle," she ended, and advanced on her victims without further ado.

Ann addressed herself distressfully to Allan—Dennys, in compliance with Sybil's request, having retired from sight (if not from hearing) in the painful fastnesses of the monkey puzzle.

"Sybil *is* an idiot," she said. "She knows better than anyone that Daddy'll be simply lepping with rage if he has to play with Tessie Jeeves. She screams so, and it puts him off his game, he says."

"Poor Cousin Ronnie! Bad luck!" Allan murmured feelingly, while he fitted a cigarette into an amber holder with consummate tenderness.

"Oh, I'll play if you like." Dennys had recovered the ball and joined once more in the conversation. "No trouble—pleasure," he reassured his hostess, anent his recent experiences in the monkey puzzle. "I don't mind Tessie; it'd take more than her to put me off to-day—any more than I am, I mean—so let me play, Ann," he finished slightly incoherently.

"Too late, thanks muchly all the same," Ann smiled at him nicely. "Sybil's attacked them all now. Come to the stables and have a look at that big fetlock of Garry Owen's—I told you about it, didn't I?"

They drifted away, followed ecstatically by the virtual master and mistress of Ballinrath—Twink and Jibber— two white West Highland terriers, whose hatred of tennis parties—beastly functions, where safety from hurtling missiles was well-nigh impossible—was only equalled by their love for the dainties and extravagant petting lavished upon them so profusely, especially by the more retiring and unconversational members of the party.

Jibber especially was past master, or rather mistress, in this, her own particular form of hostess-like diplomacy. She was lightning quick to notice the youth or maiden at a loss for conversation. When she did so, her method of proceeding was invariable. Fixing the couple with melt-ingly pathetic brown eyes, from which tears seemed not very far away, the jade would proceed to stroke a flan-nelled knee (she had a most reprehensible preference for male victims) with a nervous little paw, groaning softly the while. The ruse was invariably successful. Her small person was regaled to repletion, and she formed a well-nigh inexhaustible topic of conversation for her victims.

Twink's methods had in them less of subtlety than those of his life's partner. Let him but leap, lightly yet firmly, upon the best-cushioned laps of the assembly— belonging to those godly matrons whom he knew to have a partiality for small dogs—and he might fare as sump-tuously as he would. Tea over, however, the small con-spirators welcomed eagerly any respite from the social duties which their self-importance forbade them to desert without good and sufficient excuse. Could any better excuse be found than the departure of their own Mummy, in company with their favourite guest, both evidently bound for that happy hunting-ground—the stable yard?

This disappearance was watched with less favouring eyes by Major Hillingdon. Had he known of Dennys's recent offer of self-sacrifice in his favour, the feeling of habitual disapproval which he harboured towards that silent youth might have somewhat abated. As it was, he felt distinctly ill-used by his family, and thoroughly disgusted with Mrs Jeeves, who was at the moment screaming in his ear the glad tidings that they had won the toss. Neither was his temper improved by the discovery that three only of the six new Slazenger balls remained in the court after the last set.

Sybil, whose devilish ingenuity in getting her own back (she had not forgotten the results of her two-weeks-old escapade with the bay filly) had been employed in the partnering of her father and Mrs Jeeves, who was now cheerfully engaged upon what she termed "a foray among the matrons," amongst whom she numbered some of her most willing slaves. Having accepted an invitation to a tennis party from one, sorrowfully refused to join a "gardening picnic" to which she was asked by a second, and thoughtfully lighted a small bonfire of cigarette stumps to protect the mountainous ankles of a third from the massed attacks of midges, she slipped an arm through her cousin's and led him gently away from the vicinity of a small round table which held liquid refreshments.

"Dear boy, I want to have a little talk with you," was her motherly murmur; "shall we go into the garden and cadge a few plums off Burke?"

"Right. Just let me lap this up. Pity to waste it."

Allan drank deeply, depositing his glass at length with a regretful sigh.

"Now, I'm ready. 'Fraid we won't get much in the plum line, though. I observed my small cousin Rickard and a lady friend making tracks for the garden some time ago. What about the stables? I feel as if I'd like to look at the horses, d'you know."

"Would it, the darling! What an unobservant little

person it is! Isn't it, Benny?" She appealed to Benbow. "Never thinks about his cousin Ann, does he? Much less——"

"All right, the garden. Any old where. And on the way I propose that you unreel me this ravel. What I mean is, for goodness' sake put me wise anent these mysterious St Lawrences. What is the everlasting mystery, anyway? If I mention them at lunch, you fetch me one on the ankle-bone or tibia; if I mention them at tea, you——"

"All right, my child, don't fret." With the tail of an all-observant eye, Sybil noted a group composed of Dennys, Ann, and Garry Owen, leaving the stable yard.

"Come on," she challenged. "I'll race you to the plum trees."

She was gone like a streak, a flying vision of white pleated skirt, long white silk legs, and black bobbed hair. A charming, saucy, deliciously unexpected minx, he told himself, as he pursued; the prettiest, most alluring, indiscreet little devil, he decided, when he came upon her, flushed, a little breathless, with distinct invitation in her laughing eyes, and soft red mouth.

He kissed her, of course. Really, there was nothing else to do. And then he teased her from the lofty summit of his twenty-seven years; called her a baby, and asked her how much she liked him, and when she refused to say, sat down on the box-edging and played "She loves me, she loves me not" with dog-daisies, in his own most inimitable way. Altogether they enjoyed themselves very much, and forgot all about the plums and Benbow, who sat in the centre of the path, beaming at them in the intervals of interviewing the inhabitants of various outlying portions of his anatomy.

Now the corrugated iron roof of a pig-sty overhung this Eden, complete with Eve, and down the said roof, with thoughtful clatterings, slid Miss Elizabeth St Lawrence, and not far behind—though with more care for his gala attire (he boasted two sisters to her one indulgent brother), followed her faithful esquire, Rickard Hillingdon. Elizabeth brought up with her elbows in the gutter pipe, and her heels on an angle of some precipitance above her head.

"Hullo!" she said.

Rickard brought up beside her.

"Hullo!" he added.

"Hullo, Brats!" cried Sybil.

"Hullo!" put in Allan.

Then there was silence.

"By Jove, it *is* a hot day! I'm sweating like a two-year-old," Elizabeth was the author of this somewhat unconventional statement.

"Not 'arf, guv'nor," Rickey echoed the sentiment almost with fervour. "*I'm* sweating like——"

"Oh well, never mind." Sybil changed her position to the opposite side of the gravel path, where she could converse with the new-comers in comfort. "How are your rabbit snares getting on, Elizabeth?" she inquired diplomatically.

Elizabeth, at imminent personal risk, reached for a plum from the tree below her before replying.

"All right, thank you, Sybil. I'm after getting two this morning. To say the brutes juked! Well, it took me and Driscoll 'bout five minutes each to do them in."

"Not 'arf, guv'nor," Rickey murmured. "Mine juke, too, something awful. They juke like bleedin' stallions."

Sybil laughed. "Don't let Daddy catch you saying that," she warned him.

Rickey indicated the lady who shared his roof. "*She* says it," he averred.

"Father says it," announced Miss St Lawrence solemnly, and not at all in the tone of one who courts criticism.

Apparently there was nothing more to be said. So, after a short pause, Rickard and Elizabeth climbed once more to the summit of the pig-sty roof, and disappeared down the steep incline on the farther side.

"'Strewth! what a lovely little lady!" Allan flicked open his cigarette case. "Smoke? No? Quite right, they *are* only Americans. Tell me, does 'Father' really say things like that?"

"Mr St Lawrence," Sybil gazed reflectively at the greened toes of her tennis shoes, "is of the renowned breed of the Buckeen. Don't interrupt; I know that you're too much of a Saxon to know the meaning of a Buckeen. It's just a man who's—not quite like us. I don't mean to be a snob a bit. They explain the difference very well themselves when they call us the 'county families,' or say that we're 'stuck-up.' 'Course they're awfully good sportsmen and all that, and can generally judge a horse backwards on a dark night. And most of them have been in the country since the earliest ages, and lots of 'em are related to big Irish names, you know. But still . . . oh, you know . . . they're different, somehow. They pronounce castle to rhyme with tassle and dance with pants . . . the things you wear. Sorry—I should spare your maiden blushes, shouldn't I, *mon ami*?"

"I wouldn't have dreamt of bothering you about them. Still, perhaps you *would* remember next time. However, let's resume. 'Miss Hillingdon on the Buckeen.' Personally, though all you've told me is consumingly interesting, I don't quite see the connection between it and your father's antipathy to the St Lawrence family." Allan was slightly bored.

"Patience. We're nearly there." Sybil laced her hands round her knees, and fixing her eyes on the pig-sty roof, continued. "You see, darling, there are nice buckeens and nasty buckeens, *and* the nasty ones are horrid. Old Johnny St Lawrence is peculiarly beastly. He's a tremendous horse-coper, and he's done Daddy—and lots of people all over Ireland—up most foully, heaps of times. He took the hounds, too, when Dad gave them up, though Lord knows how he does it—or why—'cept that MFH sounds so blinking respectable to people who don't know him." Sybil paused for breath.

"I see," said Allan solemnly. "But how about the 'and Son' part? I presume Mrs St Lawrence has—er—conked?" he observed delicately.

"Yes, she's dead." Sybil had her second wind now. "It was rather a romantic sort of runaway match. She was Mummy's greatest friend, and that's why Dad tolerates Dennys at all. He dislikes him awfully, really, specially since he and Ann——" Miss Hillingdon paused in diplomatic confusion.

"Yes, since he and Ann—— Well?" Allan concentrated his entire attention on the blade of grass which he was chewing.

"Well," Sybil went on reluctantly, "I should have thought the most inadequate baby could have seen—er—how it is, between those two. Still, even Daddy doesn't really see, even though he loathes poor Dennys."

"Quite useless, I suppose." The grass-stem continued to engross Allan's entire attention.

"Oh, not altogether," Sybil answered with some haste. "Ann's a deuced determined little person, you know, an' she—— Oh, hullo, Burke!" she broke off. "We aren't stealing your plums."

"Ah, God help ye, ye may take them, ye may take them," wheezed the decrepit old gardener, who, armed with basket and ladder, had just made his appearance. "It's what it is there's a glut of fruit in the country, me lady," he went on conversationally, "God knows how, with all the apples he drew out of it. For ye could *not* sell them. Sure, 'twas only to-day the Master was at me about it. 'See here, Burke,' says he, 'thim blazing pears on the big tree below, they're droppin' in a mummy at me feet. Look at that now,' says he, and him dancin' mad." Burke paused dramatically. Sybil, who knew of old the dire necessity of making swift use of such pauses, rose to her feet.

"He must have been in the devil's own wax," she said. "Come on, Allan, for the love of Mick, the rabbits ought to be through with their set by now."

They returned to the tennis court in time to witness a general upheaval among the matrons, each of whom was intent on capturing and bearing off her young before all or any of them could be included in the new set. Allan found himself carefully buttoning the prettier girls into their coats. They were all very kind to him. A charming people, the Irish.

"Mummy," said a tall girl, for whom he had just fastened innumerable buttons, "here's a real live man for our dance. Ask him at once."

41

"Ah!" A lady who appeared absurdly young to be the mummy of the tall girl, looked at him with lively interest. "Would you be here then, Mr Hillingdon? It's not for a month or two. But you *must* come if you are. We're so lamentably short of men since the soldiers left, that we clutch at positively *any* straws, months ahead." The deep and friendly earnestness of her manner overlaid with kindliness her remarkably tactless speech. Allan accepted gratefully—provided he was still in the country.

"Goodness knows if we'll be here ourselves by then, or burnt out again to-morrow." Lady Glencurry laughed lightly. "Is it true that Moyra Bridge was blown up last night? I wanted to drive home that way."

"I believe it is. Seems rather appalling, doesn't it?" Allan was deeply in earnest.

"Oh, you won't take these things half so seriously when you've been here a little longer," he was told. "They are a nuisance, of course, still—— Oh! there's the mare, simply dancing. Muriel never can hold her. *Good*-bye, Mr Hillingdon. So glad to have met you." Lady Glencurry scrambled most efficiently into her high dog-cart and was driven off by the tall daughter.

"Hullo! you look warm. Come and have some sluicing."

Allan addressed this invitation to Dennys St Lawrence some ten minutes later. The said gentleman, who had spent the half-hour previous to the invitation in starting the engines of the departing guests' Ford cars, and clinging to the heads of horses who appeared as determined to start for home as the Fords were to remain if possible till the moon rose, accepted gratefully. The two men drank deep.

"'Fraid we must be going now," announced Dennys regretfully. "You don't happen to have seen my sister Elizabeth, do you? However, it doesn't matter; she'll turn up. I must go and say good-bye to Ann now." He pushed himself into an old tweed coat, wound a white silk scarf round his neck, and departed as on business bent.

Allan stooped to flick at a smear of green on his otherwise immaculate white flannels. "Funny thing," he soliloquised disconsolately, "but I wish he wouldn't call her—Ann. She calls him Dennys too. But then they all do, so they do... We-ell. ..." At this point in his reflections, Allan, being at no time overfond of his own undiluted company, sauntered back to the house to seek his fellow-men.

He did not find any fellow-men in the hall, nor yet in the library, but in the billiard room he discovered Captain St Lawrence making his adieux.

"Well, come over the first soft day and we'll give him a bit of a school," he heard Ann's soft voice say. Then came Dennys's indescribable monotone.

"Yes, rather. Good-bye—er—good-bye. Thanks awfully! Please don't bother; I'll let myself out this way. I see Elizabeth over there." And he left the room by the open french window.

Allan advanced. "I say, let's lead Garry out for a bite of grass," he suggested. "That fetlock'll be all the better for a little exercise."

Ann regarded her cousin for a moment with dreaming eyes. Then, with a slight start, she answered:

"*Garry*! Oh, Dennys said he'll be better left quiet for a couple of days. He and I—we took him out this after-noon, that is."

"Oh," said her cousin rather sourly. "I see."

He repented the acidity of his tone an instant later when Ann, for no apparent reason, grew pink up to the eyes, swung herself off the edge of the table on which she had been perching, and left the room precipitantly, murmuring something inaudible about the ordering of dinner. Allan picked up a cue; then, deciding that knocking balls about alone was not worth while, he lounged out of the window, whistling disconsolately for Benbow.

Rounding the corner of the house which hid from view the tennis courts, Allan came upon his host and cousin, employed in a so-far fruitless search for lost tennis balls. His offer of help (rather to his disappointment) having been accepted, he proceeded to quarter and search methodically over the ground which had been already scrutinized by Major Hillingdon, who, exhausted apparently by his previous efforts, sat upon the roller, and, lighting a cigarette, watched his young and muscular relative's operations in somewhat dour silence. Silence, however, never reigned for very long when Allan was anywhere about.

"Jolly successful little what-not, what?" he observed affably, by way of starting the conversation.

"I don't know what the devil you're chattering about," responded the Major. This reply, though unencouraging, did not depress Allan at all. He made another start.

"Jolly lot of people you have round here. Nice and affable and all that, aren't they?"

"Oh, affable!" The Major snorted querulously. "Bit too affable. There's not one decent family left in the country, except the Glencurrys—you met Muriel Dane and her mother this afternoon—and ourselves. As for the St Lawrences, and that poisonous Tessie Jeeves and her meek little husband, 'pon my soul, it makes me sick to see the girls making friends with that lot! But they say they can't get up a four for tennis without them, and of course *my* wishes are of no account about that or anything else. Old St Lawrence is the blackest old scoundrel in Ireland. Oh, a dirty little brute!" Here the Major's scorn nearly choked him. "And I've good reason to believe that the son's tarred with the same brush. Has he tried to sell you a horse yet? No? Well, don't let him. He'd stick you up with something nasty, I tell you. It's in the blood. I don't like the fellow; never did. He's like old Soapy Sponge—'Too much of a gentleman.'" The Major laughed immoderately at his own jest, then getting up from the roller, threw away the stump of his cigarette and departed.

Allan watched the cigarette end for a moment, glowing where it fell, as he reflected on a half-promise he had given to go over, in the course of a few days, to the stronghold of the St Lawrences and take a look at hounds, horses and polo ponies. Of course there was no necessity to buy a hunter for the winter. Indeed, he was not at all sure that an urgent telegram would not arrive at any moment to summon him back to England—Ireland, for no particular reason, having suddenly become rather a flat, stale, and profitless proposition.

That same evening, however, as he leant out of his bedroom window, smoking a last cigarette into the scented night, he quite changed his mind about the telegram which was to summon him away. It was only a small thing that had altered the course of his thoughts; just an after-dinner walk—a walk through long, wet-brushing grass, over bare stubble fields, lifting their cool airy scent to the moon, a walk through dark and gleaming beech trees, very slippery under foot. It was when climbing a steep slope in their friendly shelter, that Ann (who was sharing in the rabbit-straafe-object of this expedition) slipped and would have fallen had not Allan caught her and held her, one warm little moment, in his arms. She had slipped from him as hastily as any well-brought up girl would under like circumstances; but, was it fancy or fact that she had proved extra-specially kind and sweet that God-given evening?

Allan didn't know. But certainly his hand shook in a most ridiculous fashion in lighting his cigarette, as he thought of her—especially when he thought of her in connection with that blighter St Lawrence. At any rate, *that* was quite impossible. Had not even Sybil said so? And he, Allan Hillingdon—he flattered himself rather ingenuously—was no bad parti for his Irish cousin. Considering that no man on earth could count himself worthy of her, it was as well that he, having assumed to aspire, should have at least the wherewithal to give her pretty things. . . . How he would love to buy pretty things for Ann! His thoughts wandered far afield to a certain bungalow at his Hill Station. Surely a setting worthy . . . he thought of its rooms, but could remember none distinctly, save only the bath-room. A beauteous place this, once shown him by its late owners with some pardonable pride. Visions of Ann wearing the deep blue kimono, clad in which he sometimes saw her flitting about of a morning, came to him.

Ann, Ann, Ann . . .

The thought of her filled him with a deep, a most wondrous emotion, a boundless reverence and tenderness. This, then, was the Real Thing. Of course he had imagined himself in love heaps of times before. But like this, never. It was, of course, quite different from any previous experience. Why, it was Elysium when she smiled, and plain hell when the St Lawrence, and not he, took the lame Garry out for her. Dash St Lawrence any way!

"Bedtime, I *think*, Georgie dear." A soft yet firm voice from above broke in upon his meditations. Allan started back, bumping his head against his window sash with some violence, and dropping his cigarette, which spun through space like a shooting star, and glowed at him with its one fiery eye from the darkness into which it had fallen.

"Now, now, now," continued the voice. "Tut, tut, tut! I *am* surprised. But why don't you go to sleep, Allan— instead of sighing into the night like that?" Sybil's voice was sweet and soft as melted honey.

"Run away, Sybil," he answered her peevishly. "Run away! Ooze off and drown yourself, or get back to bed, or something. Only lemme alone like a dear. I'm—I'm rather busy."

Much to his surprise, Sybil acted on the second of his suggestions and withdrew from her window. His surprise would have been still greater could he have seen her cast her pyjama-clad form upon the floor of her bedroom; or heard the sobs, childlike in their abandonment and intensity, which shook her slight body so cruelly.

"Damn Ann!" she moaned between her tears. "But he shan't care for her. He mustn't. Oh God, please! *Please!* You *know* I love him. I love him. . . . Poor little Sybil. . . ." She mopped her eyes, then wept again, for the sheer heartrending pathos of her position.

CHAPTER IV

The House of St Lawrence

"WHAT'S this you say, Master Dennys? Miss Elizabeth after having a sick stomach, is it? Ah, God help her, the creature! But it's no wonder—what with that trash of taking her to tea-parties, let alone her running after yourself and the master, ever and always in them dirty kennels. I suppose the poor child will hardly be using food this morning—or will I take her up a fresh duck egg?"

Dennys rose from his seat on the kitchen table, and, after a cursory glance at some pots of linseed on the back of the range, he diffidently negatived the idea of a duck's egg for the invalid's breakfast, and suggested dry toast and tea as a suitable substitute.

"Ah, what nonsense ye have, you and your toast! The egg'll do her no harm. Amn't I delicate meself that way? And I know an egg'll not sicken her."

The light of battle burned in the eyes of Lizzie, the general servant, and absolute ruler of Cloonbeg and its owners, the St Lawrences. An answering light sprang into the eyes of her employer's son, and his native brogue obtruded itself rather more than usual in his slow and pleasant voice, as he made reply.

"Well, she'll not have an egg. Give me here that fork and I'll toast the bread for her myself, if you won't do it."

He conducted the operation of toasting several slices of bread in a masterly fashion. Then, putting them on a plate, he made his way upstairs to his small sister's room. He found the patient sitting up in bed, and looking remarkably cheerful for one in her condition. Beside her was a tray upon which languished the remains of a seemingly hearty meal. On her brother's entrance, Miss St Lawrence lay back among the pillows, and, assuming an expression of extreme langour, sniffed delicately at a grubby pocket-handkerchief, from which emanated suffocatingly a strong odour of that scent more noxious than all others to the cultured sense—namely, Californian Poppy.

"Hullo!" Dennys surveyed the debris of her meal with hopeless disapproval. "You seem to have done pretty well for yourself, don't you? I told Lizzie I was bringing you up your breakfast. Good heavens!" he stooped to examine the empty plates, "you don't mean to say she's been giving you bloater? That woman is the icy limit."

Miss St Lawrence regarded her brother in a bored manner, from beneath long eyelashes.

"It was father gave me my breakfast," she announced at last. "And he said I was to eat it all, too. He said I'd need a good one after——" She paused suggestively and with extreme delicacy. "He gave me this lovely perfume too," she continued. "It's simply exquisite. Lizzy says so. Do smell it, Dennys."

"No, thanks." Dennys picked up her tray and started to the door. Half way there he paused, and, turning to the languid maiden in the bed, observed in a slightly constrained manner:

"I say, old thing, I wish you wouldn't say 'perfume.' Sounds rather sickly, doesn't it, when you come to think of it."

Elizabeth turned on her brother a look full of scornful incomprehension.

"Ah, go on," she said. "How grand you are, I *don't* think!"

Dennys closed her door and trod heavily down the linoleum-covered stairs to the dining-room. Depositing the tray, with the debris of Elizabeth's repast, on the sideboard, he proceeded to investigate the breakfast dishes. In one was a jagged slab of oatmeal porridge; in the other, a tepid bloater. Mr St Lawrence, who had put down his newspaper as his son came into the room, now took it up again, speaking sombrely from its depths.

"Slim Chance didn't even get placed, confound the brute!"

His son helped himself to porridge, before answering.

"Of course she didn't. Any ass'd've known she wouldn't. She wasn't meant to."

"Oh, you're damned sharp—it's a pity you didn't know that so well a little while ago."

Mr St Lawrence returned morosely to his newspaper. Dennys rose, put his porridge plate, and those containing the untidy remains of his father's meal, on the side table. He did not speak again until he was half-way through his bloater.

"Did you plunge heavily on Slim Chance, father?" he asked.

"I stood to win a hundred and fifty."

Mr St Lawrence smiled, the bitter smile of the well-intentioned man, against whom—for no fault of his own—the stars work mightily in their courses.

Dennys, who knew of old the difficulties of elucidating from his father the exact extent of his financial losess, helped himself to marmalade.

"What odds did you get?"

"I got three to one."

"Oh!" Dennys looked up quickly. "Maurice Dempsey's asking fifty for that big brown of his—one that ran second in the point-to-points this year."

Mr St Lawrence wiped his too abundant black moustache with a highly scented and rather grubby silk handkerchief.

"Well, if I bought him itself I haven't a buyer for him. I'm sick to death," he continued plaintively, "of seeing horses standing idle in the stables from month's end to month's end, and not a soul so much as coming in to have a look at them. It's—it's perfectly heart-breaking."

Dennys eyed his parent as, his plaint ended, he trumpeted mournfully into his handkerchief.

"The chap staying with the Hillingdons—cousin of theirs—I asked him to come over and look at the horses," he announced. "But what's the use when there's nothing but old screws and a couple of vicious youngsters in the place?"

Mr St Lawrence brightened perceptibly.

"Ah, what matter," he said, putting away the handkerchief and pouring himself out a cup of weak, sweet tea. "Tell me," he continued, "do you think does he know a horse from a cow, or could we sell him old Hawthorn? I had Johnny Brien boiling the hock off her all yesterday— we might be able to keep it down, so, till we have his cheque. . . . Or there's that yellow four-year-old brute. He has a nasty way of taking his banks, but he's a nice horse."

For some five minutes Mr St Lawrence expatiated hopefully on the merits of every animal in his possession; then he bethought him to inquire when the prospective buyer might be expected to arrive, but without waiting for a reply, rose from his seat and made for the door, loudly expressing his determination to have "every bandage in the stable out of sight in half an hour."

Dennys said nothing. He rolled up his napkin, and disentangling his father's from the legs of the chair lately occupied by that gentleman, he rolled it up too. Then he busied himself in making a breakfast for his dog, Driscoll, the eldest-born son of Twink and Jibber. Driscoll's complete adoration of his master was equalled only by his contempt for the hounds and the kennel terriers. To-day he left his breakfast no more than half finished, in his fear that the beloved—carelessly forgetting his little Driscoll—might go down to the stables, and even start out exercising without his small guardian. For Driscoll knew well how to take care of his belongings. Once, when Dennys had taken a heavy fall off a young horse he was schooling, and had lain very still on the ground for a long time, had not Driscoll sat upon his chest most lovingly, for at least half an hour? And at the end of that time, when some confounded interfering people had come along and tried to lift him away, he had jolly well bitten one of them before he'd allow himself to be moved. It was quite unthinkable that Master should go out without him.

So Driscoll left the porridge and less succulent portions of his meal till another time, and pattered into the hall, where his claws made a tremendous clattering on the linoleum, in search of his idol. His idol wasn't in the hall, but his old blackened riding crop lay across one of the chairs and also his hat. So that was all right. He must be in the library. Driscoll went in there to see, and, sure enough, there was his own one, sitting on the arm of a chair, making excruciating noises with a pocket-knife, in the bowl of his pipe.

Driscoll leaped into the arms of his master to express his joy at this unexpected reunion, after their long parting; and Dennys, having duly acknowledged the touching greeting, knocked the bowl of his pipe against the fireplace, and, turning to his father—who had postponed his visit to the stables, and was now seated at his writing-table, morosely tearing up bills—spoke with some finality.

"Well, all I can say is that you'll be an old fool if you try to sell him any of the brutes you have in the stable now—bar the ponies, and they'll be no good to him. He hasn't come here to play polo. Besides, do you think old Ronnie Hillingdon's likely to let him be stuck with one of your famous deals, because I don't. If you hadn't made such a precious ass of yourself over backing Slim Chance, you'd have that fifty now this minute. You'd be able to get that brown of Maurice Dempsey's and make as much more on the deal. Now, I suppose, Charlie Jeeves'll have him snapped up. It's a pity. I wouldn't mind unloading one of the screws on young Hillingdon, if I sold him a decent animal like that brown, at the same time, to take the edge off, as it were."

Dennys's long speech, delivered in a regretful monotone, roused his parent to something like cold fury.

"Ah, shut up," he said. "You and your fifty pounds! Whether I backed the horse or not, I wouldn't have fifty pounds here, or in the bank, this minute. No, nor fifteen. Nor yet the money to pay this bill." He jabbed it viciously on to an over-full file as he spoke. "And it's the hell of a long one from old McKeogh the butcher, too."

Mr St Lawrence continued his filing and docketing. He was the most methodical of men, and it was, perhaps, owing to this quality that he kept himself and his family afloat, under a load of indebtedness that would certainly have sunk any ordinary man in fraudulent bankruptcy, long since. He had, indeed, intervals of exceeding prosperity, and it was during one of these that he had taken the hounds; an enterprise which he never regretted, for his love of hounds and hunting was the only great love of his life. And his genius as a huntsman was only equalled by his genius for raking in large subscriptions while reducing hunt expenses by about one half.

Dennys continued to survey his father, and his father continued his task of tearing up bills and noting down figures, for some minutes. Then, opening a drawer in his writing-table, he took out of it a cheque-book and carefully wrote out a cheque for forty-five pounds, which he signed, blotted, and handed to his son. Dennys glanced at it expressionlessly and handed it back.

"Don't be a bally fool," he said. "What earthly use d'you suppose that is, considering you're overdrawn already, as you say?"

Mr St Lawrence turned round in his chair, so as almost to face his son. He wore that expression of kind condescension, which it is the invariable custom of parents to assume when stooping to explanations of their own conduct or procedure, with their offspring. Then, cocking one knee over the other, and emphasizing his points by beating the chubby fist of his right hand into the soft and yielding palm of his left, he uplifted his voice in plausible explanation.

"Well, my dear boy," be began confidentially, "I don't

mind admitting to you that I'm damned tight for money at the present moment. At the same time"—he paused to laugh reassuringly—"I don't say that things are in as bad a way as I made out a minute ago, though these devilish bills are piling up fast enough, Lord knows. Still, we can put 'em off till we get rid of a couple of horses to young Hillingdon, and then we'll be all right. Sure, I have it figured out to the last penny. We'll get eighty, anyway, for that brown of Dempsey's, and we should get a nice bit for the yellow brute too—I'll put in the next few days schooling the tricks out of him. Well, then"—he picked up the cheque—"you'd better ride over to Lisogue this morning, and getta hold of that animal. And don't forget to bring a receipt back with you for the money—Dempsey's a slippery customer."

Dennys rose to his feet, put down Driscoll, whom he had been nursing during the interview, flicked some white hairs off his coat, and slipped his pipe into his pocket.

"All right," he said. "Glad it's not as bad as you pretended. You'd better make out the receipt for Dempsey to sign, for as smart as he is, it takes him a donkey's years to write his own name. I'm going up now to see if Elizabeth has died of the bloater you gave her for breakfast." He snapped his fingers to Driscoll, and left the room.

When the door had closed, Mr St Lawrence took out another cheque-book and wrote out another cheque. In every detail it was the same as the first, save for one slight omission, namely that of his signature at the bottom right-hand corner. He folded the piece of paper in three, in such a manner as to render it unnecessary to open more than the first fold to glance at the amount. Having done this, he wrote out a receipt for forty-five pounds, received from John St Lawrence by—— He then put both cheque and receipt in an envelope, which he placed beside his son's hat and crop on the hall table, before leaving the house in the direction of the training paddock.

Let it not be thought for a moment that this fraud which he was endeavouring to perpetrate weighed at all heavily with him. Time, he would have argued pleasantly, in horse-dealing as in other matters of business, is everything. If you have not at one time the wherewithal to pay for a horse, you will have it at another. Wherefore any means, no matter how crooked, to gain time, time being money, is amply justified.

The son of a sporting Irish country doctor, who had in his time saved as many horses as he had lost human lives, Johnny St Lawrence, from his earliest days, had lived and breathed in an atmosphere of horse and horse-coping. In this atmosphere he had learned to ride straight to hounds, to ride the slug with the spur, and the baulker with something beyond severity; to get the utmost ounce from the aged, and to match the subtleties of the vicious with subtleties deeper far. His veterinary skill was supreme. Perhaps his two hectic years as a medical student, in Trinity College, Dublin, helped him there. Be that as it may, his infinite care and patience cured many a horse, given up by more certified skill than his.

After two years, devoted to the study of medicine, Johnny St Lawrence had decided that the calling of his father was not for him; so, shaking the dust of Dublin from his feet—though not, it is regrettable to state, the speech of Dublin from his tongue—he returned to his own country, and, taking up his residence in his father's house, commenced in a small way the horse business which was to be his life's work.

Horse-coping is at once the most alluring and, at the same time, quite the most unstable business in which any man can sink his money and his unsparing energies. It is a business in which, before all else, appearances must be kept up. The home of the dealer may be almost without bread, but it cannot be without the inevitable drink which cements a deal. Good clothes must be worn, and the outward semblance of easy circumstances put before all else.

Johnny St Lawrence was a clever man. More, he was blessed with good looks, and Irish good looks at that—the startling, blue-eyed, dark-haired, good looks which are so fascinatingly irresistible to pretty eighteen. And it was to a pretty eighteen-year-old that John—after successfully combating the advances of the young ladies of his own strata of country society for nearly four years—finally succumbed.

Joan Charmian, third and youngest daughter of Sir Julian Charmian of Cloneen House, fell equally in love with Johnny St Lawrence; or she fancied that she did, which comes to much the same thing at eighteen. At any rate, she found stolen meetings with her fascinating, adoring lover a delightful change from the Cloneen *ménage*, in which she, younger by eight years than her sisters, ranked still as an unsophisticated flapper. The chain of events which finally led to her runaway match with a man whom, in sane moments, she would have classed as an unmitigated bounder, was complicated by:

(1) A heavy father's crude methods for the correction of an erring daughter.

(2) Her sisters' coldly expressed scorn of such methods as totally unnecessary, inasmuch as "Joan would never have the nerve to do it." And lastly by a week, reft from the middle of the hunting season, and spent with a godmother at Shankill, from whose eminently respectable roof she fled, first to a registry office in Dublin, and later to the arms of Johnny St Lawrence.

Less than a year afterwards, she looked back, with incredulous bitterness of spirit, on her action. "How could I?" was the question she asked herself continuously, and with an ever-deepening amazement at the fool, the idiot, that had been herself. What had she ever seen in this man, who could speak to her of the vilest of his horse-coping frauds, as "good business," who used scent, on whose tongue was the light-clipping speech of Dublin—what had she ever seen in him, to make her do this mad, wild, incredible, yet too terribly real and binding thing? His good looks? What were they to her now? Custom had staled them, and she saw only the vulgarity which under-lay them. His horsemanship? She had once thought that she loved it almost better than anything about him. What difference did it make now? His hands might be perfect on a horse's mouth, but they were so fat that she detested the thought of them holding her.

Poor little Joan! She was foolish, desperately foolish, perhaps, but, withal, a foolish child. A child who had been in love with love, and had mistaken that for the real thing. A rather fatal mistake, and one easier to rectify in the aftermath of married life, when the two people involved have utterly different souls, than when they have slightly different social outlooks.

Everything Johnny did jarred upon Joan, horribly,

gratingly. His turns of speech, his pleasantries, often coarse, always vulgar, the unnecessary gestures of those fat white hands of his. Every mood of his mind was antipathetic to her own. Above and beyond everything, his friends were awful! Yet she had to entertain them, and suffer the gallantries of the men, and the criticism of their women-kind, who considered her both "slow" and "stuck-up"—a truly fatal combination of bad qualities, which debarred her completely from any popularity in her present *milieu*. Seek the company of her own familiar friends, she would not. She was too proud for that. Let them accept her with the husband she had chosen, if they would; without him she would have none of them, though with him they would have none of her—Agnes Hillingdon being the one exception. Wide indeed was the barrier which, in Ireland, at that time, separated the county families from the "buckeen." Joan had jumped far beyond it, and might now remain with those with whom she had cast in her lot.

A short time after the birth of her son, her father died, leaving a sum of money, securely tied up, for the education of his only grandchild at one of the English public schools. That and nothing more. It was sufficient to widen the breach between Joan St Lawrence and her husband. After an interval of ten years, Joan gave birth to another child—a daughter whom she called Elizabeth Charmian—before she gave up her losing fight with life, and died, leaving the little boy of ten years old, and the tiny Elizabeth.

In due course Dennys was sent to the public school specified in his grandfather's will. There he learnt many things outside the curriculum, things which made him sick when he thought of his father's shady methods of horse-coping, things that removed him a hundred miles from his home life. In short, the great public school had him for her own, and continued to exercise an ever-increasing influence over him, even after he had left school and the lean years of the war far behind, and quite spoilt him for his present post as assistant in his father's horse-dealing business.

CHAPTER V

A Morning's Horse-coping

DENNYS watched one of the stable hands, for the third time, drive a soured youngster at the furze hurdles in the training paddock; and for the third time the youngster swerved—snorting in well-simulated panic.

"Here, get down now, Hefferney." Dennys laid a soothing hand on the little mare's hot neck. "Give me the rope, we'll lunge her over it quietly a bit, and see if she will do it."

Hefferney descended gratefully, observing as he did so that that one was the devil's own and as cute as a witch, and if it wasn't for the "howlt he had on the pedals he was a dead man."

"You're about as much use as a dead cat, as it is," rejoined his master amiably. "Take the crop now, and if she offers to refuse again, lace her well."

"I will, Misther Dennys, I will," responded the dead cat, in tones of suppressed ardour, as he moved in the background, ready to strike should Aurora—such being the poetical, though misleading name of the filly—continue her follies.

The mare, however, realizing pretty swiftly that resistance was, in this case, futile, jumped faultlessly back and forth over the furze, some seven or eight times; after which Dennys rode her over it without the smallest trouble. Hefferney, regarding the proceedingss, told himself, for the hundredth time, that Masther Dennys had the way of a horse in his knees. Aloud he observed it was a wonder for the mare to be so cross and she able to lep sticks the same way a pig'd gallop.

"Well, gallop up to the house yourself now," responded his master, "and get me the note that's on the oak chest in the hall, along with my hat and crop. And hurry yourself."

He slackened his rein and allowed Aurora to snatch hurried mouthfuls of grass as he awaited Hefferney's return. Sitting thus loosely in his saddle, long limbs, long stirrups, and looking as much a lithe part of his horse now as when the animal was moving, Dennys St Lawrence presented as good a picture of young manhood as one could wish to see on any glorious summer morning. With his bare dark head and his grey eyes, his handsome horse, and his easy seat in the saddle, he belonged to this Irish morning with complete entirety.

The setting was perfect, nor was the man found wanting. So, at least, thought Ann, as she drew rein in the narrow lane which skirted the training paddock, and called a greeting to the figure, seated with its back to her. Dennys turned swiftly at the sound of her voice, and rode over to the dividing wall.

"Morning," he said. "Topping day, isn't it?"

"Ripping," assented Ann. She rubbed Pet Girl's hogged mane pensively with the handle of her crop, feeling rather more conscious of Dennys's eyes than she liked. She raised her own with something of an effort.

"I'm going over to Dempsey's of Lisogue, to see about some duck eggs. Care to come?"

"I'd love to, Ann," he told her in his grave voice, which made his lightest remark to err on the side of solemnity. "Here's Hefferney now with my hat and crop. I'll meet you at the north gate. S'long."

Ann rode off down the lane with the tone of his "S'long" lingering like a kiss in her memory. She had never known a man to have so many tones of voice as Dennys. But there was one tone that she knew was kept for her only, and it was the one in which he had said "S'long." She was beginning to recognize that tone rather too frequently for her peace of mind, of late. It was one thing to like Dennys frightfully and—as Sybil would have put it—"Buzz round some with the che-ild"; it was quite another thing to allow him to exercise proprietary claims towards her. More especially since in her heart of hearts, where she didn't even own it to herself, she distinctly liked Dennys's way of being proprietary. It was not one bit pushing or ostentatious. It was just—Dennys's way, and that she should esteem his way above and beyond the ways of other men was a danger which, vaguely, she was beginning to recognize.

Somehow, the fact of its being scarcely fair to give to Dennys St Lawrence what would have constituted distinct encouragement to a man of her own caste, never occurred to Ann. She had not, up to the present, contemplated the possibility of losing her heart to him, but it did not follow that he was capable of keeping his emotions in the same fine, careless control as his lady. She found in Dennys a splendid pal and promptly adopted him as such; the ridiculously inadequate supply of men in the country, available for such purposes as tennis and dancing, enabling her to do this without exciting undue comment; save, indeed, from parental head-quarters, for Major Hillingdon had never accepted the St Lawrence family, as they had lately been accepted, or rather, tolerated *faute de mieux*, by that which remained of county society after three years of systematic attack upon landed property. He had, however, learned to endure, though scarcely to welcome, the not infrequent presence of Dennys St Lawrence in his house.

He would, however, scarcely have relished the spectacle presented by his elder daughter some half an hour later, as the said lady, having a moment previously parted company with her horse, picked herself out of the brambly ditch, into which Pet Girl had fallen, in a bored fashion, while giving a lead to Captain St Lawrence's Aurora. After which exhibition, in a sudden onrush of idiotic enthusiasm, the mare had flung her heels to heaven and galloped hard for an open gate leading on to the road.

"Oh, Dennys, wasn't that a toss and a half?" called Ann. "Will we ever catch her? Why"— horror dawned in her voice—"we've left the gate open and there's a traction engine down the road!"

Ann started to run, in the futile hope of cutting off the mare, when she became aware of Dennys's voice shouting to her from seemingly half-way across the field, to run to the gate. She reached it in time to see Aurora jump out into the road, and Dennys catch Pet Girl's rein as she galloped headlong for the traction engine, which completely blocked the narrow road a hundred yards farther on. Some three minutes later they met; Ann, adorably flushed, and rather diffident—inasmuch as she "had made a frightful fool of herself"—mounting the once more demure Pet Girl with the minimum of assistance from Dennys. As they rode on, she laid an impulsive hand on his mare's neck and spoke quickly, confusedly.

"Dennys, you were perfectly—absolutely ripping. I don't know how you were so quick, I—you don't know what it'd 've meant to me if anything had happened to the mare. It'd 've been perfectly awful."

By a supreme effort Dennys refrained from covering the small hand with his own, and telling its owner of his immense love for it, and herself, and everything appertaining thereto. But he loved rather proudly, did Dennys, and the very thought of Ann sharing his present position of dependence upon his father was anathema, not to be entertained for a moment. Tell her of his love and he felt convinced that he would lose her; hug the secret jealously to himself, and they twain might at least continue in their present joyous companionship. In this case half a loaf was, to Dennys, incomparably better than no bread. So all he said was:

"Good thing for us this mare didn't turn nasty and refuse the bank. As it was, we nearly parted company. Did you see the way she slipped up on her landing? I don't know how she managed to get her legs under her again at all."

"Pet Girl's worse," responded Ann. "The way she went asleep on the top of that bank!" She flicked Pet Girl disapprovingly with her crop. "But, sure, what horse could jump decently in cold blood, on a boiling day like this?" she inquired extenuatingly.

"Yes, that's so," agreed Dennys.

From this their talk drifted comfortably to other matters, circling amicably round such subjects as hounds, horses, hunting, and polo. And if Dennys's conversational range did not extend much further, why, neither did Ann's.

Many tortuous stone-fenced lanes, winding their lonesome way through tiny scorched fields, where Bolahauns—which being translated reads Fairy Horses, and is the Irish name for yellow ragweed—alone made brave show, brought them at length to heather, and whin-grown upland. There, in the distance, great blown white clouds laid their full breasts to the rim of that barren land, and no sound—till their horses' feet jarred upon it—broke the stillness, save only the whimpering gurgle of a burn, hiding its golden waters low down between boulders and the dark stems of the purple heather.

In silence Dennys and Ann rode beneath that wide and friendly sky; a silence which neither of them attempted to break, till signs of life—in the shape of two draggled goats, spancelled together, and each pulling separate ways across the road—warned them that human habitation of sorts was at hand.

"Here we are now," said Dennys, giving a crack with the thong of his crop to the goat which seemed, of the two, the more determined to spend the remainder of its natural life under the nose of the snorting Pet Girl. "Your duck eggs should be good, after you coming all this way for them."

Their horses picked out an intricate path, which led through and round mountainous manure heaps to the dwelling-house of the clan Dempsey. A long, low building, this, which had once been whitewashed, but could now only be distinguished from the darksome cowsheds, which surrounded it on all sides, by a chimney, from which issued fragrantly, as a faintly distilled essence above the complex farmyard smells, a thin blue trail of turf smoke.

Dennys dismounted, and tapped with the handle of his crop upon the door. From within the house, as if in answer, came an agonized cry, and a large and palely inadequate looking turkey hen rose from the floor, balancing an instant, with frenzied flappings of her wings, upon the half-door, before hurling herself with one last despairing shriek into the outraged face of the palpitating Aurora— whose subsequent behaviour provided good if not ample excuse, for the language used by her owner in the presence of a lady.

Peace restored once more, Ann became aware of two small children lurking in giggling confusion round an angle of the all-pervading manure heap; she rode up to them, and, tuning her voice to the key favoured by the cooing doves, inquired of a violet-eyed little girl whether her mother was in.

"She is not, Miss," murmured the little girl.

"She's in th' asylum," volunteered violet-eyes No. 2.

"Oh, dear, I'm sorry to hear that." Ann's voice was all sympathy, but it did not for an instant move the two violet eyes to further confidences. "Is there anyone in who could sell me some duck eggs?"

The little girls conferred together for some moments; then informing Ann of their intention of fetching their auntie, they left the yard by some vague route, via the manure heaps.

Dennys lit a cigarette, and adjusting himself with the maximum of comfort to Aurora's nervous sidlings, he turned to Ann.

"There's a horse here I was thinking of taking a look at—you might remember him. Ran second in our point-to-points—farmer's race—this year. A nice horse. . . . Hullo! here's herself. You put your eggs through first. Morning, Miss Dempsey. Grand day, isn't it?"

"It is, thank God, your honour, sir," replied the tall, slatternly woman, who, followed by violet eyes one and two, had just made her appearance. "A rare day, only for the blasht that's in it." A glance from her fine blue eyes included Ann in the conversation, before they swept devastatingly towards the two little girls, who had remained unostentatiously in the background.

"Get out, get out o' this, ye little devils ye, and don't be thronging the gentry this way." She spoke evenly and without rancour, much as some other mother might have said, "Run away and play, dears." The two little girls having faded obediently round a distant angle of the manure heap, she turned apologetically to Ann.

"Children's very wayward," she explained. "Sure the face of the globe might be before them, and if there was a horse walking from them a mile off, they'd be in undther his feet. God knows I was heart-scalded with them, the time the mother was took off, but I have them well regulated now." She flicked a satisfied eye after the retreating little girls.

Ann laughed sympathetically and broached the subject of the duck eggs. Before long, however, the intricacies of the deal were rudely interrupted by the precipitate arrival of a large brown horse. Pet Girl and Aurora viewed his advent with lady-like decorum, until he advanced upon them with whinnyings and snortings of friendship, at which the ladylike decorum gave place to coquettish disapproval, from which state they progressed rapidly to one of uncontrolled and well-simulated excitement. Round the manure heaps waltzed Pet Girl; into an open shed, well-stocked with angular farm machinery, backed Aurora; while the brown, evidently well satisfied with the disturbance he had caused, jumped an awkwardly filled gap, and careered off down the lane which it divided from the yard, at a useful gallop, and without ceasing to yodel encouragingly to his new acquaintances.

In the yard Dennys was anxiously scanning Aurora's legs for cuts, whilst Miss Dempsey held forth on the subject of the brown horse.

"That one's the finished rogue," she wound up a lengthy harangue on the heart-scaldings she had suffered from the behaviour of the finished rogue since her brother left her with the farm.

"Is it the Free Staters have your brother prisoner now, or the Republicans?" Dennys asked, with all the semblance of carelessness at this juncture. Instantly the woman's eyes became suspicious—haunted. In a flash her demeanour changed, she was anxious—the dread in her eyes was manifest.

"What did ye hear?" She spoke swiftly, looking behind and around her for possible eavesdroppers. "Did ye hear they came for him e'er it making day lasht Friday? They dragged him from the bedeen—six o' them, and took him off." She pointed to the bhorieen. "An' he let one bawl out of him—Oh God!" She put a hand up to her shivering grey face. "He's living," she went on. "I got word from him e'er yesterday. But sure they have him back in the mountains. . . . May God keep him; God is good. He is good. . . ."

"But," Ann's voice was full of horror, "why don't you represent your case to the Free State troops in Bungarvin? Surely Captain O'Connor'd do something."

"Is it him?" The woman laughed harshly. "Sure isn't he own brother to the O'Connor that Maurice had a little disagreement with in regard o' the land north." She jerked her thumb to indicate the direction. "It's little I'd get from that one. And if I went to the soldiers itself, thim lads from the hills'd be down on me like flies. Ah meself is the finished fool to be talkin' to yez this way, but yez is the old stock."

Dennys laughed shortly.

"A lot of use you had for us when we were over you! Oh, well, those days are done with now—I'm terribly sorry to hear of your troubles." He paused. "Look here, Miss Dempsey, I'd like a look at this brown of yours. Have you a place I could put this mare into?"

Aurora safely incarcerated in a black and noxious-smelling shed, the trio set off to capture the brown, Dennys carrying his mare's saddle and bridle. The horse was caught and saddled. Dennys, after a perfunctory school and examination, progressed by almost imperceptible degrees to ownership; his final possession secured by the signature of Mary Dempsey, scrawled below the receipt for forty-five pounds made out by his father.

Some twenty minutes later they headed for home, Ann leading Aurora, and Dennys riding his new purchase. Back across the lonely bog land they rode, and home by an intricate maze of by-lanes and cross cuts. At the back gate of Cloonbeg, Ann gave up Aurora's leading rein.

"I expect she'll go quietly with that brute now," she said, "Or would you rather I took her up to the yard for you?"

"No, thanks most awfully. They'll be all right now." Dennys patted the brown's neck soothingly. "Whoa, pet. Thank you ever so much. It—it was simply great. Good-bye."

"Good-bye. Hope you'll have luck with him. I'll have to beat it or I'll be late for lunch."

Ann rode quietly till out of earshot of Dennys's two restless horses; then, coming to a long stretch of turf at the side of the road, she put Pet Girl into a canter and kept her at it for a good mile. Pulling up, she bent down and put her cheek close to the mare's neck.

"You *are* hot, darling," she breathed. "My pet, Pet Girl—mother's beautiful mare. . . . I *am* a fool amn't I? Yes, I am, I *am*, Pet Girl; and I'm so peeved with every one in the whole world, but still——"

Ann bit into the handle of her crop, deeply occupied with her thoughts, and digging Pet Girl in the ribs with her boot, she proceeded at a more leisurely pace in the direction of home.

In the stable yard she met Allan. He emerged from Garry Owen's box in time to render superfluous assistance in her dismounting.

"Where are the men, old boy?" she inquired, as, leaning against the stable door, she watched him inexpertly rubbing down Pet Girl with a wisp of hay. "Look out," she continued, noting a gleam in the mare's eyes, "she's apt to kick in the stable."

"I'll kick her back if she does, only way to teach 'em. Hull-*up*, Girl!" Allan bent down to lift Pet Girl's reluctant near fore. As he did so, she craned a snake-like neck and bit heavily into the seat of his expensive and well-cut riding breeches. It was not dignified. It was, in fact, the reverse. Still Ann might, of her kindness, have enjoyed the situation more soberly.

"Oh, Allan," she moaned, when speech was possible to her, "bite her back, dear, bite her back. That'll teach her!"

Allan eyed Pet Girl in silence, and a thought sourly. Then, with unwonted perseverance, he returned once more to his attack on that more than ever reluctant near fore.

Ann, recovering herself, summoned Aiden to complete the mare's toilet, and led the way into Garry Owen's box; remarking, as she stooped under the iron cross-bars, that the poor darling had had blue stone on his fetlock the morning long to take off proud flesh. And that was very, *very* sore, wasn't it, *avick*? She bent down as she finished her sentence to examine the injured fetlock.

Allan felt rather uncomfortable. At Sybil's instigation, he had put in the half-hour previous to Ann's return in careful stuping of the wound; the bandaging, too, had really been rather neatly done. In fact, he had quite expected a charming comment on his diligence, from Ann. But now he seemed (with his usual cursed luck) to have done the wrong thing again.

"Some ass has taken off the blue-stone!" cried Ann. "D'you know if Sybil was mucking round? I suppose she meant well, but——"

"Well, as a matter of fact, old thing, it was I—as it were; you see, I thought—— Oh, dash it! I'm frightfully sorry, Ann," he finished penitently.

Ann assured him that it did not matter in the least; that, most stinging of all, he couldn't have known, or he wouldn't have done it; and, as she deftly unwound the bandage, she asked him to get the blue bag and hold it for her. Allan, as he obediently shook blue-stone into Ann's hard little palm, felt both foolish and young, also inexperienced; all three being sensations to which he was entirely unaccustomed.

From the loft above them, Sybil overheard every word of their discourse. She even succeeded—by lying on her front upon the floor—in witnessing Allan's discomfort with the blue-stone bag. Chuckling maliciously, she returned to the perusal of one of the more sultry passages of a novel by Cynthia Stockley. At the sound of the luncheon gong, which rang very soon after, she rose to her feet, and standing a-tiptoe, put the book behind a beam. From a window she saw Allan and her sister leave the yard by different routes.

"M'm, yes," she murmured pensively, "I think I really must have been one of those snake-women in a former life. I call that neat—veh-ry neat." She let herself down into an empty loose-box and repaired to her room to powder her small nose for lunch.

CHAPTER VI

Grouse, Girls and Guns

FAIR weather is to be found the world over, and at all times and seasons; but at no place and in no season is the sun kinder than he is to Ireland in the month of September. Nine Septembers out of ten are truly "seasons of mist and mellow fruitfulness." Morning mists lift their grey smoke reluctantly from the tender green of the after-grass; the early sun dries the grey veils of dew on the ripening apples, but not until he is high in his heaven do the silver traceries woven by the fairies' workmen from spike to spike of the tall box edging in the Irish gardens, fade away. If you are not up and out before this happens, you have missed quite the best part of the day.

All the dews and mists and morning mazery had long disappeared when Allan—after a late breakfast—left the house to seek other company than that of Benbow, who had succeeded in obtaining a quite supernumerary meal, by the simple expedient of gazing with anguished eyes at every mouthful which his master swallowed.

"Well, I suppose you *must* have something, but—dash it all, man!—don't slobber in that abandoned manner," Allan had said as he put down a porridge plate of bacon rinds and toast crusts for Benbow's consumption. Then, after a futile search for the more expensive brand of cigarette, jealously guarded by Ann for her tennis parties, he lit a "Players," and strolled out of the house and towards the tennis court, of which he had (at the time much against his will) been appointed keeper.

But now things were very different! Every wormcast

flattened, was flattened for Ann, so the roller was pulled slowly and conscientiously down and up, up and down.

Benbow, having finished his breakfast, lay in the sun and watched his master's unwonted energy with some consternation. His meditations, however, were before long rudely interrupted by the precipitate arrival of the latest comers to Ballinrath—namely two idiotic hound pups yclept Rachel and Ravager. Benbow bore their attentions with patience for some minutes, then rising with dignity, he clearly intimated that the interview was closed. The puppies, delighted with their success in moving so large and important a personage, pursued him with galumphing caracolings and yelps of excitement. Experience told Benbow that in another moment his admirers would be clinging to his ears. Turning, he rushed upon them open-mouthed. Allan saw a flying medly of black, tan, white, brindle; then Ravager, detaching himself from the mêlée, sat down, put his head in the air, and proceeded to howl.

Never had Allan heard such wailing. Each note was of penetrating intensity and nicely calculated to travel to the kitchen regions, where Ann was even now interviewing the cook.

As Allan had foreseen, she came—hurrying. To feel her precious tenderly all over and assure herself that the little beast was frightened, not hurt, was but the work of a moment. The comforting proved a lengthier affair. In fact Ravager was only visibly cheered after an invitation to "come and see the lovely sheep's head mother had for her own," had been issued.

The trio departed, and Allan was left once more to his meditations, the lawn-roller and Benbow. Benbow loved him—yes. But Benbow had also let him in for this—this hideous business. He must speak to Benbow seriously. Happy thought, that.

"Benny," he called, seating himself upon the rollers, "Ben, me boy, come here. No, funny-face, no. You don't imagine you deserve a rib-scratch, do you? Massage your front, is it? Damned if I do. Now, sit up, Glaxo, and take notice. You—are—to—leave—those—poisonous—little—beasts—alone! Understand? They may put their beastly big feet in your mouth, or use you as a nest for rest, or an air-cushion, or any old thing. But I won't have you playing shark with them. It's a good game, I know; but they don't understand it. See? Neither does Ann—she thinks you wanted to bite them. Nobody understands us. We're a misunderstood pair. Nobody loves us. We aren't loveable, that's why—oh, good morning! Nice day, isn't it? Nice horse, that. Nice—oh, everything in the hen-run is exquisite." Allan laughed in what he deemed a hollow and mirthless manner, as he shook hands with Captain St Lawrence.

Dennys regarded him with a hint of austerity.

"Yes, he's a good horse," he admitted. "Ran second in a point-to-point this year. Pretty rotten course too. We've only had him a short time. Came over to try him round Ann's school. Care to see how he does it?"

Allan assented, and together they made their way round the series of small fields and over a number of intricate fences which bounded them; such being Ann's school. The brown horse acquitted himself well on the whole, making no very flagrant error, and when the round of fly, bank, double, wall, and water jump had been completed,

Allan felt emboldened to try the animal himself; so stirrups were lengthened and places were changed.

A horse between your knees is a good thing, yea, very good. By the time the big brown had done the round of the jumps and galloped the mile in the big lawn, Allan felt towards him as a friend and brother.

"Well, how d'you like him?" Dennys knocked out his pipe, and descended from the railings of the big lawn.

"I think he's a good one." Allan dismounted to look wisely and as appraisingly as might be at his late steed. Really—dash it all—he knew that he knew less than nothing about a horse, but St Lawrence needn't look at him as if he was the type of worm which can't recognize a good thing when it sees it.

"Er, sound?" he asked perfunctorily.

Dennys silently passed a hand down the inside of the big horse's near hind.

"Just the smallest sign of a spavin," he said at last. "It'll never come against him, and that's absolutely the only thing. Of course you can have him vetted if you like. He won't pass. But I happen to know the vet has had his eye on him this long time—so——" Dennys laughed, a short expressionless bark.

There was a long pause. Then, in a rush of enthusiasm, Allan answered:

"I like the horse most awfully, I do really, though I needn't tell you I'm not much of a judge. Still I—what d'you want for him?" he ended, his enthusiasm fizzling out before Denny's imperturbability.

"A hundred's what father's asking for him now. But I daresay if we waited till the season started we'd get better offers," replied "father's" son, lighting a cigarette as he spoke, in his most unemotional manner. Inwardly he thought—"What a marvellous ass! Begad, it's lucky for him he didn't come and see father."

Allan, who had lately seen his uncle, Lord Semple-Maughan, unhesitatingly hand out one-fifty for a park hack for his fair daughter Dillys, closed on the deal without a stagger.

Sybil entered the billiard room as he blotted the counterfoil in his cheque-book. Seating herself upon the arm of his chair, she ruffled his hair with slim brown fingers.

"Good morning, Dennys," she began; "it's always a pleasure to see your bonny face. Allan, old friend, what on earth have you been spending a hundred pounds on. Don't tell me—let me think it out; it—it's good for my brain. You've bought a gramophone—or a wife for Benbow? Or is it a bottle of eye-lash manure? Or face-fodder? No, I know what it is! It's half a dozen of those fascinating Milanese silk vests you always wear——Ah no! Allan, don't—— Shut up!—Stop!—Allan—not—not before the child!'

Sybil wriggled out of the undignified position in which she had been placed (upside down in a deep arm-chair) and proceeded to repair the ravages on her appearance. Standing a-tiptoe before the old Chippendale mirror, which hung over the high mantelpiece, she wielded a scrap of swansdown to some effect; well aware that the pose showed off to perfection the charming immature graces of her figure.

"Hullo!" she turned swiftly from the mirror, "here's father. Oh, it's only Ann, still my beating heart. You look harrowed, little sister. Has Mrs Burke been worrying you? Fancy that, Dennys, fancy anyone harrowing Ann."

"Oh, do shut up." Ann, able no longer to ignore the flow of her sister's conversation, turned upon her. "If you'd let me get a word in edgeways, I'd tell you that there's not a thing to eat in the house; Mrs Burke says the teeth are going to and fro in her mouth with neuralgia; and altogether I think we might have a day on mountain. The birds ought to be lying pretty well, and father's away—which is a pity, of course," added Miss Hillingdon in tones of filial piety.

As Allan tramped up the steep road which led from the woods of Ballinrath to Locklin's hill, he reflected with inward amazement on the spirit of innate devilment to which Ann, no less than Sybil, so frequently gave ear. After all, why should they have chosen this particular day to bring four guns on to the mountain? They knew that their father intended to have a shoot of eight guns before the end of the week; they knew there would be a parental storm of grave proportions to face later on. They knew that if the house was out of food, no game shot that afternoon would be eatable for days; yet knowing all these things, they still persisted in defiance, or seemingly in oblivion of retribution to come, in having this day on the mountain. It was just their Irish love of doing things out of order, he supposed; that, or natural perversity—which was much the same thing anyway.

"Penny for your thoughts," Ann offered idly.

"Wondering if I'd made a conspicuous ass of myself this morning." Allan frowned heavily as he spoke. Now Ann found him distinctly attractive when he frowned; it lent to his fair and boyish countenance a not unpleasing and certainly unusual severity.

"Well, if you'll tell me what you've been an' gone an'

done, I'll be delighted to tell you that you're not—haven't been, I mean." She encouraged him with one of her rare and for that reason all the more desirable smiles.

"Bought a horse." Allan made the admission almost shamefacedly.

"No. Did you really? From Dennys? A brown five-year-old brute?" Her questions came tumbling in her eagerness.

"Yes. What do *you* think? Cousin Ronnie advised me not to buy from the St. Lawrences. But dash it all, I'm not a fool, and in spite of what Cousin Ronnie says, I'm sure St Lawrence is—well—you know what I mean——" Allan, remembering some hints which the inimitable Sybil had let fall anent the relations between Dennys and her elder sister, floundered uncomfortably.

Ann came to his aid instantly. It was characteristic of her that she hated to see people flounder in the conversational pitfalls they had digged for themselves.

"That he is straight, you mean." She finished his speech for him with another of her charming smiles. "Yes, I know he is. And I'm sure you weren't a fool, Allan. If it's the brown I mean, you've got a real good thing. We ought to have some great hunts together with him and Garry Owen this winter."

Such a simple speech, yet spoken so sweetly that it warmed Allan's very heart to remember it.

"Rather!" he assented, while a glow of enthusiasm, in which Ann, the brown horse, and Dennys were comingled, rose exultingly within him.

"Here we are at last!" Ann climbed the gate which separated the stony bhoireen from the open mountain beyond, and sat on the top bar with her gun across her knees. "We may as well wait for Sybil and Dennys here, they'll be some time before they can get Hefferney." Hefferney combined the duties of herd and gamekeeper on the Hillingdon estate. "Have one of my cigarettes." She tendered him her flat, engine-turned silver case. "They're decent, I know, because Dennys gave them to me this morning. What are they?" She stooped to examine the gold stamp before lighting up at the match he held for her. "Russian. Aren't they good?"

Leaning against the rough granite gate-post, Ann gave herself up entirely to the lazy pleasure of enjoying a good cigarette. Quite unconscious of the grace of her attitude, perched as she was with a delicious back-ground of hazel copse, the dull green of which mirrored itself deeply in her thoughtful eyes, Ann merely felt pleasure in that the sun warmed her back, and that Dennys had brought her these excellent cigarettes, and that Allan was such a dear boy—really a perfect dear. So sensible of him not to have minded father's nasty remarks about Dennys. Father *would* be bound to say something beastly, of course. . . .

Allan, leaning on the gate at her side, his gun in the crook of his arm, found the lady passing sweet. The setting suited her to perfection . . . those masses of glorious heather in front . . . and what neat feet she had, excellently shod. The strong morning light turned her hair to gold, while it discovered no fault in her evenly tanned skin.

A discreet cough broke the silence.

"Yes, we're here," came Sybil's voice. "May we come in? We're all of a dither. Hefferney was manicuring the sheep's feet, but he's going to join us at lunch time at the herd's cottage. So we'd better shoot the western end now, an' join him there. He's bringing the lunch with him. Let's get into line now, and it's only birds remember, because Dad imagines he's going to have a hare drive next week, and there aren't more than eighteen hares if you beat the mountains from here to Ballinove. See? Right! Come on, then."

Allan, stationed next to Sybil in the line of four guns, found himself wondering if her shooting was as good as her dancing or as erratic as her tennis. Here a covey of five rose seemingly from beneath his feet—a fluff of feathers wandering down the wind was the only result of his two barrels. The birds swung down towards Sybil. She couldn't, of course—— By Jove! she had though—and another. Pretty good that—pretty good.

"I simply hate it when they get up under my feet," said Sybil, as he wrung the neck of a still flapping old cock bird, and shoved her brace into his game bag. "I like other people's birds so much better. I think they're awful shots when they get up the way these did." Allan resumed his place in the line, feeling not at all so bad as he might have felt, about his two flagrant misses.

By lunch time they had walked about four miles, and the bag totalled two and a half brace of grouse and a couple of snipe. The snipe, brought down by brilliant, if fluky shots, were Allan's contribution to the bag.

Lunch, partaken of by the waters of the hurrying mountain burn, was a cheerful meal. Despite the alleged poverty of the commissariat, Mrs Burke had managed to produce some excellent sandwiches, also enormous hunks of rich black cake, almond iced.

"Truly a fair prospect. Yes, and warm."

Allan, stretched at full length in the heather, gazed with

rapt concentration into the cloudless heaven. A slight mist
dimmed the brightness of distant heather, and Ballinove
burn was "running, rippling, singing, through the heat."

"By Jove! What a day! What a whopping day!" Hullo!
what was Dennys saying about cubbing to-morrow?—it
couldn't be!

"You're not in earnest?" He roused himself to ask.
"Heavens! I've lost track of time, but I suppose it is about
the middle of the month. Fancy that now. Well, well."

"You might take the brown out, Allan," Ann suggested,
"and I'll have Fenian. Pity Garry isn't fit. . . ." She and
Dennys were soon thick in technical intricacies.

Sybil turned to Allan, removing the stump of her
cigarette from the long holder, which she affected at all
times.

"I like optimism," she observed sweetly; "it's one of
the qualities I shall insist on when selecting a husband."

"I shouldn't mind that so much," Ann took her up
eagerly, "but he *must* know how to speak to dogs. There's
a lot in that." She pondered the thought gravely.

"Another thing." Sybil announced it severely. "Mine
mustn't sing in his bath. I can't stand that; specially when
the plug is up. This here"—she indicated her cousin with
the stem of her cigarette holder—"sings 'O lovely night,'
regularly every morning."

"Pity you hit on that one," returned Allan quite
unmoved. "It's one of the few tunes I *don't* profess to
massacre. Besides, one must do something to keep one's
heart up in a cold bath."

"I knew a chap once," Dennys's gentle tones made
themselves heard, "who had a filthy habit of smoking
scented cigarettes in his bath."

"Well, God pity *his* wife!" spake Sybil severely.

"I think it was from his wife he learnt it. Anyway, it's not as bad as what Elizabeth does. I found her the other day with Driscoll—my little dog, you know—in the bath with her. She said it was the easiest way to wash him."

"Do you bath Elizabeth?" Sybil put the question, wide-eyed.

"No, of course not. But some one has to see that she washes behind her ears, and Lizzie's hopeless about it." A slight blush of modesty became visible beneath Dennys's tan, and his excursions into the conversation having (as usual) resulted in confusion for himself, he relapsed into silence and reflected on the extreme smallness of his hostess's brogues, till called upon to rise and resume his place in the line of guns.

During the afternoon they covered perhaps another four miles, all rough walking over heather, bog, and bracken, and added another brace of birds, and a hare— shot by Allan in a moment of abstraction—to the bag.

Six o'clock found them partaking of a late tea. Tired, but happy in a consciousness of a toil completed, a sensation none the less potent for the fact that the toil had been both enjoyable and illicit. Allan uncurled his long legs from the rungs of his chair, and, rising, brought his cup round to Ann, to be filled for the fourth time.

"Well," he observed thoughtfully, his eye on Sybil, who was abstractedly helping herself to the last of the jam, "I'd say it had been a good day—even a damn good day—but for one thing. That is, that Sybil——"

"Yes—Sybil what!" inquired the lady.

Allan took his cup from Ann's hand and returned to his seat.

"Sybil," he announced consequentially, "is a child in years. But in years only. In reality, her ways are devious, and she knows far more than she ought to know. She——"

Sybil favoured him with a glance from her green eyes. "Shut up," she said sweetly. "You dither!"

She looked round the table, and then proceeded to give the conversation a personal tone. This is a matter which presents no difficulties to the Sybils of this world; it is done by an imperceptible movement of the shoulders and a slight wavering of the eyelashes. Bold indeed the next-door-neighbour who ventures to join in a *tête-à-tête* from which he is thus pointedly though delicately excluded.

"I have," she continued, "a very old soul. I was told so by the last person who read my hand. Perhaps I was an Egyptian once; perhaps——" She paused.

"Cleopatra reincarnate," murmured her cousin, "you—you shrimp!" He finished his tea, helped himself to a cigarette, with a murmured, "Not for children," pushed the box across the table towards Dennys, and proceeded to search his person fruitlessly for matches.

"D'you know I haven't got a match, Sybil," he announced plaintively. "Get me the box off the mantel-shelf, like a good little thing," he finished with superb insolence.

Sybil rose obediently, even with alacrity.

"I think," she observed half a minute later, as she surveyed with satisfaction a reddening mark upon her cousin's square chin, "I might almost say that my eye was in to-day. In fact, it was what you might call shooting. I——"

But her soliloquy was interrupted, and her departure from the scene accelerated, by the arrival of Major Hillingdon. Allan left the room soon after, and tracking the lady to the hay-loft, there made his peace.

CHAPTER VII

The Greater Call

ANN was fed up, utterly and completely. It is not an elegant expression, nevertheless it is the one she used. And that was how she was feeling.

Everything, since that jolly old tea at six o'clock, had seemed to go wrong. Nothing, in fact, had gone right. From seven of the clock until seven-thirty that evening, she had heard her doings of the day described as iniquitous; and indeed, seen in the lurid limelight of parental disapproval, they appeared heinous enough. A daughter who will defy her aged father to the extent of bringing every idler in the country on to his mountain, to shoot *his* birds; who will allow—without protest—a spavined cart-horse to be foisted by a rogue upon a fool; one who spends her time giving tea and the parental cigarettes to a nasty bounder, against whom she has been warned, not once, but many times, by a devoted parent—a daughter who will do all these things—yea and more also—one who will not only permit, but encourage her hound puppies to leave long defunct cats where the unwary may tread upon their corpses—surely such a one is far gone in evil courses.

Ann didn't think so, but for all that it was very depressing, very. More, it was beastly unfair! She was no child of seventeen, to be hauled over the coals for every misdemeanour. She was a grown woman; and twenty-three is no mean age to have attained unto . . . woman's estate . . .she was pretty to. Leaving the deep arm-chair in which she was huddled, Ann crossed over to the dressing-table and sat long, very long, staring sombrely into her mirror.

Time passed. Her father came up to bed at eleven o'clock. She heard his step on the stairs and his voice speaking to the dogs. Ann sighed, and stood upright, raising her hands to ruffle her short hair pensively. The candle-light shadowed the curves where a black frock clung round her young slimness. Yes, she was good to look upon, was Ann. Very sweet and fair. Then, on a sudden, the night sent an errant mischief-making breeze, to blow in at her window, and stir to dissatisfied longings all her half-awakened senses. Her hands dropped from her hair, and she stood, deeply considering. Then, crossing over to the window, she leant her warm arms on the sash, and leaned out, listening to the night, sniffling the air delicately—head up, like a thoroughbred horse.

To the left of her window lay the soft depths of a fir-tree; below her, a vague white rose glimmered on its climbing stem, wantoning, listlessly; and to her came faintly the elusive scent of the late mignonette in the beds below.

Ann looked, and hearkened to all the voices of the night. And as she waited . . . listening . . . all the voices and scents sang together; calling to her, whispering, urging the sweetness of things undreamed.

Ann turned from them with a soft cry, and flung herself on her bed.

"I *want* him so," she cried. "Oh, why is Daddy such a pig!"

Five minutes later she had decided that bed was a banal place, more especially as it was the place her father would undoubtedly expect her to occupy at this hour. She sat on the edge of the banal bed for a few moments, in order to entertain the idea and consider her toes. Then she laughed, and opening her door very gently, crept downstairs, shoes in hand. How damnably the boards creaked! It would be just like father to come out and stop her, now that she was determined to go out and think all her new thoughts, quite alone, under the sky. Ann caught her breath as she heard a door-handle click loudly on the landing above— but no prosaic, pyjama-clad papa appeared.

Cautiously the girl bestrode the bannisters and slid silently to the foot of the stairs. With huge care she opened one of the billiard-room windows and was out on the lawn at last. Swiftly she gained the shelter of the laurels, and ran through them by the short cuts known to her childhood.

Something tugged at her heart and subdued her will, something which said "Come"—so she came. Frightened rabbits bounced in terror from her path; sleepy blackbirds made an unearthly noise, so indignant were they at being awakened; and sappy laurel boughs clapped back at her bare arms and face. But she didn't care! She laughed and ran on, deliciously, unreasonably happy, and anxious to "get there."

At last she reached the edge of the shrubbery, and climbing the fence which separated it from the river field, sat on the top strand of wire for a moment, poised against the sky in slim young grace. Then she jumped down, and her feet—quite of their own accord—found the trampled path that led to the seat under the cedar tree, with a view of river and mountain.

Ann walked into the deep gloom quietly, as if she was walking into church; and there, standing so as to obstruct her view of the mountains, was a man. Ann's first thought, and the one she acted on, was to say, "What are you doing under my cedar tree?" Her second thought, which arrived when it was too late—a habit second thoughts have—was to say nothing, but run away very quickly. For the man, instead of just answering that he was sorry, he'd only been snaring rabbits, turned round and said instead:

"Ann, Ann!"

The woman walked up to him, and slipped her hand into his and stood with her bare shoulder against his tweed arm, and—looked at the mountains.

This time the breeze came with a tang of wood-smoke, the first smell that the first man and woman smelled, when they set up house for the first time together. A very primeval smell of earth, warm, well-baked earth, while the spices of the cedar tree flowed forth and mingled with the murmuring wind. High up, a sleepy wood-pigeon clucked softly to himself before moving a little distance along his perching bough . . . it was a beautiful magic that the night wind was weaving. When she had made it very strong, she whispered in the ear of a fat trout in the river below, and he rose with an obedient plop at a fly which was not there. But the noise he made just completed the wind's spell, for when he heard it, Dennys said a very foolish and hackneyed word; though for all that it was the word the breeze had wanted him to say all along, and Ann too, for that matter.

"Darling!" was what he said; and Ann made answer, "Darling!" which was equally unoriginal. But she got no further, for after that the lips that he loved belonged to Dennys, for a short space, altogether. So did her hair, and the place on the nape of her neck that he had waited so long to kiss . . . and her round sweet throat and fast shut eyes . . . for a short space they were his and she was his.

There was no moon, though she is at best an indifferent chaperon; only one large star shone out, and it winked its eye, thoughtfully, from time to time. So they were quite, quite alone.

All the seeds which the night wind had sown in Ann's heart rooted and flowered in a moment. Their scent rushed through her, sweeping away in a little moment all the prejudices of years. She only knew that she was blindly, wonderfully, ecstatically happy, and that it was the most marvellous thing in the world to stand a-tiptoe between Dennys's fishing boots, and to feel his arms close, so close, and his beloved face in her hair.

Soon, from no particular direction, there came to them a straying, haunting, gay melody—a sound of pipes, thin, reedy, and elfin. Their happiness mounted to ecstasy as they listened. Then, subtly, the glad tune changed to wailing, and halted and broke. Ann shivered involuntarily.

"Are you cold, my dear?" Dennys asked her. "Ann, you precious thing, what a thoughtless brute I am! I shouldn't keep you out here, should I?"

"It's not that, my—*Dennys*!" For an instant she was close in his arms again, a blind ecstatic moment of exquisite surrender. It left her dizzy, shattered, and the man white and shaken. . . .Then she moved away, and picking up his old felt hat from the ground, fiddled softly with the dent in its crown.

"Look out," he warned her, "it's full of flies and tackle." Ann depositied a careful kiss in the dent she had made, and gave it back to him.

"Darling, I must go," she said. "Dennys, I—I *do* love

you." Then she turned and ran back down the path, climbed the fence and was lost to sight among the laurels.

Dennys came out from under the cedar tree and stood where he could see the path by which she must leave the shrubbery. He waited a good many minutes. The moon came out and flooded with light the spot where he had hoped to glimpse his lady-love. Why didn't she come? Ah, there was her shadow, lying long before her in the pool of moonlight. No, two shadows. It was his lady and some other person as well; a man—Allan Hillingdon! Dennys doubled his fists and took three long strides in the direction of the shrubberies; then his hands dropped to his sides, he faced about, picked up his rod and fishing basket, whistled softly to Driscoll, and turned towards home.

The sight of Allan's tall figure, lounging down the shrubbery path, came as something of a surprise to Ann, scuttling with haste up the same path. She paused uncertainly, waiting for him to speak.

"Hullo, Iseult!" he said. He had forgotten who Iseult was, but the name seemed to suit this moonlit maiden, with her radiant face. "Enjoying the moonlight like myself?"

Ann came back with a whirr to every-day life.

"Is there a moon?" she asked; adding confusedly: "Oh, yes, I am. It's such a heavenly night, bed seems impossible somehow. Father'd be inexpressibly shocked, though. Come on in."

"Oh, must we?" Allan was distressed. "What about the river, Ann? Hasn't it any attractions?"

"No," she said, "none, none!"

"God gi' ye good even then, m'lady." Allan bent over her hands. "I wish I had a *chapeau bras*," he murmured plaintively, "then perhaps you'd be kind to me."

"I wouldn't like to be unkind to anybody," she told him softly. "My aunt! There's Dad opening the billiard-room window. What sort of a row will I get now?"

Miss Hillingdon and her cousin crossed the lawn intervening between moonlight and the wrath-to-come, in silence and very demurely. On the ancient precept of a soft answer turning away wrath, Ann had formulated, by the time the billiard-room window was reached, a pretty enough apology.

"Yes, I know, darling," she said, "my aunts would be horrified, and I shouldn't be gadding round at this time of night. It was very, very wrong, but not at all chilly, and"—she held up a dutiful cheek for the parental salute—"good night, Daddy dear; good night, Allan. I may have something to break to you all in the morning, when you're feeling strong."

She smiled at them radiantly and was gone, having spiked her parent's gun, neatly enough.

"Well, I'm damned!" said the Major hopelessly. He stood looking out on the lawn for a moment, listening to the sound of galloping hoofs which came from the direction of the river field. "What the deuce has got those horses?" He closed the window. "Well, there's no wire there, so it doesn't much matter. Good night, my boy. Time to turn in, eh?"

"Quite, sir." Allan held the door open for his elderly cousin, and followed him upstairs.

"Now what the devil was up with Ann to-night?" he

asked of the hair-brushes on his dressing-table. "Turned me down, of course, but she seemed rather uplifted about something. Girls are splendid—girls are simply splendid—rule us, and fool us, as every fellow knows. . . . What the dickens am I quoting from? Cousin Ronnie was confoundedly genial, too—can't think why. The dear old lad's been almost frosty to me occasionally lately. Well, bed, I suppose."

Allan yawned enormously and proceeded to divest himself of his clothes.

CHAPTER VIII

Six O'clock Sport

DESPITE the late hours she had kept the previous evening, Ann awoke at the grey gloomy hour of five a.m. It would perhaps be more correct to say that her slumbers were broken by the arrival in her bedroom of her small brother, Rickey, fully dressed and in somewhat sporting attire. So much was apparent to Ann as she sat up, rubbing her eyes, for she was very sleepy.

"Oh, cubbing, of course. Rick, what on earth are you doing in those clothes?" she inquired, when she had fully taken in the extravagances of her brother's costume, for he wore, in addition to a remarkably neat pair of breeches, made for him at his own particular request by the village tailor, an old black hunting coat of his father's. Now Major Hillingdon was a small man, while Rickey, though tall for his twelve years, was hardly of a height to prevent the tails of the coat from trailing behind in a manner at once ridiculous and pathetic. In his button-hole was a small bunch of violets, and round his inadequate calves twined and romped a pair of Fox's puttees. His neck was innocent of collar and tie, and it was on this omission that Ann first remarked. In criticizing the vagaries of Richard's attire, it was always as well to start carefully at some point the eccentricity of which he could not argue.

"What price a clean collar, old man?"

"Oh, that'll be all right." Rickey left the bedside, and striding over to the chest of drawers, proceeded to make a thorough search in the top drawer.

"Where the deuce d'you keep your hunting stocks,

Ann? I tried one of Daddy's, but they're all that beastly old-fashioned sort that holds your chin up. You know! Ah! here we are. Will you tie it for me like a dear. I can't get the hang of the rotten thing."

Ann took the proffered band of linen and looked at her brother in a propitiating fashion.

"You know that a collar and tie are more correct for cubbing," she told him.

"Rot! Elizabeth's going to wear a stock," announced Rickey with great decision; "one of Dennys's."

"Oh, very well." Ann surrendered unconditionally. "Stand still, old man, or how can I tie it. There—go and look at yourself."

Rickey surveyed himself in the cheval glass for several moments. Apparently his toilet did not give him quite the glow of satisfaction he had anticipated when designing it. Turning to his sister he inquired with abandon: "Tell me, Ann—do I look an ass behind?"

"Well, darling, it is very long. I think, really, one of your own coats'd be more the thing," she told him eagerly.

"Oh, you won't notice that once I'm up on Juniper. She's so deuced fat, she'll sort of hold the tails out with her sides. And I say, Ann, *will* you lend me your mauve mouche rag? Thanks awfully. You know, I think the towt ensembly's rather fine."

After another prolonged prink, Beau Brummel made tracks for the door, pausing *en route* to give his sister the opportunity of making one of her encouragingly flattering remarks. She did not fail him.

"It's jolly nice," she said, "and those violets and the mauve hankey give quite the right touch of subdued colour. Just see that Sybil gets up, will you, darling, or we shan't get off till ten o'clock."

"I'll see that Allan gets up, if you like," he answered, "but I'm not going near Sybil. Think I want to have her bagging her yellow waistcoat off me—not much!"

With which he closed the door firmly, and Ann got out of bed and said her prayers, repeating over and over:

"Thank you very much—I thank Thee, Lord. . . . Dennys will be at the meet. . . .Dennys will be at the meet. . . .Dennys will . . ." She gave it up in despair.

At about a quarter to six, Ann and Allan and Rickey were in the loose-boxes of their mounts. Ann and Rickey were putting the finishing touches to unruly manes, while Allan was leaning against the stable-door, very much in Fox's way, as he trotted and ran, in and out, back and forth.

"Yez had a right to be off out o' this half an hour ago," he announced. "The way ye'll not be destroyin' the horses and you beltin' them along the hard road to Knockure. God knows they're in a bad way altogether, without this trash o' hunting before it'd be making day."

"Why, what's the matter with them?"

Sybil had just arrived on the scene, and now stood in the open stable-door, straightening her felt hat, and buttoning her gloves. "They sure look a bit jaded. Maybe it was yourself and Aiden had them out last night, Fox, going to Johnny Byrne's wake."

"When I came in the yard this morning," Fox pointedly ignored Sybil's innuendo, "I declare to you, Miss Ann, there wasn't one o' them horses but was drenched down with the sweat. And as for the big fella beyont"—he indicated Garry Owen's box—"he was that strange in himself ye couldn' shpit on him—ye could not lay a hand on him," he amended hastily.

"Why, what was up with them? Had they seen a ghost or what?" Allan inquired.

"Arrah, what ghost?" Fox broke in almost angrily. Then he spat secretively behind his hand, and continued in a hushed voice: "It's what th' ould woman I have was saying, she heard *that one* lasht night, and he piping down by the river, the way ye'd fill yer heart lish'ning to him. An' sure the world knows that's very unhealthy for horses—God save them! Meself I think they'd have enough done if ye brought them the length of the meet, and back, itself, miss," he finished, as he held the new brown, looking in truth deplorable enough, for Allan to mount.

"Ah, maybe the ride'll freshen them, Fox," Ann answered, seating herself neatly in the side saddle and squaring off her reins.

Sybil was the last to mount. Fox held her off stirrup in sour disapproval.

"I'd say 'twas a dangerous thing for a young lady to sit above on a horse that way," he told her, as he watched the youthful exuberances of Pet Girl, who seemed less affected by the general blight than her fellows, "and very ugly. I'd sooner have the way Miss Ann rides, and she's able to sit a damn sight tighter over her fences than what you are, Miss Sybil."

Sybil laughed. "What an old grouser you are, Fox! It's a long time now since I've cut a voluntary!"

"Well, maybe, maybe," Fox stooped to pluck a wad of bedding out of the mare's hoof, "but for all, a pairson'd be able to shoot shnipes very handy betuxsht youself and the saddle, and you going over a two-foot wall. Mind youself, now," he called, as the four rose out of the yard, "that's a terrible loose mare to shy."

They rode single-file along the narrow back avenue. Ann, ahead of the others, sang aloud for very gladness of heart. Was not the sun shining? Was not the first nip of frost in the air? And wasn't she going to see Dennys . . . to see Dennys . . . to see Dennys. . . .? The thought sang in her brain and flowered in her heart. She wanted to gallop Fenian all the way to the meet, that she might see him and hear him speak the sooner. She wanted to feel the wind strong in her face, shouting to her of the greatness of her happiness. Forgotten was old Johnny St Lawrence and all his vulgarities and bestialities; forgotten the thought of what every one would say when it was known that she was to marry "old St Lawrence's boy." "What, that old ruffian?" "Not really." "Good Lord!"

Well, let them! She didn't care. She wasn't marrying old St Lawrence, or his family, or his friends—she was marrying Dennys. "He didn't ask me to," she gurgled inwardly, "but I'm dashed if I don't." She felt suddenly an overwhelming desire to tell the others, Allan, Sybil, and Rickey; to say, "Dennys and I are engaged. Isn't it ripping? Isn't it splendid? Isn't he a darling?" Then she thought, "No, I won't tell them yet. I hope Dennys hasn't told his father either. He'll be so—so dashed jovial when he hears." Hullo, what was Sybil saying? Ann detached her mind from the subject of Dennys with something of an effort.

"Yes, Sybil, what?"

". . . if you don't send him home, you jolly well ought too. He's perfectly disgraceful. How could you let him come out like that?" This was evidently the winding up of some comments on the extravagance of Rickey's attire.

"Oh, he's all right," Ann answered tolerantly, surveying Rickard's coat, the long tails of which were not appreciably shortened by Juniper's portly barrel. "I think he's rather chic. Don't you, Allan?"

Allan looked his young cousin over judicially, from romping stock to winding puttees. "Distinctly tricky— one might almost say passionate," was his verdict. "I like the nuance round his neck. What is it? Ah yes, a stock. Well, at least the waistcoat is past reproach. Who's the lady anyway, Rickey?"

"Oh, you're a smelly lot. Awfully funny, aren't you?" burst forth the overwrought Rickard. "All jolly fine for you! *You'll* be hunting all the winter, and when I come back, you'll probably have Juniper lamed on me, like last time; Ann won't have a clean stock left in the world, and Daddy'll've decided this is the only coat that fits him, just because it happens to fit me. Sybil calls me a fool to wear it—jolly sight fatter fool she is herself. Elizabeth says so and Fox says so. So fat sucks, Miss Hillingdon— juicy sucks!"

"Oh, look here," interrupted Allan, "that's a thing no perfect gentleman says to a lady, however great the provocation."

"And anyway," said Ann, bringing her lump of putty to cement the breach in the family harmony, "according to Fox, we'll break our necks to-day, so you needn't worry about our laming Juniper for you during the term, Rickey."

"Did Fox say that?" Allan inquired, as the brown shied lavishly at some water spilled in the road. "This animal seems a bit nervy somehow. What was Fox chattering about anyway? A lot of rot about a piper or something, wasn't it?"

The three Irish Hillingdons looked at each other and then between their horses' ears—not at Allan. Then Sybil laughed, she never could stay silent for two minutes together, and spoke the thing that was:

"We are asses!" she said.

"Oh, I wouldn't go so far as to say that," Allan reassured her; "it's only this Celtic mystery that's a bit beyond a mere Saxon like myself. I don't want to butt in on the family skeleton, believe me."

Ann pulled her horse into a walk. "There's no mystery about it," she said, "only Dad doesn't like it talked about; it upsets the maids, and you noticed how queer Fox was to-day."

"Do stop saying 'it,' like a good girl. It makes me feel all prickly. What is 'it' anyway?"

"He's the piper," Rickey broke in suddenly, and they all turned to look at him.

Allan thought the boy's face looked smaller than usual. "Kid's scared! Better not ask any more," he decided. "Dashed funny though!"

But Rickey continued of his own accord. "He doesn't often pipe," he said, "but he's always around some place. Pipes sound awfully queer; jolly at first, and then rotten. I heard him once when I was hiding from Burke under the gooseberry bushes. Burke was awfully waxy . . . and then the piper began to play, in the nut-walk somewhere, and Burke started to spit like anything . . . that was just before I broke my arm this summer."

"I say, let's canter along here."

Ann interrupted Rickey's long discourse, and suggested with the heel of a small boot that Fenian might leave the hard macadam, which he preferred to the strip of grass by the roadside. Shaking him into a canter. Allan followed her. Sybil and Rickey, remaining behind, shouted virtuously that that was no way to ride to a meet, cubbing or no.

About half a mile further on, Ann pulled up and turned to Allan a flushed and glowing face.

"Wasn't that glorious? Why is it one never gets tired of a horse? Tennis and golf and every game—yes! But a horse just puts you in tune again every time." There was exaltation in her voice. "Look out! here's a motor. That beast hates 'em." Laughingly she laid a hand on her cousin's rein, and he removed it with some care. As the car passed them, she recognized the driver as Dennys; he raised his hat politely, gave the horses a wide berth, and drove on.

"Let's wait for the others," said Ann. She dropped her reins on Fenian's neck and allowed him to snatch mouthfuls of green wayside grass. The brown followed his example as voraciously as if his last meal had happened a week past. Allan put his reins over his crop, stuck the crop under his knee, and lit a cigarette. Ann thoughtfully watched him smoke for a few minutes, wondering idly why Dennys had driven the car to the meet. Allan interrupted her reverie.

"Wonder why the St Lawrence chap isn't hunting?" he observed.

"Oh, but I'm sure he is—he'd 've said so if he wasn't."

"Well, he was wearing trousers, so he can't be hunting," said Allan conclusively. "Nice chap, but fearfully pig-headed, I should think," he continued. "Does he run the hounds or does 'Father'?"

"Oh, he does everything, he and Johnny Brien between them. 'Father' pays the piper—or doesn't pay as the case may be. Hullo! here are the others."

"Well, *mes enfants*," Sybil pulled Pet Girl up and sat half round in her saddle, "you look devilish romantic, I must say, and the autumnal woods surely make a fair background for so pretty a picture. Pet Girl's sensing you with her nostrils—the way horses in books do. By the way, did Dennys pass you?" she inquired, as they jogged along the last half-mile to Knockure. "He told us that he was going to Meath to look at a horse that ran second in some point-to-point or other. Rather rot, I call it! We won't get out of the woods to-day."

"Did he say that he was going to Meath, Sybil?" Ann felt puzzled and rather hurt. "Then he won't be out this morning. Funny he didn't tell us."

"Probably thought you were too engrossed in your own affairs to worry about any little thing like that. Were you cantering joyfully along, or just resting your horses in that jolly little hole in the hedge where we found you, when he passed?"

Sybil possessed in a large measure the art of saying nasty things with their edge off; consequently to Allan, this speech conveyed nothing but "Sybil's usual rot," while with Ann it bit and stung as her sister had meant it to do. Ann did not have to think out an adequate reply, however, as at that moment they were joined by two other riders, Lady Muriel Dane and her brother John.

"Hallo—'allo—'allo!" Sybil greeted them cheerfully. "What's my son John doing so far from home?"

"He's very busy riding," answered the Honourable John, a youth whose one redemption from complete plainness was a charming smile. "When fourteen days, three times a year, are all the leave the exigencies of the Service permit a fella, a brute like this thing old St Lawrence sold Muriel as a lady's patent safety, requires all the spare parts of one's attention. I haven't time to flirt with you, Sybil!" he finished regretfully.

His mount, a very light middled chestnut mare, with a wild eye and a wild mane, here made a determined effort to kick the spruce Pet Girl.

"Here, you're not nice to know!" Sybil pulled out to the far side of the road. "Why not tie some red tape on that wild woman's tail? She nearly killed us that time. Hullo! here are the hounds. Nice of the master to wait! Oh, he's holding forth about something. Did you know that Dennys'd gone buying horses? Are there any cubs about? Hello, Jimmy! Lovely morning, isn't it?"

Sybil greeted another member of her train of willing slaves, a train which made up in devotion what it lacked in numbers, and one which was handled by the object of its devotion with a finesse, and withal a kindliness, not often found in one so young—one might almost say so inexperienced, but for the undoubted fact that Sybil had arrived at her present incarnation endowed with a subtlety and gift for intrigue which could easily have afforded points to a successful twenty-eight-year-old player of the game.

"I say, Ann," Rickey rode up to his sister, who was walking her excited youngster round in circles, "he's going to put the hounds in at the bottom of Knockure Woods. I vote we move on now—if he breaks at all, it'll be over the hill he'll go."

"I don't think I will, Rick. They'll not leave the woods for hours, and—and I want to see how Deemster's entered." She hesitated. "By the way, did Dennys tell you why he was going to Meath? Stand, boy! Quiet, can't you!"

Rickey eyed his sister and her restless mount for a moment.

"If you'd let the curb alone, he'd stand all right," he suggested tactlessly. "No, I don't know why he went; horses, I suppose. Oh, he'll tell you—I say, Mr St Lawrence, Ann wants to know why Dennys has gone to Meath."

Ann, who had failed to notice that worthy's approach, was covered with confusion. Had she had any more powerful weapon in her hand than a crop, it would have gone hard with the tactless, though well-meaning Rickard. His clear, boyish voice had been plainly audible to all and sundry, as were also the Master's lengthy explanations of his son's absence.

"As if it were anything to me," thought poor Ann, "whether he's here or not." But all the time she knew that it meant a great deal more to her than she cared to own.

"Well, he'll be most gratified to hear that you were asking for him." The Master concluded his harangue and moved off, leaving Ann happier, inasmuch as she now knew that what his father specified as "urgent business" had taken Dennys to Meath, whence he was returning in the course of a few days.

Being fully occupied with Fenian's misdemeanours—

having recovered from his lethargy, he was showing a marked disposition to buck—Ann, like a wise girl, put the matter out of her mind—and, as the big four-year-old jumped "the height of himself" over two foot of a furze-filled gap into Knockure Woods, most of Ann's early morning light-heartedness returned. Why should there be any bad luck or evil fortune to touch her in this best of all possible worlds? Anyway, what did she care—so long as she had her hunting? "The fox, the 'ound, the 'orse"— where could you find anything to touch it? In her way, Ann was as single-minded a sportsman even as Dennys.

Cubbing is a form of sport which appeals most strongly to those who love hounds as well as hunting. These enthusiasts may at their leisure appreciate the beauties of hound work in covert; the initiation, sometimes painful, of the young entry, and the unhurried wisdom of their seniors.

The many rides which crossed and recrossed in Knockure Woods made perfect places from which to see hounds work; but their treacherous mazeries also provided snares innumerable for the unwary. At any moment an irate master might appear, seemingly from nowhere, to damn and denounce all who stood in his path; the next instant to be lost to sight, while his field, hovering uncertainly amidst the treacherous rides, heard his horn and his "gone away," as the fox broke far from where they were. Ensued fruitless gallopings up rides and down rides, and by the time the blown horses were clear of the hill-side, to their riders came faintly the heart-searching cry of hounds, who have missed blood by the length of a brush and put their fox to ground somewhere in the fastnesses of his home coverts. Moral, stay on the hillside! Yes, pursue this course if you will, and the chances are ten to one your fox breaks—if a fox he be and not an untutored cub—at the bottom, and the anxious watchers on the hillside see hounds and hunt streaming away down the valley, while they are left as badly as when previously they stuck to the woods.

But this was cubbing—a very different matter. Ann was expounding these difficulties while they waited on the outskirts of the wood, listening to old St Lawrence's voice as it rose and fell in encouragement to his young entry.

'Troi f'r 'im Woodbine . . . troi—troi—troi . . . eleu in Ravager . . . ge-et 'in t'cover, Spinster . . . *Spinster*! . . . Hangin' around . . . Hangin' around. . . .Yo-oi, *Woodbine*. . . .' His voice grew fainter in the distance. A hound strayed across the ride a hundred yards from where Ann and her cousin sat on their horse, another and another, nosing interestedly at bracken tufts and tree-stumps, feathering ever so slightly.

"That's Deemster," Ann indicated a small hound dog. "Puppy I walked—by Jove! you'd almost say——"

A bare-footed lad leapt on the fence behind them and pointed across the grey-dewed field. "Oh, look! Look! Look at he, how cute he is! He has the dogs bet. Look at he sneakin' off!"

Ann swung Fenian round.

"Did you see the fox?"

"I did, miss. Oh, oh, oh, look below!"

Ann, following the direction of the pointing finger, made out a slim moving form slipping quietly along the edge of the field, almost invisible in the early morning murk.

Even as Allan crooked his finger behind his ear and gave vent to a piercing Tally, Deemster—best entered puppy of the lot—flung his beautiful head up, owning to scent with one melodious howl; then together with seven couples more, he scrambled through the fence, tried for a moment, then hurled himself on to the line.

As Fenian galloped with her over the first field, pulling all he knew, Ann was aware of the Master hurtling past on his big grey.

"It's early days to ride the country!" he called jovially. "It's for the old kiln he'll make. Stick to me now!"

"If I don't ride over you," thought Ann, as Fenian, dragging his head away, galloped wildly at a small bank. The next thing Ann was aware of was the ground which rose at her in the most unprovoked manner, and hit her a terrific whack on the head. There followed a period of oblivion, from which she awoke to find herself lying on a lumpy sofa, one that smelt abominbly musty, in a room quite unknown to her. With a jerk, the oil-cloth covered table and garish pictures of saints which hung upon the walls swam back into their places, and Ann recognized her surroundings. Of course—she was "back in the room" in the covert keeper's cottage, with Mrs Hanlon watching her face, and murmuring, "God help us—the creature!" at decent intervals.

Ann choked and sat up. "I've had a fall?" she asked stupidly.

"Yes, the deuce of a toss!" It was Allan's voice that answered her. "Drink this, and I'll tell you about it."

While she drank out of an enormous wine-glass something which tasted inconceivably nasty, her cousin informed her of the facts:—

(*a*) That he had never felt so shaken in his life;

(*b*) That concussion was the least of the evils he had feared for her before she had deigned to sit up and take notice;

(*c*) That Fenian had obviously shut his eyes and taken the bank with his chest.

"Has he hurt himself?" interpolated Ann.

"Right as rain!" replied her cousin cheerily. Reassured on this point, Ann rose somewhat unsteadily to her feet, and announced her intention of remounting and finding the hounds.

Her temporary hostess, groaning heavily, protested against such wanton, nay sinful, flying in the face of Providence.

"And it only God's mercy she wasn't stretched a corpse at me feet!"—thus spoke Mrs Hanlon, recounting the incident later in the day to her husband,—"and she to defy all the way she did. 'I'll go folly the dogs,' she said. 'Twas then the Captain was with her proved very good. 'Ye will not,' he said. 'In God's name,' says he, 'let us come on home out o' this to your da. He'll skin the two of us surely. It's what we'd be no more than straws to him in his passion.'" Here Mrs Hanlon paused to give due weight to the next development in her story. "Oh, the *look* he left on her. She went then."

James Hanlon lit his pipe, with slow smacking noises, before permitting himself his only comment on the story.

"She had a right to be killed," he said.

"Oh God!" remarked his wife, conclusively and with befitting reverence. "Did ye get the lend of the horse and car off Mary Dempsey?" she inquired after a pause.

"I did not," returned Jamsey a thought morosely. "I

seen herself and one o' poor Maurice's little gerrls drivin' the ould pony up the long yellow hill to Lisogue. 'It's a pet day,' I said to her. She passed no remark at all, only to give a belt to th'ould pony. 'Me aunt's very vexed,' said the little one was with her then. 'Oh, why so?' I said. 'Isn't it what the people says she's the qui'test woman in three parishes.' She pulled up the pony with that and she gave me one look. Christians! She had a face on her as black as the Earl o' Hell's riding boot!"

Jamsey paused at the psychologically perfect moment, to light his pipe, before resuming.

"'Isn't it a quare thing,' she said to me, 'with all the chat they have they'd pairsecute a poor woman the way they're after doing it to meself. Never mind them that took Maurice, they are poor people and God will surely punish them. But there's others—may the devil poach them,' she said, 'and they having their two fists full o' gold, and the grandest o' clothes on them, and they rolling in riches, and wouldn't think hard to thrick a poor woman of her little share.' I declare now, the sweat was coming from her with the passion.

"'Oh, oh,' I said. 'Well, well, isn't that too bad?' I asked her then what way was the brown horse she had; for I wouldn't choose to have the people on the roads hear he drawing up poor Maurice's name to me—tho' indeed I had a great wish for Maurice always. Well, when I asked after the brown horse she went clean mad altogether. She laughed in my face. 'I sowld him,' she said 'and look what the devil' pup gev me for him.' She showed me a bank paper then with forty-five pounds on it. 'That was a hell of a good horse to go for forty-five pounds,' I said, the way I qui'ten her like. 'Is it forty-five pounds,' she squealed at me, the very same as a pig. 'No, nor forty-five pence. And devil dom the justice you'd get in this world and you a lone tormented woman.' She tore up the bit o' paper then, a bank cheque it was, like. Well, I allowed that was foolidge thing for her to go do; so with that, she gave taste o' the stick to th'ould hairo under the cart and took herself off. Faith I was as glad. That one's a great tease."

"God help poor Mary! It's great annoyance she got." Mrs Hanlon rose ponderously from her seat, and proceeded to clear the kitchen table of the debris of her husband's tea. Her task finished, she seated herself once more by the low-burning turf fire, a coarse woollen sock in her hand, and resumed the discussion.

"Ah, Mary's got great hardship always. Surely when the sister-in-law was put in th'asylum, ye'd say 'twas a pity of her; let alone them scab devils from the mountains taking poor Maurice, and he as good a pathriot as any of them."

Jamsey's eyes travelled round the small kitchen and came to rest again on his wife's face. He leant towards her and spoke in a low voice, punctuating his words with stabs of his pipe-stem.

"Isn't it what they're saying," he said, "that them as dhragged poor Maurice from the bed that night is the very same ones as is looking for him now."

"The Military?" murmured his wife interrogatively.

"Sure the world knows," James spoke with a rising tone of indignation in his voice, "that the little fella in the barracks—that—what's this I'll call him?—that *Captain* O'Connor is own brother to the man Jamsey fell out with in regard o' the bit o' land north of Lisogue. Faith herself was in the right of it! Devil dom the justice she'd see from them O'Connors. Sure there's a hell o' a click o' them up in the hills. And isn't Lisogue now the frightful place for a lone woman?"

"Oh, God be good to Mary!" moaned his wife. "And was it to the likes of them she'd go sell the horse?"

"It was not, then," returned Jamsey mysteriously. "It's one that's better able to pay for it tricked her of the money. A low, perverted, dirty schamer—and may the luck o' hell folly him!" With which pious sentiment, Jamsey rose and left the house.

"Oh my, isn't the world a fright!" commented Mrs Hanlon, as she leaned over the half-door to bid one Maggie to put in the turkeys from the foxes.

CHAPTER IX

Dancing Shadows

WRAPPING herself in her kimono—the blue kimono of Allan's dreams—Ann picked up a brass can and ran light-foot down the wide, dark corridor to the bath-room. There she found Allan shaving, Sybil being rude, and Rickard, girt in a towel, demanding the privacy every fellow has a right to expect in his perishing bath.

As she filled her can, Ann soothed, as best she might, the aggrieved Rickard, and admonished Sybil for lack of modesty—that young lady, attired in a shoulder strap and a few yards of flesh-coloured crêpe-de-chine, was endeavouring to study in her cousin's shaving mirror the effect of a deep red velvet rose against her black hair. Allan found shaving a difficult operation; though he allowed the situation to be piquant, it stopped short, he averred, on this side of being pleasing. Sybil, as she tilted the mirror to the light, reviled him in a few well-chosen words. Followed a distinctly one-sided contest, from which emerged a tumbled Sybil, who fled to her room, pursued by maledictions and a wet sponge, and ornamented lavishly with shaving lather.

An hour later, clothed and in her right mind, Sybil descended to the billiard-room, there to await the arrival of the rest of the party. If Ann was pleasing to the eye, Sybil was equally so. Taller than her sister, and longer on the leg, she was graceful as a young fawn. Her small dark head was deliciously poised on a rounded throat; her pointed face might have been cut from white marble, so pale was it that her undeniably attractive mouth took redder values in contrast. Her green eyes said a thousand things to the moment, nine hundred and ninety-nine of which had better been left unsaid. Her feet were charming—her ankles things to dream on.

To-night, as she sat on the old leather fender-seat in the billiard-room, delicately smoking one of Ann's Russian cigarettes and listening equally to the chaff and thinly veiled admiration showered upon her by her father, she looked, and felt, her very best.

"What's that dress going to cost me, I'd like to know?"

Sybil glanced down at the slim silken thing she wore, at her flesh-silk-clad legs and red-heeled shoes. She put up a hand to feel the red velvet rose in her smooth black hair. Then she raised her eyes trustfully to her father's face.

"Not so very much, Daddy dear," she reassured him. "Not so much"—she hesitated, ending with a rush—"not so much as my new habit."

For a moment, astonishment took the place of wrath in the Major's tones; this, however, was soon displaced by cold fury.

"May I ask," he inquired, rising as he spoke to hurl three inches of expensive cigar into the fire, "your reasons for ordering a new habit without consulting me on the subject? I suppose you know that habits cost money? I should think not less than——"

"Fifteen guineas!" supplemented his daughter, unabashed. "That is, astride ones. Side-saddle, they run up to almost any price."

"Good God!" shouted the Major, finally losing control of his hard-held temper, "do you imagine for a moment that I'm going to pay fifteen guineas for a perfectly indecent riding habit? Don't tell me it's not indecent; I know the beastly garments too well. Why the blazes can't you be content to ride side-saddle, and wear one of your poor mother's old habits? There are half a dozen of them lying idle this minute, good habits too. None of this beastly expanse of breeches about them."

Sybil faced the storm calmly. When it had somewhat expended itself, she informed her father, between puffs of smoke, that she had already received the habit in question from its makers; that she had worn it twice and had one fall in it, therefore she regretted her inability to return it; that he was a darling and she knew he wouldn't mind.

She ended by producing an undeniable bill for fifteen guineas.

"It's all very well, Sybil," Major Hillingdon remarked lugubriously, "but calling me a darling won't pay the blooming bill. And I may as well tell you now that I'm financially in no condition to have shocks of this sort sprung on me. I'm dam' hard up, and little trifles of fifteen-guinea habits, let alone eight guineas ... am I right? Yes, I thought so, eight-guinea dresses! Fact is, me dear child, if I could get Ann off my chest, I'd feel better."

Major Hillingdon, after making this somewhat surprising announcement, proceeded to pace up and down the hearthrug, much to the discomfort of the two little dogs.

"It'd be a good thing if she and Allan managed to hit it off, eh? Fact, that was largely in my mind when I asked him to stay here for the hunting." Major Hillingdon laughed, delightedly as a child, at his own consummate wiliness. "We must contrive, Sybil"—here he picked up one of the white dogs, and seated himself on the fender beside his daughter—"to throw 'em together more, as it were. To let them see a good bit of each other. You know

what I mean—let 'em go out after snipe alone, occasionally. A little tact is always necessary on these occasions."

"Quite," agreed his daughter cheerfully. "There's only
one thing you've forgotten, and that is that Ann doesn't
care a rap about him."

"Well, why doesn't she?" demanded Ann's justly irri-
tated parent. "After all the trouble I've taken about it, she
ought to. Nothing to do with that St Lawrence fella, I
hope?" he demanded suspiciously.

Sybil dropped her cigarette into the fire and stared at
her father coolly.

"My dear Dad—well, hardly!"

Her tone implied that such a suspicion was unworthy
of the parent who fostered it, and next door to an
aspersion on Ann's sense of what could, and could not, be
done.

"Oh, of course not, of course not! Thing's impossible!
He hasn't been here for some weeks now, either, has he?
All the better. Well, don't forget what I've told you," he
added in an obvious aside, as Ann, followed by her cousin,
entered the room.

Allan drove the Ford to Aidens Mount, the home of
Mr and Mrs Jeeves, and the scene of the dance. A rather
silent Ann sat beside him; an Ann who told herself over
and over again that she was going to see Dennys at the
dance, and then the silence of the last weeks would be
explained. To think that she had scarcely seen him since
that precious half-hour, now so long ago! Ann glowed, as
she did fifty times a day, at the remembrance of it. To-
night the anticipation of seeing him again, of holding his
dear face near hers, of hearing him say silly darling things
in his earnest voice, filled her blood with a wild sweet

surging, which reduced the 25 m.p.h. of stout Henry Ford to a sorry jog-trot indeed.

The three occasions upon which they had met since that memorable evening had proved inauspicious for any renewal of the theme uppermost in the mind of each. Upon one, her father had been present; on another, Elizabeth had flatly refused to be shaken off; while on yet a third—well, the exigencies of a morning's cubbing permit of few interruptions. But to-night—tonight! a ripple of irrepressible laughter rose in Ann's throat as she thought of the hours that would be theirs.

Half an hour later, Ann, Sybil, Allan and John Dane (Sybil's partner) were responding suitably to their hostess's rapturous greeting. As they made their way from the stair-foot, where Mrs. Jeeves—terribly resplendent in pink satin—received her guests, to the already crowded ball-room, John Dane ostentatiously loosened his collar.

"Sybil, my girl, lend me your programme an instant," he implored.

"No, dear, I think *not*." Sybil paused and wrote hastily on her slip of pasteboard. "But you may have 1, 4, 7, 11 and the extras."

"They're at No. 3 already," expostulated John Dane, "and if you don't let me have a few more, I shall have to dance with some of the young ladies Tessie's imported from Newbury. Didn't you hear her being jovial about them, a minute ago?"

"Hardly worse than the young men from Dublin I'll be introduced to? Last dance here, one of 'em asked me if I liked jazzing, and wanted to know if I was a keen follower of the hounds. Ye gods! Here's Charlie Jeeves charging down with one now. Quick, John!"

"How delicious you smell," observed John softly, a moment later, as they joined the tide of dancers, "but have you really forgotten your socks, or is it only in my heated imagination that your adorable understandings are bare and pink? Tell me, Sybil."

Sybil's dark eyelashes drooped provokingly. Her rose-red feather fan posed artistically behind the Hon. John's dark head, while her red-heeled shoes and lissom young body moved entrancingly to the syncopations of the band. She was absolutely and completely in her element.

Dennys—as he put his Rover 8 into second on the last of the hills on the road from Cloonbeg to Aidens Mount—asked himself savagely, and for the hundredth time, why he was going to this confounded show. The answer was the same as it had been for the ninety and nine previous times of asking—because he must see Ann, must find out, once and for all, how matters stood between them, must know the reason of the meeting he had witnessed between herself and Allan, after she had left him that precious night, which now seemed such infinite worlds away.

All very ridiculous, doubtless, but it should be borne in mind that Dennys was young, that he took the inferiority of his social standing as compared with Ann's, very hardly. And further, he was passionately aware of the advantages which would be hers as the wife of Allan Hillingdon, compared with those which he, Dennys St Lawrence, with nothing but an MC and a good war record, had to offer.

And yet . . . and yet . . . she was so much the lady of his heart, and he had hoped, if only the horse business would look up, that in a year or two, perhaps . . . he had hoped, well, that she would ride into his life and that thenceforth all their riding would be done together—dreams—damned idle dreams!

Dennys parked the little Rover, and went into the house. The strains of the band came faintly to the lamp-lit hall where he stood. A couple, seeking seclusion, passed him and entered one of the cars outside the door.

"Dennys, me dear boy," his hostess's voice boomed greetings. "Aren't you very late? I declare that's aw'fly naughty of you! There's the sweetest little girl here from Newbury, and I won't introduce you in punishment for your sins."

Dennys found himself laboriously forging a reply to the effect that a dance with his hostess would amply compensate him for the loss of the Newbury charmer, and a moment later they were fox-trotting together. As he gloomily pushed his partner through the crowd, Dennys looked everywhere for Ann, but without success. It was not till the end of his dance with the sweet little girl from Newbury—to whom his hostess, willy-nilly, had introduced him—that he saw her. She was dancing with Allan, her curly pate about on a level with her partner's middle stud. Dennys could see that they were executing some intricate step, and laughing over it like two children. Allan was dancing with her as if she was something immensely precious and fragile; more—as if she was *his* to take care of. As they passed one of the exits which opened on to the side of the house where were parked the long line of motors, he saw them stop dancing, and go out into the comparative shadow of the porch. Then he saw Allan pick up his partner as though her eight stone odd had been but two, and stride off with her into the darkness.

"Oh, *did* you see that cave-man stunt?" the Newbury girl wanted to know.

"No, I missed it," returned her partner in his most leisurely tones. "What's that new thing you were trying to show me—not that—the other one where you pause forward . . . have I got it now? You know, you really are a priceless little dancer."

The yellow-haired girl fluffed. This silent, though undoubtedly good-to-look-at young man was at last coming on.

Ann's bouffant pale pink skirts took up most of the space in the Danes' big car, into which her cousin had lifted her—the remainder was occupied by a strangely elated Allan. In his hand was a minute pink and silver brocaded slipper, on his face an expression of the utmost solicitude.

"How's it feel now?" he inquired for the twentieth time. "Shall I get you a drink?"

Ann's interest in a slim left ankle, poised across her right knee, temporarily elapsed.

"No, thanks, old thing," she responded; "I'll be as right as rain in a moment. Awfully silly of me to fuss, but I've wrenched this ankle before, and it's the mischief and all the first minute or so. Fact,"—she laughed a little shakily—"it was all I could do not to sit down on the floor and howl when it happened. Your assistance was most prompt, though. And now," she ended hastily, "if you have such a thing as a cigarette on you, all would be bliss."

Allan produced one, lit it for her, and sat in silence for several minutes, watching her delicious profile outline and fade, as the tip of her cigarette glowed and paled. At last Allan cleared his throat ominously, and leant towards the pink figure beside him.

"Ann," he began, "I——"

"D'you know, Allan," she interrupted, "there's one thing I really want at this moment, and that's an ice. Do go and get *two*—one for you and one for me. And mine's a pink one."

It was not until he had reached the buffet to fulfil her behest in the matter of pink ice, that Allan became aware that the pink shoe was still in his hand. When he awoke to the fact, he slipped it into his pocket unconcernedly as if it had been his handkerchief.

As Ann sat in the car, gently massaging her injured ankle, she felt distinctly worried. She liked Allan, and therefore did not wish him to propose to her, a declaration to which, her unerring instinct told her, he was about to commit himself. But there was a far more important matter—Dennys had not yet turned up to claim the dances left blank for him on her programme! Up to date, she had danced two of them with Allan, and another with one of Tessie's appalling importations from Dublin, when by rights she should have been sitting them out with her Dennys.

Dash it! There she was, shoeless, and virtually chained to this blessed car, while he was probably looking everywhere for her. It was at this juncture that the subject of her meditations passed her, walking rather fast in the direction of the avenue gate. Ann wrestled desperately with the window strap for an instant, then put her fair head out into the thick drizzle which was falling at the moment.

"Dennys!" she called. "Captain St Lawrence!" But no answer came out of the mist.

She pulled up the window, and stared blankly at the plate glass opposite. What the deuce was the matter?

Allan's return, with two brimming glasses of champagne, cheered her considerably, and during the next quarter of an hour she was fully occupied in staving off the proposal which she now realized to be inevitable.

"By Jove! I've missed Sybil's dance!" Allan exclaimed in horror, after his many fruitless efforts to give the conversation a more personal turn had been baulked.

"You'll look after me, won't you, Ann, if she's annoyed?"

"I will! But I shouldn't worry over it if I were you; she's probably forgotten it was yours. So occupied with the Naval Dane to-night, y'know."

"I wish you'd be just a little occupied——" began Allan, but Ann interrupted him swiftly.

"My shoe, please," she demanded.

"How," inquired her cousin, as he placed the flimsy article upon her outstretched foot, "does one fasten all these innumerable gadgets? Don't hurry me; let me think it out. It's as good as fifteen quid's worth of Pelmanism any day. Besides, your foot is so very lovely. You know, Ann——"

"I know that I'll never get my shoe on if I leave it to you, partner." Ann bent to the task of weaving an intricate pattern in silver ribbon round her ankle. "Listen! Aren't they playing that thing from 'Laughing April'? Let's go in and dance. Yes, the ankle's quite all right, thanks. Please, Allan—if you're going to be foolish, I won't dance with you."

When they re-entered the ball-room, the fun was becoming both fast and furious. Was this owing to the matrons having deserted their bridge tables for the maze of the dance? Partly perhaps, and partly to the excellent champagne provided by Mr Jeeves.

Lady Muriel Dane hissed into Ann's ear a tale of supper speechifiers, whose efforts to propose toasts had stuck in their throats.

"That old ruffian John Lynch"—she indicated for Allan's benefit a purple-faced individual in the hunt coat, who was at the moment using his partner as a battering ram with which to cleave his not over-steady way through the dancers—"got up to propose Charlie Jeeves' health, only his wife who was sitting beside him kept clutching him by the coat-tails and imploring him to shut his mouth and come home for God's sake."

"They're taking bets now on how long he'll stand up," volunteered Lady Muriel's partner.

"*No!* Go and put something on for me, Jimmy." She turned to Allan. "You must think us perfectly mad, Mr Hillingdon, but as a matter of fact all our dances aren't as amusing as Tessie's. Oh, Ann, guess what I heard one of the matrons say to a pal—'Well, Mrs. Kennedy, what do *you* think of the new naked backs?' Quite good, wasn't it? I must say, Tessie's yellow charmer from Newbury had rather over-done it. Let's go and get some more supper—I didn't eat a thing last time I went in, I was laughing too much."

As he seated himself beside Muriel Dane at the supper-table, Allan was aware of a man and a slender dark-haired girl who shared a tiny table in a secluded corner. On it stood a gold-necked bottle, which perhaps accounted for the brightness of Sybil's eyes and the slight flush on her cheeks. John Dane was cautiously examining the contents of a small, silken, and beribboned wallet, from which he produced a morsel of swansdown, a minute ivory comb, also a tiny brocade-backed mirror, while asking obviously inane questions as to their uses. Finally he tied the ribbon fastenings with elaborate pains, and, despite the protests of its owner, placed the vanity in his pocket. Later, the couple rose and made their way to the ball-room.

"That been going on all the evening?" Ann indicated the departing backs.

Muriel nodded, and laughed. "It's the last night of John's leave," she explained, "and—how extra-ordinarily pretty that child is growing!" Thus lightly does twenty-one speak of her sister seventeen.

It was not until five o'clock that Ann finally extricated her young sister from the mazes of the extras in which she had enmeshed herself, enveigled her into her white fur wrap, and presented her to their hostess to make her adieux.

"Oh, you're not going yet, surely?" exclaimed that hospitable lady. "Why, the fun's only starting now, and most of them won't be out of this till seven o'clock. Can't you really manage to stop on a bit? Well, I'm awfully sorry you can't stay. I suppose we'll see you at the top of the hunt to-morrow, Mr Hillingdon! Did you hear that the Master's away and Dennys is hunting the hounds? Well, he is! I don't know what was the matter with that boy this evening—he arrived as late as the goats and left in an hour. Oh, he had some grand long excuse made up to me about it, but I could see there was something wrong. Well, good-bye now! I'm delighted you could come. Safe home! I hope you kept Mr Hillingdon from the champagne, the way he won't wreck you all!" This last sally was screamed above the concentrated din of the Ford's protesting engine.

"And he only danced three with me," remarked Sybil bitterly to the darkness around her, as she snuggled down beneath her blue eider-down. "But I fancy I showed him that I didn't care!" She straightened her slight form rigidly beneath the bedclothes. "But I *do*." Her murmur found sympathy in the friendly dark, the recipient of many such confidences from Sybil and her like.

Ann, in the adjoining room, slid into bed. She pulled Jibber, who was sleeping at her feet, up beside her, and laid her face against the rough white hair of the best little pal that ever was.

"Jib, what was the matter?" she breathed. Jibber opened one sapient eye, licked her mistress's neck and slept again. "You don't help me much, do you?"—Ann surveyed the white atom—"but you're a great comfort, old girl."

CHAPTER X

The First of the Season

ALLAN was tying an immaculate white hunting stock on the grey and murky morning of the opening meet. Despite, or perhaps because of his love-sick state, he performed the rite with almost lavish care.

"Right over left, divide——" He found himself murmuring his father's old formula for the successful tying of a stock.

"Dash the thing, that's not got it!" He tried again, and at last tied it to his satisfaction. Then he sat down and confronted his boots, which stared at him unsympathetically, and, in all senses of the word, unreceptively.

The breakfast bell boomed as his right foot, halfway into its boot, reached that almost impassable gully which is in all hunting boots, and through which the human foot invariably refuses to go without long persuasion, vocal and otherwise. On this occasion, the vocal persuasion used by Allan was such as to crinkle the air around him.

Late for breakfast again, and Ann was always so mad with people when they were late! Oh, curse that boot! If he could only get some one to come and give him a hand, all might still be well. Even in such matters as the pulling on of his hunting boots, Allan invariably required "a hand" of some sort. As he opened his door to call Brien, the pantry boy, to his aid, Sybil passed down the passage.

"Sybil," he hailed her, "you're invaluable. Just come and give me a hand with these boots, will you, dear?"

Sybil complied, and hauled at the recalcitrant boots with a good will and to some effect. The task was over sooner than she could have wished—she loved his boots, she told herself, simply loved them. And his dearness, and his nearness. Yes, she was cat-like in that. Or was it just the smell of his shaving soap she loved? She didn't know. All of it, probably!

She finished fastening the stiff buckle of his spurs and stood up. She looked such a kid in her short riding-coat, just a charming girl, one would have said, with a mind as clean as her long limbs. But she was hardly that. She was one of the precocious sisterhood of flappers; girls thoroughly awake to their sex and its attractions, yet pitiably childish in their three-quarter knowledge of the ways of men.

"That's that!" She straightened out her stoop. "Quite the lady of old and her knight, what? Your spurs, I mean."

Allan, though hurried, made, as was his wont, courteous and appropriate reply.

"Iss fegs! I thank thee, good madonna." He bent him over her slim brown fingers, and was rather surprised when she snatched her hand away. "Dash it! I mean Tut— or Pish—I thought you were in pretty fooling."

"You're always fooling. I hate it!" Sybil felt unaccountably angry. Not so did Allan thank Ann for any small act she might perform in his service. She wanted to hurt him for his unintentional hurting of her, but all she could think of to say was:

"My dear old thing, you simply mustn't wear pink to-day. You're not in the shires and it's not done here much." She added that only one who was born a fool would wear new boots to an opening meet, and further observed acidly that Sailor (the brown he had brought from

Dennys) had been raising hell in his box all the morning, and that she (Sybil) hoped he (Allan) would enjoy himself.

When she left his room, she was inwardly seething with annoyance against herself and Allan, and all the world. When, a little later, she saw Ann giving him a sisterly morning greeting and a bunch of violets, in the hall, and noted Allan's reverent reception of both, she felt a great agony rising in her throat and an awful ache behind her eyes. When the modern flapper falls very much in love, she may be a laughable figure, but she is, none the less, pitiable. Her jealousy belongs nearly as much to her childhood as her love does to her too early developed womanhood. Anyhow, she decided that she would ride them all down that day, and jolly well show Allan . . . she didn't quite know what.

Poor Sybil! Her high courage abated somewhat when Pet Girl, with Fox at her head, emerged alertly from her box and sidled obstinately away from the mounting block. Once up, however, and out of the yard, all her accustomed confidence returned, while she sat lithe and close to Pet Girl's extravagant early morning enthusiasms.

Allan, considering her as deeply as Sailor's overflowing spirits would permit, compared her mentally—and enthusiastically—to the cover design of a Christmas annual. His meditations were interrupted by Ann riding up beside him. Her perfect hands were very light on the snaffle, her hot youngster answering at her least touch on the reins.

"I didn't see Cousin Ronnie about when we started." Allan said it for something to say.

"No, didn't you?" said Ann. She did not add that she had seen her father looking out at the start from the bath-room window, and had understood, with that peculiar sympathy which was hers, the travail of mind he suffered in realizing the bitter fact that his nerve was gone. It was cruelly hard, he who had been the best man to hounds in the country, and now—well, the very sight of a plunging horse made him feel cold and sick. Ann, who had never known fear or funked horse or a fence, could understand, whilst hating herself for pitying him.

"He'll spend the morning cursing the gardeners," she thought, "and then have a beastly, dull lunch alone. Poor Dad, poor Dad! Oh, it *is* rotten."

At this point her meditations were interrupted by the arrival of Mrs Jeeves, accompanied by a husband of frostbitten appearance. Tessie, as usual, was in rude health and the best of spirits. She greeted Ann and then turned immediately to Allan.

"Good morning, Mr Hillingdon. How are you after the dance? Charlie's feet are all swollen, but I see that you squeezed yours into a lovely pair of new boots. Oh, you're too much of a swell for us altogether!" She ran a laughing and thoroughly approving eye over him, from his deliciously sleek silk hat, and his brown hatchet-like profile—split by a large white grin at what he considered the licensed insanity of this mad Irish woman—down to his stiff and gleaming boots.

"Oh, look here," said Allan, "I think you're distinctly unkind. I want some one to mother me to-day, you know; shepherd me over a strange country, and what not. I was hoping you'd be nice to me."

"Of course I will!" Tessie's bray of laughter nearly made the horses shy. "But really, Mr Hillingdon, you might have put it better—mother you, indeed!"

They drifted into further and more intricate badinage. It was characteristic of Allan that, though his precious *tête-à-tête* with Ann had been so rudely interrupted, he showed no whit morose towards the interrupter thereof, hardly even cursing her inwardly. There was more of the gentleman than of the primeval man about Allan.

Meanwhile, Sybil having ridden on ahead, Ann gravely discussed the day's prospects with Charlie Jeeves. He liked Ann, though as a general rule he preferred girls with more "go" about them. Thus they progressed for some little way, till on the crest of a shriek of mirth, Tessie turned to Ann.

"Did ye hear what he said to me? Oh, I'm afraid he's a naughty boy! Well, good-bye now; Charlie and I have to go up here to see some rotten farmer." She turned her horse up a side road. "See you later!" she called.

Charlie Jeeves lifted his hat and followed his spouse at a shattering trot, up a steep and stony lane. Though he had a strong dislike for battering his horses along the road, in this, as in all other matters, he followed the pace set by his wife.

Ann and Allan rode the remaining mile to Glencurry, the scene of the meet, in silence; Ann because she was thinking of Dennys, thinking and wondering, trying to dispossess her mind of a horrid little devil of doubt and perplexity—which had established itself when Dennys strode away into the rain—to return as often as routed by common-sense arguments. Allan was silent because the sight of Ann filled his mind, and as he might not talk to her of herself, no other subject seemed worthy of consideration.

As they passed the kennels, Ann pulled up, wondering

if the hounds had gone on, and finally asked Allan to get down and tighten her girths. A most unnecessary operation this, and one which she could have accomplished herself with considerably greater expedition, for Allan lingered long over each buckle, his head pressed close to her saddle-flap. Ann hummed a fragment of a tune; her eyes were far away, her hand in its yellow chamois leather glove rubbed soothingly along her horse's neck. The movement was so careless, and so kind, so precisely typical of her treatment of himself, that for the moment it filled the man with an almost wild self-forgetfulness. As he caught and kissed the careless fingers, his love for her rose surging in his throat . . . to his dying day, the slight smell of soap on newly-washed chamois gloves caused him an indefinite sense of pain and disappointment.

Ann removed her hand swiftly, and her surprised eyes looked down into Allan's.

"Ann," he said, "Ann dear——"

"Allan dear," she answered, "don't be a—don't be silly. Oh, here are the hounds. Thanks be!" she added mentally; and as Dennys rose out of the kennel yard, with the pack round his horse, she raised her crop in cheerful greeting.

Dennys touched his old velvet cap, and would have gone on without waiting for them—Allan was something of a strategist even in his worst moments, and was feverishly altering every buckle in her girths—but that Ann, determined once and for all to chase that little bogey of doubt and fear, called after him in honeyed tones.

"Hullo! Feeling fit after last night?" She accompanied the words with a dazzling smile, which accentuated, while it in no wise dispersed, the gloom which dwelt on her admirer's countenance, like thunder-clouds before an impending storm.

"Awfully fit, thanks. We're late! Co-oop hounds!" He cut savagely at one of the young entry straying up the bank of the road towards some rabbit-holes, and rode on, a dour and silent knight.

Ann's chin was high in air as she turned to Allan.

"Don't hurry," she said caressingly. When they finally arrived at the meet, the place was completely deserted.

"The dogs is gone wesht to Riley's Knock." They were informed of this fact by a grey-bearded patriarch, who left his occupation of propping up the walls of his house in order to come forward and answer Allan's "Which way?"

Ann gathered up her reins.

"Come on," she said, "we must hit it up. There's a short cut here."

Garry Owen slipped over a low bank, Sailor following with a good deal of superfluous energy. As they cantered across the intervening fields to the covert, their progress was watched with some interest by at least two members of the hunt. One of these was Sybil and the other Tessie Jeeves—Dennys at the time being fully occupied in putting his hounds through covert; a serious business compared to which all earthly thoughts, in which category even Ann was included, very properly took a back seat in his mind.

Ann and Allan joined a group of riders, which numbered amongst its members Sybil and Tessie.

"Well, you're a nice late pair," Sybil greeted them tactlessly. "They started out with me." She turned to Tessie, asking, and not in vain, for condemnation for the culprits. Tessie laughed broadly.

"Oh, they're a nice brace of babies to be trusted by themselves," she proclaimed, "and only this morning he was asking me to mother him. How bad he is!" She turned on the motherless one a hard brown eye, shining with comprehension and sympathy. Allan, who considered his inanities verging on bad form, laughed idiotically and forgave her, because doubtless here was a truly Irish form of wit.

The sun broke through the swathes of mist, tempering the moist chill of the air with a semblance of warmth; occasional gleams of grass shone out of the uniform dulness of the stubble fields, and far away the mountains lost themselves in remote grey.

The gathering at the covert side was motley in the extreme. Very little of the picturesque correctness of attire to be met with in an English field was to be seen. Most of the horses, however, were good; a few exceptionally so. Nearly all were clever fencers, as indeed they have need to be, to get unscathed through a country where narrow stone-faced, briar-wreathed banks occurred at almost unbelievably close intervals. Their riders ranged in caste from the Hillingdons and their likes, through the intricate mazery of the class, half farmer, half horse-coper, generally entirely good sportsmen and excellent horsemen—of which Charlie Jeeves and old Johnny St Lawrence were typical examples—down to the undisguised farmers. The latter were mounted for the most part on hairy youngsters, or aged half clipped animals, collar marked, and with the traces of shafts on their fat sides, yet showing a wonderful dexterity and facility in getting across country; their hunting kit was uncomplicated to a degree, consisting as it did in the mooring of the trouser leg in the vicinity of the ankle by a bicycle clip.

A group of this class was discussing the day's prospects, the vagaries of the weather, the horses out, and their riders, all in passionate undertones. The undertones were due to the fact of Master Dennys being—as an old offender put it—"as good a man to curse as the father." An aged votary of the chase spat contemptuously and silencingly.

"It is thim curse," he said; "there's nothin' only chat out o' thim. God knows when 'twas poor Major Hillingdon had the hounds, he'd rain curses the way ye'd dhry down before him." The exponent of the time-that-were paused. His iron-grey brows projected like hoods over yellow falcon eyes which held a challenge. In Ireland a conversational challenge is never disregarded. The glove of contest was picked up immediately by a meek little man, with a rat-like and not over-clean profile.

"Well then," he snickered, "it's pity of the Major if all the people's sayings about him now is true."

"And what the hell has they to say about him?" There was hostility in the yellow eyes.

"It's what Aiden Nolan above at the house was tellin' me—he wouldn't throw a leg on a horse now, not for love nor gold. Sure meself lasht year I thought him gone very dashed like, and an eye out for the small little places in a fince always." Mr Kelly contemplated benignly the orange red of his new pig-skin gaiters, clamped immovably against his horse's withers; then, picking up his single rein, he trotted off to a place of further vantage.

"That's an ugly little, dirty little fella for ye." Matty Devlin of the falcon eyes denounced the detractor of the Major's prowess in calm and measured tones, and having thus summarily and most truthfully disposed of his opponent, he continued his saga in praise of the Major and his lovely family.

"A good decent man that never did a sup o' harm with his tongue, for all he cursed. And a half-crown he'd have always for thim that'd knock a gap for him, though God knew 'twas seldom he'd ask to get that done. A gentleman that would pay on the nail for whatever he'd buy, horse or oats, one that—unlike some who should be nameless—would never do a poor neighbour of his little share."

The encomium rambled on its way through the family, reaching its summit of eloquence upon Ann—"a fine, lovely lump o' a girrl."

"Well, well, Matty," broke in a bored member of the audience, "and isn't it a great pity of her, and she so comely as she is, and they not to have a match made up for her yet."

The eyes of Matty swooped to those of the interrupter, and carried them with his own to the spot further down the hillside where Ann's and Allan's horses stood together—in that semblance of boredom affected by young horses at the covert side.

"Now, I'd say that was as smart a young chap as ever I see, that Mr Hillingdon"—his even voice rose on a note of triumph—"an' a dam nice match for her. I have a great wish for Miss Ann always, and I'd say she could not ask better."

"*Less noise there!*" The huntsman's voice on the far side of the hedge spoke like the crack of a leather thong. The group of farmers withered away from its vicinity, but not before Matty had gathered every eye to his with one portentous wink.

Dennys called himself several sorts of idiot for paying

the least attention to the rot those old fools talked. Still, his jaw grew heavier as he looked down the hill, and saw Ann piloting Allan to a good getting away place which he remembered having shown her himself, one day when they had had the deuce of a smart run out of this very covert. They had talked over every fence afterwards, on their way home, he remembered; why their fox had taken that particular line; who was responsible for the non-stoppage of the earth when he had got to ground; but especially that this particular getting away place was one to remember in a nasty bit of country.

At this point in his reflections, a hound spoke in the undergrowth near him; a delicate whimper of expectation, and at the sound the huntsman reigned supreme in Dennys's soul, the lover in him, for the time being, very properly dead.

It was old Dextress who had found a scent. She ran it carefully across an open patch of grey-dewed grass, spoke once, and again more decidely. She was a hound to be trusted; Dennys put the others on to her quietly.

"Ge-et t'Dextress. Eleu in there, Ravager, *Ravager*!" They certainly had a line of some sort, he thought, as he watched them anxiously. Yes, good old Dextress was heaving her portly person up the bank. Dennys broke down a gap and the pack poured through, a beautiful wave of tan, and white, and rich black. Now Dextress had it. She threw up her head with one melodious howl, then settled to the line in a way which meant business. Now Ravager and Druid, two old hounds, spoke; and now with yelps of inexperienced joy, Daisy and Dammit flung themselves on the line.

"Oh, beautiful! Beautiful!" sang Dennys's soul, in

union with that of the immortal John. The hat of a watcher far out to the left was lifted high in air, and Dennys's eyes, following the direction, made out a slither of yellow rust, slipping across the end of a pale stubble field—his fox. "Gone away!" he sounded. "Gone away!" Johnny Brien hustled his old grey cob out of covert, flogging on the tail hounds, and settled down to get the utmost out of his old screw.

Five hectic minutes later, as his hounds bore well away left-handed, Dennys reflected pleasurably on the fact that he was, at any rate for the present, well rid of the crowd, which had nearly all been left on the wrong side of the hill. Nearly, but not quite all, for Ann and Allan, thanks to their good start, were coming on well.

Sailor was coming on, if anything, too well. In fact, to Dennys's experienced eye, matters looked as if the big brown was taking charge completely. He galloped straight and wicked as a bee, with a determined eye on hounds, and took some nasty places in a most dangerous way. Dennys heard Ann shout some remark to her cousin about keeping to the left, but he was too much interested in his hounds to pay much attention to that mad galloping Saxon—as he mentally labelled Allan. That is, until he was unpleasantly aware that the fellow was distinctly too close to his hounds.

"Hold hard, man!" he roared. "Pull out to your right, can't you?"

How ridiculous of Ann to call out again: "Keep to your left—your *left*, Allan!" Why on earth—God! he remembered now—it was the Focher's Leap—a ghastly drop, with an unbelievably bad landing off an innocent-looking bank; and that idiot was riding straight for it. A man had been killed there once before; a man and his horse. Now it was to be the turn of Ann's cousin—the man she loved. And it would be his fault . . . his . . . he had ordered him to keep to the right. The thought whirled through his brain in the sickening instant while he watched Sailor raking his head away, gallop at the fence, saw him change feet on top, and jumping out with a great bound, disappear from sight on the far side . . . a big-hearted horse. . . .

Ann, her face white and strained, rode past him, and steadying her horse at a place well to the left of the Focher's Leap, jumped into the next field to see what remained of her cousin.

Dennys came after her quickly, calling to her to hold on. He knew better than she how horrible is the sight of a broken man under a twisted horse. . . .Catching her up, he rose first round the corner of the field, which hid from view they knew not what. . . .

As a matter of fact, the ground below the Focher's Leap revealed nothing more than some very deep hoof-marks, for Allan and Sailor, now a field and a half ahead, were going amiably enough together, well to the right of hounds.

"Curse the fellow!" muttered Dennys as he caught hold of his horse's head and rode hard to make up for lost time. "He's the deuce of a lot too lucky. Wonder if Ann'd've looked like that if I'd made such a hare of myself."

Hounds checked for a short time where a flock of sheep had crossed the line, but it was long enough to permit Charlie Jeeves and some others to come up.

"By Jove, you dam nearly slipped away from us that time," he puffed, as he dismounted from his small four-year-old throughbred, much as though she had been a bicycle. "It's the devil's own place to get away from—that Riley's Knock. But this little lady's real cute." He patted her wet neck affectionately.

"Well, you know, she hardly looks up to your weight, Charlie," Ann observed gravely.

Mr Jeeves, who rode perhaps nine stone, surveyed his mount with an indulgent eye.

"May be," he answered. "However, she'll carry me as far as the next horse, and devilish well at that." He hoisted himself into his saddle without ceremony, his eye on the hounds. "I'd say old Druid had a line," he remarked.

"Ah, that's a dam good hound," Ann overheard a farmer observe to one of his fellows. "I reared him meself for the hunt, when the Major was in it, himself and the sister; the sister died on me, thought. I dunno what should have happened to her, unless 'twas the dose o' methylated me little girl gave her one time in mistake for turpentine."

Ann stored the tale in her mind; then she rode up to Allan, who was having a conversation with Sailor.

"I suppose you don't realize that you've been making history this morning," she began. "At least, Sailor has—the darling, the——"

"Oh, I suppose you mean the time we were nearly into the hounds," Allan interrupted. "I know! Don't rub it in, old thing. This blinking animal pulled like a blessed steam-engine the first couple of fields. Hullo! we're off. No. we're not! Yes, we are. . . .Steady, Boy!"

Hounds ran steadily for about twenty minutes, across a series of small fields, fenced by preposterously tall thin banks, trying to the temper of a big galloping, big jumped horse like Sailor. Allan sighed with relief when a great field spread itself invitingly before him. "Now, old man!"

He sat forward as Sailor sprang into his beautiful stretching gallop. As the good green fields flowed past, Allan's heart sang paeans of praise to the makers of the broad, firm banks which fenced them—banks that Sailor took faultlessly, one after another, galloping with his heart before him over the wide fields.

But the broad fields and banks narrowed all too soon. Sound grass gave place to the treacherous gleaming emerald of bog-land, and here it was that hounds lost their well-deserved fox, after fifty minutes of the best, and over the finest bit of going in the country.

Men dropped their reins on their horses' lathering necks, shoved their hats to the backs of their heads, and lit cigarettes. Women pushed loosened hair under their hats, and chattered ecstatically.

As Allan dismounted, in order to scan Sailor's legs for cuts, a feeling rose in his heart akin to adoration for the horse which had carried him so well. Sybil rose up to him. her cheeks were glowing, and she was very muddy.

"Wasn't that the father and mother of a run?" she called. "You know, I think it must have been the vixen Johnny Brien was buying all the old hens in the country for last summer. I suppose she took that ripping line out of gratitude. I think we've lost her, though."

Allan cocked an expressive eye at old Dextress, sitting down to scratch—a clear indication that she considered that the game was up.

Heley's gorse—a snug patch of furze on a neighbouring hillside—was next drawn blank. As they jogged along the roads to the next draw, Tessie ranged up alongside Allan.

"Well, wasn't that a grand hunt?" she remarked. "You'd think it might have sweetened the Master a bit, but he's just black with rage. I wouldn't go near him for a pension, though I assure you I've dandled that same boy on my knees, when he was a small kid."

"Lucky blighter!" murmured Allan politely, turning to listen to some man who was making remarks into his other ear. Tessie seemed to have heard that better than he had.

"The what?" she screamed. "The Focher's Leap below Riley's! My God! d'ye mean to tell me you went over such an *awful* place?"

"Sorry, but I don't fathom all this chatter." Allan was puzzled. "I sort of remember a pretty devilish steep drop below Riley's, but I hadn't time to look back at it. Right of the third field from the covert, was it? Yes, I remember it now, all right. My cousin shouted to me to keep to the left, but the Master and I both thought I'd be into hounds if I did, so I acted on his advice and pulled out to the right. No stopping this lad; I could hardly steady him at it."

"Well, I'm damned!" said the young man. "That's some gee-gee."

"Now Tommy! Tommy!" Tessie admonished him.

"Well, but fancy telling a chap to ride straight into a place like that. I mean, think of the horse—what if he *had* ridden over a couple of hounds?"

"Thanks," said Allan dryly. "But one would rather risk the horse, you know."

"Well, if I don't give Dennys a piece of my mind before I go home to-day!" Tessie resolved loudly, riding off to spread the news of the incident among all and sundry.

Her opportunity occurred as they were going home that evening. Dennys—despite two nice little gallops in the afternoon—had estranged all men by his extreme bitterness, and was riding alone at the head of his hounds, thinking hard thoughts of all the world, but most especially of himself. His gloomy reverie was cheerfully interrupted by Tessie. Curse the woman! What rot was she talking now?

The harsh timbre of his hound voice still lingered when he spoke to Tessie, though his words were polite enough. "I beg your pardon—who? Hillingdon? Goes well, does he? Can't say I noticed him, except when he nearly laid out the tail hounds coming out of Riley's."

His laugh was not of an encouraging variety, but its only effect upon Tessie was to barb the badinage of her ready tongue.

"Oh, I suppose there's more room where he comes from." She excused her protégé. "Though I don't suppose he's really used to places like Focher's Leap. Ann Hillingdon's raging; she's telling every one 'twas you sent him into it. Is that so?"

Dennys's short, unpleasant laugh was not good to hear. He broke it off to cut ineffectually at a loitering hound.

"Well?" Tessie evidently was not going without her answer.

"Oh, she can say what she damn well chooses—especially as it's more than half true." Dennys spurred his tired horse and rode unceremoniously away.

It proved a more arduous matter to ride away from his own thoughts. No sooner did he half-heartedly resolve to banish all memory of Ann, than each tiniest incident that cropped up reminded him most forcibly of her. When he dismounted in the kennel yard, Driscoll, son of Twink and Jibber, detached himself importantly from the bourgeois company of the kennel terriers, to greet him with effusive adoration not to be denied. He held the ecstatic white body and filthy feet against his old pink coat, as he examined the contents of the hounds' feeding troughs with a parent's searching eye. Then slipping on a linen kennel coat, he went into the wire enclosure to watch his hounds feed—noisily and furtively—as Johnny called them by name, the weakest first.

"Dammit's going very lame. Did you notice him?" He indicated a young hound who had just slunk off into a corner, there to bolt some choice morsel in sunken-eyed, jealous greed.

"Yes, Mister Dennys. Good 'ound that. One o' the puppies Miss 'Illingdon walked. Went very sick once too, but 'er pulled 'im round, she did." In common with many another Irish whip, Johnny had adopted the speech of that country which had known him during his best years.

Dennys left the stable yard and walked up to the house, to partake meditatively of toast and poached eggs in that man's room—so untidy, without being comfortable—which they called the library.

His tea over, there was Driscoll to be considered—Driscoll, whose hungry brown eyes cried aloud for nourishment, albeit his rejection of toast crusts spoke volumes for the occupation he had followed that afternoon, in the company of the despised kennel terriers.

"Not hungry, old man? Right! Come and talk to your poor old master, honey boy!"

Driscoll, in willing obedience to the invitation, leapt lightly from the floor to the arm of the chair, and thence to his master's waistcoat; there to curl himself with sensuous joy, and, after indicating unmistakably that his

143

master might profitably fill a few unoccupied moments in scratching his (Driscoll's) front, proceeded to listen with a semblance of deep interest for any remarks which his oracle and deity might deign to let fall.

But everything was all wrong to-night—somehow. The friction on his chest, though methodical, was not so delightfully searching as a thoughtful master knew well how to make it. The waistcoat too—that acknowleged nest for rest of small dogs—proved unyielding in the extreme. The entire atmosphere, indeed, was less soothing than usual. In fact, there was something wrong, and Driscoll grew every minute more firmly convinced of the fact. Raising himself as if to scratch, he gazed earnestly into the adored face, of whose smallest change of expression he was adept interpreter. But now its expression was beyond measure troubled, and the dear eyes looked past him into the fire's heart.

Driscoll raised a tiny, tentative paw and brought it down nervously on a big brown hand. No answer! He must try again—no—none! Then Master had no use for his little Driscoll; there was trouble, and he was a mere outsider. Perhaps the adored one was feeling as bad as he himself remembered to have felt, after a prolonged orgy with the kennel terriers . . . the thought was unbearable. With a tiny heart-rending sob, Driscoll buried his face in the folds of Dennys's white stock, though a gold safety-pin pressed cruelly hard on a wet black nose.

Ah! at last.

"Why, Driscoll, Driscoll pet!" Dennys plucked the little face from his stock and held it softly against his own. "Was my little dog crying? Sure, you know poor old master loves you. Yes, but she doesn't care one bit about him, and says beastly things. But women are always like that, aren't they, Driscoll? And we won't have anything more to say to them, will we, Driscoll? No, old man, not ever."

Driscoll signified his passionate assent, before contentedly resuming his place on the waistcoat that was all the world to him—a world in which everything was now beautiful, since he had been some help when Master was feeling bad. Dennys stretched out a long arm and scooped the post, which had arrived while he was out, from a distant table. Then lighting a cigarette, he leant back in his chair to read.

He chuckled joyously over a letter from Elizabeth. She told him how the school had played the staff—and licked it too—and of her own hopes of the second eleven. Followed a detailed account of some complicated school row, then inquiries for the hounds and horses, and stern injunctions not to let Johnny have Dimpey—an old and useless hunter—for the hounds. The letter ended with a pious wish that Miss Pratt might not open and read it, and a P.S. which said:

"Love to Daddy and tell Ann she's a pig not to write after she said she would."

Dennys smiled as he replaced it in its envelope. After all, there was always Elizabeth! The next missive was in his father's writing. From it he learned that St. Lawrence senior had picked up a nice little bunch of horses, dirt cheap, from two old ladies, who for political reasons, were obliged to clear out of their home and leave Ireland. The date of his return was fixed vaguely as next week—or the week after. Dennys threw the letter into the fire, and turned over the last item of his correspondence before opening it. Probably a notice about a dead horse, or a fowl claim, he thought, as he glanced at the illiterate writing on a sheet of copy-book paper. It proved to be the latter. Dennys put it aside with other unanswered fowl claims, and, changing his pen, addressed himself heavily to the task of composing an epistle to Elizabeth. The letter finished and addressed in his neat, ridiculously boyish writing, he tramped heavily upstairs to take off his boots.

The moon glinted the light of her virginal first quarter through the unshuttered window of his room. He crossed over to sniff the frosty air, and as he did so, a great loneliness, correspondingly chill, swept devastatingly through him. He leant his head against the window-sash, and his soul refused comfort, whilst it cried bitterly on the name of the girl he believed as far removed from him as the white new moon. . . . He was of the ranks of those who love greatly and are exceedingly proud.

Three miles away, Ann tugged desperately at her hunting boots, while great bitter tears chased each other down her cheeks.

CHAPTER XI
And They Also Said . . .

IT was Major Hillingdon's invariable custom to go the rounds of stables, garden, and farm-yard, immediately after breakfast. He was on these occasions accompanied by Twink and Jibber, who enjoyed an hour or so of the Major's company, and spent their time chasing cats, sniffing importantly at rat-holes, and generally attending to the affairs of the universe.

On the morning of the sixth of November, the Major tapped the glass, called to the dogs—whose affected languor over their breakfasts immediately turned to voracious haste—and started the round of inspection at the loose-box wherein Allan's big brown was housed.

"Well, Fox," began the Major, as he eyed Sailor with some approval, "that horse carried Mr Allan well on Friday, I believe."

"I heard so," returned Fox, unmoved. Followed a lengthy pause, broken only by Sailor's ceaseless biting at the manger, in his efforts to relieve his feelings under the tickle of the curry-comb. "It'd be a job now for God Almighty to send us a wet day," observed Fox suddenly.

"Why?" inquired his master, with some curiosity.

"The way I'd get to take the hair off o' the bay filly," replied the single-minded Fox. "Sure ye couldn't get ne'er a one o' thim lads off the farm when the fine weather's in it. And the sight of the clippin' machine itself is able to destroy that mare. I'd want two houldin' her."

"Well, the men are very busy at present, but Miss Ann and Mr Allan'll come out and give you a hand some day soon."

Fox laughed sardonically.

"Is it Miss Ann? Miss Ann'd go away out of the stable altogether if ye went to put the touch on the mare. Sure, she wouldn't care to see a fly hurted, never mind a horse. Hullup, big fella!" This was to the horse. "That one's able to bet a kick that'd sphlit a stone."

"He carried Mr Allan very well last Friday. Lord knows how the pair of them didn't break their necks at Focher's Leap, though. He should win some big point-to-points in England next year."

"That'd be the quare change for him." Fox opened the stable door on the pretence of getting a brush, and took a swift look round the yard to make sure that no myrmidon was lurking within earshot. He then followed his master into the next box—Garry Owen's. "Did your honour happen to hear," he began unconcernedly, "where Mr St Lawrence got that horse?"

"Didn't inquire. It had nothing to do with me. Entirely Mr Allan's buy," replied the Major; he had a sure presentiment that he was about to hear something unpleasant—nor did Fox fail him.

"Well, it's what the people's saying that the young fella got him from Miss Dempsey above at Lisogue; and divil a ha'penny he ped for him, only to give her an old bank cheque was what he done. And when she went to put it in the bank at Bungarvin, the lads was in it split theirselves laughing at her. 'Twas what they told her 'twas worth no more than the bit of paper he had it wrote out on."

To himself Major Hillingdon exclaimed: "Well, of all the dam dirty acts I ever heard of!" Aloud, all he said was: "People'll say a lot more than their prayers, Fox. Was that the poor woman whose brother was taken by the Republicans last month?"

"The very same—God help her!"

"Bad business. Rotten bad business!" muttered the Major, turning to leave the stable. "Did you see Miss Ann anywhere, Fox?"

"She was out here feeding the hound pups afther her breakfish," responded Fox. Then in tones of unalloyed bitterness, he added: "Them's the rogues o' the world. Ye couldn't put a thing out o' yer hand but it's gone from you. They med off with the dendther brush e'er yesterday; well I eat the place for the dendther brush, and in the latter end Miss Sybil got it in the laurels. Oh, thim's the finished article! Sure my woman couldn't hang as much as a little chemisette out on the line that me brave boys wouldn't have it down; and then to have it strewn round the hall-door steps is what they'd go do. They'd have a pairson annoyed."

"Confounded nuisance, Fox! I'll send them back to the kennels. I'll make Miss Ann shut them up. Here, Jib! Twink! Come here, sir!"

Whistling for the two little white terriers, the Major left the yard. As he walked along the muddy lane towards the farm, it came to him as a brilliant inspiration to tell Ann the story he had just heard from Fox. "Put any thought of the chap out of her head; not that there was ever anything in it. Couldn't have been anything in it. . . . Motherless girls, though . . . can't be too careful, Jove, no." Thus meditating, the Major opened the farm-yard gate and stepped into the region of concentrated wet mud enclosed within.

Seated upon the shaft of a cart, he perceived his elder

daughter. Beside her stood a disreputable figure which he recognized as a local poacher—one Mike Dooney. Ann appeared to be cheerfully haggling with him over the price of a ferret which he held aloft, just out of reach of the two enraptured hound puppies.

"Two bob's all I'll give you," he heard Ann say. "Here it is. You can go and put the little brute in the ferret's hutch."

"I will, me lady. I thank your honour, miss," returned Mike Dooney with dignity. "Sure that's the grand ferret, and the nosey ferret, and the great thraveller——"

It was at this point that the ferret's nerve gave out under the strain of the hound puppies' prolonged attentions. It bit Mike Dooney's hand, ran up his arm, and hung itself like a stole about his neck. Mike Dooney, with a yelp of horror, flung off his coat and hurled it, together with the ferret, far from him. Like two flashes of lightning, the little dogs were upon it, ably seconded by the nearly delirious hound puppies. Major Hillingdon intervened with a stick, Mike Dooney called upon his Deity, but it was Ann who plunged dauntlessly into the thick of the fray, and with extraordinary speed and dexterity succeeded in rescuing her purchase from the very jaws of death.

"Well now, Mike, weren't you the big fool" inquired Ann pleasantly, when the ferret had been safely incarcerated in its new home. Mike surveyed this small, pink-cheeked lady in silence for a moment. When he spoke, it was with strong emotion.

"I've thravelled Ireland," he said, "but ye're the hardest woman I ever seen. If I had the price of a drink on me this minute, I'd go drink a health to yer honour's Ladyship. Ye have great courage surely!"

Ann laughed her appreciation of the compliment and ran off after her father, whom she found contemplatively scratching the back of an elderly sow, that sprawled among her numerous progeny in the pig-sty.

"More money to be made out of pigs than horses. Far more," said he, as Ann came and leant over the door beside him. "And that reminds me—I've just heard a devilish nasty story about that St Lawrence crew of horse-copers. Bad lot, that! Bad lot! All tarred with the same brush. Never trust these gentlemanly horse-dealers; sure to do you up, or do you down, or do you dirt some way. Sure to!"

"What did you hear, father?" inquired Ann, endeavouring to keep her voice even and unconcerned.

"Well, Fox tells me——"

"Oh, Fox!" interpolated Ann, in scathing accents.

"Fox doesn't exaggerate. Never known that fella exaggerate, always tells you a thing straight."

"And he told you?" prompted Ann.

"Well, it seems," said the Major, now fairly goaded by Ann's doubt to make the worst of the story, "it seems that this young St Lawrence fellow palmed off some sort of bogus cheque on a farmer woman for the brown horse he sold Allan. Got a receipt from her too. Bad Job! I'm sorry to see that young fellow following in his disreputable old father's footsteps. Did well in the war, too. But it's what's bred in the bone that comes out in the end. Sure to!"

The Major here ceased his unsparing attentions to the pig, and earnestly watched Ann's face for any sign of emotion.

The girl, intent on a thorn in Jibber's paw, gave no sign.

"Well, what do you think of that?" he inquired at last, a distinct note of triumph in his harsh, ringing little bark of a voice. Ann put Jibber down carefully. Inwardly she was in a tumult; outwardly, perfectly unconcerned.

"I'm sure it's a lie," she replied smoothly. "The whole story's absurd and ridiculous. Why, if they had done such a thing, the woman could easily have the matter taken up."

"Just what she could not do. It's that unfortunate Mary Dempsey, whose brother was kidnapped this summer. It was a perfect scandal the way the authorities behaved over that, and do you think they'd be any better over this business?—I don't!"

The Major lit his pipe in irritable puffs and Ann forbore from argument.

Presently, when he had stalked away, she went into the haggard and ensconced herself high up in an angle of the big hayrick. The puppies babbled deliriously at the foot of the ladder which she had climbed—Jibber under one arm—to reach her present haven; but for once Ann ignored them. She wanted, desperately, to be alone and think this new thing out. Jibber didn't count, of course; she was a great help in time of stress.

Ann lay upon her back among the choking fragrance of the hay, and gazed, solemn-eyed, into the arched, corrugated iron roof above her head. Something had to be faced; that was the point. Yes—what had to be faced? Suddenly it all swept over her in a sickening wave. Had Dennys done this thing? *Her* Dennys. Oh, surely not! Ann clenched her small fists and sat up straight in the hay.

"Jib," she spoke between shut teeth, "now I know why I haven't seen him—really, since, since that time. He must have thought I knew, and kept away on purpose. Perhaps he didn't mean it—that night. And I made a fool of myself. I made a perfect fool of myself! Oh, Jib, what a fool I was!"

Ann drew from her pocket a large and elaborately patterned silk handkerchief, into which she bit desperately for some moments. Having thus relieved her feelings, she lay silent awhile, contemplating life, which appeared at the moment very black indeed. The salient point in her reflections was a desire to hide from all—including herself—the depths of her hurt. Pride was up in arms. Pride demanded that a token of how little she cared should be given to Dennys, and to all who might concern themselves with the affair. How, then, was this to be accomplished? Ann racked her brain, and chewed many long stems of hay, in her efforts to solve the problem. The obvious idea of becoming engaged to Allan never occurred to her. Had such a course been suggested, she would have opened wide grey eyes of horror, and promptly said:

"But it wouldn't be fair; he's such a dear. And besides, I like him."

Having pondered deeply for some time, it came over Ann that she was very lonely; that, despite all things, she cared for Dennys and no one else. A thousand pictures of him came to mock her: pictures of Dennys riding at the head of his hounds; Dennys giving her leads over bad places out hunting; Dennys's badger-digs; Dennys congratulating her as he gaffed her first salmon . . . Dennys with his slow smile and inscrutable eyes . . . *her* Dennys! Surely he had not done this thing!

"I say, Ann old friend, come and straafe the wily snipe with me," suggested a plaintive voice from below.

Ann sat up, and brushed some hay from her garments. After all, why not? She didn't care. Picking up Jibber, she descended the ladder and fell into step beside Allan—the tall young man with the nice teeth and the brown sweater beneath his old shooting coat.

"Nice day," observed Allan, as they made tracks for the house.

"M'm," replied his cousin, and volunteered no further remark until they reached the gun-room. An extraordinarily untidy place this, which smelt of everything under the sun—Rangoon oil and iodine (here the Major kept stable first-aid accessories); bulbs (here also were stored the choicer tulips); and cats, who favoured the room as quiet and suitable for the production and up-bringing of vast hordes of kittens. In the gun-room, Ann squinted down the barrels of her gun.

"What a life! Don't you think so, Allan? Sybil hasn't cleaned this gun since she had it. Blast her! Ramrod, please."

Allan removed three kittens and their mother from their nest in his game-bag, slipped some cartridges in his pockets, and seating himself, contemplated his cousin in silence for a while. How small she was, and how intense! The dusty sunlight turned her tangled hair to silver, and she was simply covered with hayseed. Something immense surged up in Allan and caught devastatingly at his throat. She was so awfully sweet! Yesterday the lady had also proved wondrous kind—perhaps to-day . . . Then Jibber placed her cold little nose in his hand, and Allan awoke to mundane things once more.

"Ann," he said, "I know Jib is quite as useful on the bogs as Benny'd be—even more so, because Ben hates prickles. But—er—shall we leave her behind for once? I feel, somehow, that the snipe would be easier to hit if they weren't up six hundred yards ahead. Of course, if you think her feelings would be hurt——"

Ann's eyes travelled accusingly from her cousin's face to the small white suppliant crouched at his feet.

"I couldn't have believed you'd be so hard-hearted. Of course it shall come! Mother's only child!" This last was addressed to Jibber, in a croon of concentrated tenderness.

Twenty minutes later the trio started forth. They tramped over many brown fields of turnips, shorn bald of leaves by the insatiable wood pigeons. They toiled over plough, and pushed through briers, and covered many miles in search of a covey of partridges rumoured to be in the vicinity. Oh, the elusive partridge! Take your gun and scour their most accustomed haunts, and the chances are that you will find them not at all. Mount your horse and ride along the King's highway, with no better weapon to your hand than a hunting crop, and in all probability six plump brown birds will rise from the sheltering lee of a bank not ten yards distant, to disappear with extraordinary rapidity—their wings sounding like the beating of many carpets.

Yet, though they saw no sign of the reported covey, the going was good, this November morning was fair and passing pleasant. A hint of warmth and a breeze met and kissed in the air, and parted company, laughing. Those cravens who, at the first approach of winter, fly to sunnier climes, know not the perfect enjoyment of a morning such as this; a gun, a dog, the hope of a covey of partridges, and the right sort of pal with whom to tramp from field to field, and hill to valley. So Allan thought as he lifted

Jibber over a high wall, and encouraged her activities in a brier patch.

Ensued a terrific hunt after a rabbit. Enraptured shrieks came from Jibber, as she flung herself through heavy covert, the prelude to a mad burst down the hillside in pursuit of that swiftly doubling brown body. Then—bang! and white Scut gives a great leap forward, turns a huge somersault, and lies twitching.

"Poor little divil! Give it a biff in the neck, Allan."

Allan administered the *coup de grâce*, and suggested that they should now fulfil the original programme concerning snipe and the bogs.

"All right, let's head for Lisogue. Then we can shoot our way home down the valley," Ann said.

Ten minutes later, they crossed the last of the series of low stone walls which distinguished the sad sedgy fields from the bog proper. Tiny fields these, which scarcely had grazing for the lean goats, and strings of dispirited ducks which roamed them, yet the kind Irish sunshine turned to emerald the green places where water from the hills ran down their sides, and warmed the loose round stones of the walls which hedged the poor land in these pathetic patternings.

Ann seated herself upon a stone and tilted her chin to the sky. Her gaze, in due course wandering earthwards, fixed itself intently upon a group of low white-washed buildings on the slope opposite to them. She sniffed the turf smoke which came faintly from a fitfully smoking chimney, then pointed a small grubbily gloved hand.

"That's Lisogue—where Sailor comes from," she said. "And I believe this is Mary Dempsey coming down here now. What can she want?"

Allan looked up and saw a tall, grey-haired woman approaching them. She crossed the irregular stepping-stones of the stream which ran down the bottom, with easy, measured grace, and accosted Ann with every circumstance of dignity.

"Good evening to your honour, miss. I'm in heavy trouble this long time—if I could get speaking to your honour."

"Of course, Miss Dempsey—if I can be of any use. Have you had any news of your poor brother yet?"

Mary Dempsey raised her arms to heaven in a large gesture of despair, of abandonment. Then, folding the shawl she wore more tightly across her, she spoke in calm tones of concentrated hopelessness.

"My child, they found his body e'er yesterday thrown out on the hill of Ringfaad. 'Twas hid from them those months when the thick bracken was in it, but when that withered, they found him, and the wet leaves sticking on him. Sure I was destroyed this two months thinking him living. And now he's dead, God knows I do be thinking how 'twas happy I was to have hope in this world. When that went from me I was left a lone tormented woman surely."

The even voice faltered and ceased; Mary Dempsey looked steadfastly towards the hills. In the face of such tragedy, even Ann's ever-ready sympathy was stunned and silenced.

"It's my wish," continued the grey-haired woman, with concentrated emphasis, "that I'd never see Heaven till I'd piled the sods o' Hell on them low trash of O'Connors. And the first I'd have under my sway'd be the little fella in the barracks."

"But, Miss Dempsey, can't you do anything? I mean, it's perfectly preposterous—appalling——" Ann broke in, dismayed.

"Sure, what help'd be in it for me? I can only keep quiet and not be saying anything. 'Tis best so. God is good, and them above is blessed yet. But, Miss Ann, me darlin' girl, it wasn't to go moidther you with my troubles I put this delay on yez. But sure yourself remembers the day ye rode into my poor place last summer, yourself an' young Mister St Lawrence. I said then yez was the nicest pair ever I'd ask to see—I'd be long sorry to say it now. Can ye mind the brown horse I sowld him? Och, ye knew it well! Didn't he sell it to the Captain here the very week after? Maybe your honour could recall 'twas a bank cheque for forty-five pounds he gave me for the horse; and a paper for me to say I'd got it. Ah, divil a one so pleasant as what he was! And yourself was very good to me in my trouble too. 'Twas when poor Maurice was gone first it should happen. Well, my lady, three days afther I took the cheque into the bank in Bungarvin, and I gave it to a bit of a lad behind the counter. 'Sure that's no good,' he said to me, 'there's no name wrote on it. Who did ye get it from?' I told him that 'twas from Mr St Lawrence. Well, he laughed at me. 'That's the cute old fox,' he said. 'If you'll be said by me, don't leave him till ye have pound notes in your hands. Well, well',' he said, and looked at me the way you'd look at a fool. I was going home that same evening, and I met a chap on the road—a nice respectable, poor man, I know him this long time. I comminced to tell him what happened me in regard o' the cheque, and the poor man had me teased with the things he'd say to me, the way the passion rose in me throat, and didn't I tear the cheque across, the way he'd see how little good it was. Sure, all sense'd go from a pairson that got as great annoyance as myself."

"But it must be a mistake—I'm sure it's a mistake." Ann was pink to the roots of her curls. "Have you written to Mr St Lawrence about it?"

"Is it write? Sure me heart's broke writing to him, and I get no reply at all." Mary Dempsey shrouded herself if possible still deeper in her cloak—a perfect mantle of woe. From its depths she regarded Ann covertly. "I thought maybe yourself'd say a good word for me," she continued. "Sure 'twas the way when I seen the two of ye——"

"Er—look here, Miss Dempsey," Allan struck in suddenly, "it's a dashed sad story, and I'm sorry for you and all that. But what I mean to say is that Miss Hillingdon can't possibly do anything for you in the matter. By the way, have you written to Captain St Lawrence or to his father?"

"No, sir, but to the Captain of the dogs. Sure I thought——"

"Well, take my advice and send a line to Captain Dennys St Lawrence himself. Mr St Lawrence has been away, you know, and probably hasn't been getting his letters. I'm sure Mr Dennys'll see to it. I'm awfully sorry for you—believe me, I am. But Miss Hillingdon has absolutely no influence in the matter. Good bye, Miss Dempsey—come on, Ann, don't you think we ought to be getting on?"

Mary Dempsey watched the two fast-disappearing figures out of sight. Then she re-crossed the stepping stones—less certainly this time, because her eyes were blinded with tears.

"Try my hanky, Ann," suggested Allan some minutes later. "It's—it's drier, dear."

They were sitting in the lee of a patch of furze—at least, Allan was sitting, intent on his third cigarette, but Ann was lying face downward on the damp grass sobbing as if her heart would break. She accepted the proffered handkerchief and fought fiercely for self-control. Soon her sobs died down to a miserable sniff, and she sat up and mopped her eyes with a great show of determination. Allan ached to comfort her. He put out a large brown hand and covered her small one, lying so listlessly on the short grass and furze prickles.

"Have a smoke, dear?" he suggested at last.

Ann accepted. "Allan," she said, in a very small voice.

"Yes, old bird." Allan turned to her with his large smile, his voice studiously unconcerned.

"I'm really sure you think me a poisonous little fool, but *really* I couldn't help it. Oh, Allan, if you only knew what an awful time I've had, you'd understand."

"Suppose you tell me all about it—I mean, if I can be any help. I'd love to know, and I'm sure it would do you good to get it off your chest, Ann dear," Allan said.

"Registering sympathy," Ann flashed sweetly, almost her own self again. "Are you sure it wouldn't bore you to hear? I feel as if I must tell some one, and of course Dad is hopeless and Sybil too young." Ann sighed. "I know now," she said, "that I fell in love with Dennys long ago—oh, ages ago."

Allan started violently, but Ann did not notice. She was staring out through the grey sky into that land of long, long ago—in reality but a few short months—in which she and Dennys had fished, and shot, and ridden together, and understood one another with perfect sympathy. Allan, feeling sick and dizzy, as though—as he tersely expressed it to himself—"his best friend had bitten him in the stomach," waited to hear more.

"You see," the small sad voice continued, "we used to do everything together—everything. He used to help me with the horses, and manage my bets for me. He taught me to bat a ball off a pony too, and—oh, nearly everything I know. Besides being such a dear. 'Course father hated him, and he never could see that he was different from his family. You know, his mother was one of the Charmians of Carnahask, and she ran away to marry Johnny St Lawrence. She was a great friend of mother's, and they died within a year of each other. Then Dennys went to Winchester, and after that came the war. He did most awfully well, you know; he's an MC and a captain. He's been out in East Africa till two years ago, when his health gave out and he had to come home. Since then he's been living with his father and helping with the horses and the hounds, and we've——" Ann paused.

"Yes?" prompted her cousin.

"We've seen a great deal of each other," finished the child, with quaint dignity.

"But, Ann dear, where does the trouble come in?" Allan asked gently.

"I'll tell you." Ann summoned Jibber to her and held the rough little head close under her chin, for comfort, before continuing. "Well, you see, Allan, we were beastly happy, and then—d'you remember that day we went up the mountain—when father was so cross? Well, that evening when I was going to bed, I felt somehow—I can't describe it—as if some one had sent out a fearfully strong SOS to me; a kind of call that I *had* to answer. You wouldn't know what I mean—not being a girl yourself." Ann glanced at the tall young man beside her, who nodded his undivided assent to her last remark. "Then," she continued, in a hushed voice, "I let myself out at the billiard-room window. You'd all gone to bed—or at least I thought you had—and I ran, and ran, through the laurels, in my evening shoes and all——"

"In your evening shoes, Ann. Yes?"

"You see, something was pulling me on; something much stronger than myself. Well, there under the trees by the river I met Dennys; and he . . . and we—I mean——"

"Yes, I *quite* understand," interpolated Allan hastily.

"No, you just don't," Ann rounded on him, "and I must say it. Fact is, though he was awfully dear and sweet, I've thought since then"—Ann spoke slowly and painfully—"that perhaps I cared for him more than he did for me . . . and . . . and showed it."

"Absolutely not possible, dear," her cousin assured her, from the rock bottom of conviction.

"It's like you to say so, old man." Ann gave his tweed arm a grateful little pat. "Oh, Allan, it makes it *so* much better to tell some one. But the next day, the very next day—cubbing, you remember?—he wasn't there, and I'd been so sure of seeing him at the meet, that it was like—like a smack across the eyes to hear he'd gone to Meath. But still, Allan, I was so sure. You see, I'd been his best pal for such ages, it never struck me anything could be wrong. Even when I didn't see him properly—alone, for nearly three weeks, I still thought it was just a series of rotten accidents that prevented it. I'd've written, only, silly as it sounds, I felt shy and simply couldn't. Then there was the Jeeves' dance, and I felt quite sure everything'd be all right then. And I looked forward to it immensely." Ann heaved a retrospective sigh and spread out her hands hopelessly. "Instead, it was an utter, a complete wash-out. Dennys was there, but he never came near me, or asked me for a dance, or a—or anything. *Then*, of course, I realized that there must be some rotten misunderstanding. So next Friday—it was last Friday—what ages ago it seems!—I tried to be nice when we met him outside the kennels, but he just rode on and left me there. So I was angry, awfully angry, and I'm afraid I flirted abominably with you, Allan dear."

"Oh, don't mind me," put in her cousin hastily. "Look on me as a mere lay figure—you know, like one of those things you make blouses on."

Ann regarded him uncomprehendingly.

"You *know* that I love you," she said. "I think you're a perfect darling."

"Thanks, dear, it's very sweet of you," Allan assured her pensively. "Well, as you were saying——"

Ann clasped her hands round her knees, and gazed miserably into a neighbouring whin bush, her eyes once more filling with tears.

"There isn't anything more to say. That—that's all."

"But, Ann, if that's all, I'm sure it's nothing but some fool mistake that can easily be cleared up. You've no idea how easily these misunderstandings happen. Why, my dear girl, did I never tell you the story about Agatha and the cocktail? It happened at Simla, and I loved Agatha very much, and——" He stopped, arrested by the almost perceptible stiffening of the figure by his side.

"You heard what that woman said, Allan?"

"Insinuated pretty plainly that St Lawrence got off a bogus cheque on her, after extracting a receipt. The thing's manifestly impossible."

"It's not a bit impossible. If you knew anything about horse-dealing—especially in Ireland—you'd realize the hideous things people'll do without turning a hair. I've heard of old St Lawrence doing things every bit as bad as that. But Dennys—I thought I knew Dennys——"

"You evidently don't, if you imagine him capable of doing a thing like that. I don't pretend to have a whole lot of insight into human nature, but anyone could see that chap is straight." Allan spoke somewhat shortly.

"My dear, it's not only what the woman told me, but I heard the same story only this morning from Daddy. Besides, I saw Dennys give her the cheque with my own eyes. He must've known." With Ann, as with most women, arguments against her half-formed suspicions only served to crystalize them in her mind to irrevocable facts.

"And believing this," Allan laid an impressive forefinger on his cousin's knee, "do you—can you still care for the chap?"

Ann's face seemed to shrivel; it became pinched and white, while her grey eyes grew abnormally large. "I care for every inch of him," she spoke low, "but I'd never marry him, even if he wanted me. I *couldn't* marry a cheat."

"I'm convinced the chap is as straight as you or I," said Allan again.

"I'm not." Ann rose stiffly to her feet and picked up her gun; calling to Jibber, she walked away into the bog. Allan followed suit. So she'll never marry him, he mused, never, never! I *wonder*. What pluck that kid has! Such a tiny thing. . . . Here Allan missed an easy shot at a snipe, and cursing himself for a fool, strode deep into a bog hole.

He had been hard hit, had Allan. When the girl a man loves for the moment more than all things, treats him as her best friend, even to the extent of telling him the story of her love affair with another man, he does not feel exactly rejoiced. Uplifted perhaps, but not rejoiced. But though showing him clearly that he was a thousand miles off the road to her heart, Ann had at least convinced him of the absence of any other successful traveller along that thorny way. That was something. Allan felt distinctly sorry for that unfortunate devil St Lawrence. Surely it was not possible that he had done, or connived at the doing of such a rotten thing. Yet the evidence against him was so plausible. The strongest, to Allan's mind, being the fellow's avoidance of Ann. No one with a spark of decency in them would go near a wonderful girl like Ann, if they'd done such a thing, thought Allan; and the St Lawrence fellow *was* decent, therefore. . . . What a rotten shame, wonderful man to ride, too. Very man for old Bill Lammingham, to have out on his blessed ranch.

Raising his gun to his shoulder, Allan drew a careful bead upon a small bird of zig-zag flight. He fired, and the snipe plumped down into a whin-bush.

"Pretty good!" called Ann. "Don't pick it up yet, I want Jib to set it. She looks so sweet setting things."

He waited patiently while Jibber, encouraged by her 'mother,' methodically quartered every inch of ground between himself and the furze-bush, wherein was impaled the snipe. Arrived there, she sat up as though begging; cold nose a-tremble; bright eyes alight.

"Darling!" Ann made much of the white scrap, while Allan, whose arm was embedded up to the shoulder in furze prickles, remarked that if her retrieving instincts were as well developed as her nose, Jibber might almost be considered useful.

"Idiot!" replied his cousin shortly. "And now, come on. We really must have more than one jack and a rabbit to show for our day."

"Yes. With scoffers and mockers such as Sybil encumbering the earth," agreed Allan.

Nevertheless, when all the bog pools had turned golden and red with the evening sky, nothing further had been added to the bag. Ann, indeed, had suggested that Jibber might repose herself there for a period; Allan did not, however, for a moment seriously consider the idea.

"Had it been yourself now, little one, I should've loved it. She's dead tired, poor mite!" he added impersonally, to the world around him.

"She's *not* tired, and she's *not* a mite," returned his companion with some hauteur.

"No, she's not. She's just an atom," agreed Allan cheerfully. "That's a high wall, cousin."

"So it is." Ann surveyed it for a moment. "If you're good, you may——"

"Yes?"

"Lift Jibber over it." she ended. "I'm going by this gate, I *fink*."

They left the bogs behind them, and set off to cover the three miles to Ballinrath by road. It took them the best part of an hour, during which time Allan proved the most charming and delightful of companions. He beguiled the way with stories of India—stories of polo and races, bets and dances, and the true histories of many happenings, embellishing his own recollections, and those of other people, with a wealth of minute and piquant detail. As they walked up the dark, evergreen-shaded drive to the house, Ann slipped a small, friendly hand through her cousin's arm.

"Allan, old dear, you're the best pal ever. I'm most grateful to you. Your niceness all day's been something amazing. And—and I really couldn't help being a fool. . . ."

"Dear fool," replied her cousin, "I feel, if you know what I mean, very honoured. I should love you to do it again, just as often as ever you feel like it."

They deposited the rabbit and snipe unostentatiously in the pantry, and calling Jibber from her fruitless scouring of an empty porridge pot under the sink, made their way to the billiard-room, there to consume enormous quantities of hot, buttery potato cakes, and many cups of tea.

Sybil, seated behind the urn, dispensed tea with a grave and matronly air. When the returning hunters' heavy thirsts proved somewhat abated, she turned her attention to the gramophone. A discordant bleating of saxophones, reedy thrill of swanee whistles, and the hurrying beat of pianos, sounded in the quiet room for a space. Sybil was playing fox-trots. Followed a pause, while the lady shuffled over a heap of records in search of her special fancy.

"What's she going to give us?"

Allan lay back in his old leather arm-chair, and stared

appreciatively around the room; at the tall windows—
heavily curtained; the dark carpet and glimpses of shining
floor; chairs and settees which positively smelt of use and
comfort; the glittering array of heavy silver on the tea-
table, the large solid cake, and many kinds of jam; at the
two little white dogs, gazing with anguished eyes upon
Ann, who—seated on the leather fender-stool—gave to
each its portion in due season. The collar of her cream silk
shirt had rucked up at the back of her neck, and Allan
experienced a ridiculously keen desire to flatten it out over
her jumper. Then the first notes of Kriesler's 'Chanson
meditation' stole magically upon the air—the cry of youth,
youth ardent and seeking, hung vibrant for a moment. The
theme changed, leading through the mazeries of life to a
still content. The great full notes sounded deeply through
the room . . . the master ceased . . . a gramophone needle
ploughed gratingly, and Sybil applied the brake.

"Finis!" She flung a handful of used gramophone
needles into the heart of the turf fire. "Why, Ann!" she
exclaimed beneath her breath; but Ann rose, and fled
precipitantly from the room. "What *is* the matter?" Sybil
demanded, wide-eyed, of her cousin.

"Matter? How should I know? I suppose her feet felt
cold, or she hadn't a hankie, or something. Girls always
seem to want to cry if they've forgotten their hankies."

"Don't be childish," interrupted Sybil. "I mean what
happened to-day?"

"Don't be so infernally astute," replied her cousin, as
he tendered first one wet boot and then the other to the
roaring fire. "Why should anything have happened to-
day—anyway?"

"Silly of me. Forgive, Sweetest. Let's see—where did

you go? Walked it from here to Lisogue, didn't you? And then back through the bogs—best part of six miles. Bag— one jack and a rabbit. Then I played the Kriesler and Ann weeps. Oo-la-la! Allan isn't half a bright boy—*No!*"

"Oh, Sybil, like a good child stop scintillating for a moment. Give your stupendous intellect a rest, as it were, and come here and I'll tell you a story."

"Well!" Sybil seated herself upon the fender, and registered breathless interest. "Do begin, uncle."

"I—I can't," said her 'uncle' weakly. "Not if you look at me like that—I can't. Only one I can think of is the cocktail of the sweet young thing, and that might be a bit over your head. Too subtle!"

"Dearest, d'you feel quite well?" Sybil laid cool fingers on his forehead. "How about a nice hot bath? I know it's not your bath night, but for once we might ask nurse to stretch a point. Such a shock to the system, so complete a change of environment as—in short—a bath, would, I feel sure, be beneficial. Tone up those jaded nerves. Tootaloo, Babe! See you later." Sybil departed, whistling a cheerful stave as she went.

Allan, after gazing soulfully into the fire for some moments, went upstairs to change. The bath proved redolent of some expensive water-softener; by this Allan judged Ann to be feeling very bad. She had once told him that she reserved these bath-salts for those occasions when every man's hand was against her, and she could endure no more buffets from fate. As he passed by her door, Allan paused, and knocked.

"Feeling better, old thing?" he inquired tenderly.

"Much," replied an almost cheerful voice. "I'm brushing my hair."

"Oo! May I come in and watch you? I'd love to."

"No, not just now. Run away and dress, and don't stand about in draughts with nothing on," replied Miss Hillingdon maternally.

"Let me hasten to explain," said Allan, "that to a modest man like myself, there is something abhorrent, if not indecent, about such a proceeding. I——"

"*Will* you go away!" interrupted Ann, with a gurgle of laughter; and Allan retired, smiling softly, to his own room.

Half an hour later, he was seated before the library writing-table, deep in throes of composition, biting heavily upon the end of Ann's fountain pen, and staring morosely at the blank sheets of blue linen paper, red-stamped, which confronted him. Then, filled seemingly with sudden resolution, he hurled away his cigarette, humped his shoulders determinedly, wrote the day of the month on one of the many blank sheets before him, and proceeded to fill it, and some others, with his own peculiarly tidy and characteristic hand-writing.

This done, he heaved a sigh of immense satisfaction, collected the loose sheets, pulled forward one of the heavy candlesticks which illumined the writing-table, and proceeded to read the missive, pausing now and again to make a correction. This then, is what he read:——

BALLINRATH HOUSE,
BUNGARVIN.

DEAR BUDGE—

My excuse for a long silence must be that posts leave both Elysium and Hades but irregularly. Yes, I have explored both places pretty thoroughly of late.

Listen, Budge. She is small, but—yes, you are quite right—just the height of my heart. Her mind is serious, and a constant delight unto me. So are her feet, and neck, and chin, and eyelashes—forgive me for our friendship's sake, I maudle. More, I burble. And now let me get it over. She loves another, but will never marry him—never, never. I had it from her own lips this day. The circumstances are exceptional, which leads me to imagine that her 'never, never,' does not in this case stand for 'Tomorrow—the next day—when she will.' I would it meant that some day I might aspire; of that hope, I do not, however, flatter myself. Enough if I may serve the lady. And here, Budge, is where you come in. You do really. But don't be frightened, the way will not be hard.

In regard to your proposal that I should spend the winter with yourself and Iris on that ranch of yours in Texas, the alluring possibilities of joining forces with you thrown in. I would beg to state—

(a) That to me, cows (I beg their pardons—steers) lack subtlety.

(b) That, judging by the lurid pictures I have seen of western horses and their hideous antics, I should consider the most wild and woolly of Irish three-year-olds an infinitely preferable ride.

(c) That, hopeless backslider as you are—I feel sure of your understanding, and possibly even sympathizing with me, when I tell you, extraordinary as it may appear, that I still happen to be more or less keen on the regiment, and have not yet contemplated sending in my papers. Otherwise, the prospect of enjoying your and Iris's society for an indefinite period would probably over-ride my aforesaid objections to ranch life.

Now I come to the root fundamental of the matter. You want, you tell me, a man to join you in your work, and bear with you the burden and heat of this ranch. A man, moreover, who is one of ourselves and a competent sportsman to boot. To such an one, you would give an admirable wage as foreman; or, should he bring with him capital, instal him as your partner in the Bar V Ranch. Budge, I know of such man, in every respect the man you want. What he does not know of horses—more, of hounds—is not worth the learning. With his gun he is, well, at any rate a great deal better than myself. His schools were Winchester, the war, and East Africa; which last place he found poisonous to his system and whence he returned some two years ago, to join his father here in Ireland.

His father is an MFH, than which—we have it on the highest authority—no occupation is more honourable. He is also a horse-coper of malodorous reputation. A combination of occupations rare, I imagine, even in Ireland. This man's son is the beloved of my dear Ann. It is he whom she will never marry—never, never. And why, you ask? Because very circumstantial evidence goes to show that he—Dennys—has been in some way mixed up in a very crooked and dirty piece of business. Therefore Ann, who I feel sure would gladly die for the fellow, will yet never marry him—(at the risk of appearing monotonous let me rub it well in) never, never.

My friend Budge, I believe this man to be utterly straight. I know him for a good sort, also for the best man to hounds, and one of the finest huntsmen I've seen. I recommend him to you with all confidence. Offer him your job as foreman, I know well he has no money to buy the partnership. If he accepts, I consider you both lucky. For him it means a new beginning, very far away from his extraordinarily beastly old father's dirty habits in horse dealing and other matters. For you, it means the right man in the right place. And for Ann—well, I'm not sure, but I think it's best for Ann. If she cares a great deal, she'll marry him—anyway. If not, perhaps of her great kindness she'll marry me.

Should you decide to offer your billet to my friend, address your letter to—Captain Dennys St Lawrence, MC, Cloonbeg, Bungarvin, Ireland.

My love to Iris and my god-daughter.

Yours ever,

ALLAN.

Selecting a stout envelope, he addressed it, collected the many sheets of his letter, and placing them therein, with a heavy sigh, licked and closed the flap of the envelope. After which he extinguished the candles on the writing-table, and crossing the room to the great fireplace, remained standing awhile in deep thought—one foot upon the fender, his fair head bent, his forehead puckered.

Sybil, from where she lay—all graceful slim curves and long silk-stockinged leg—in the corner of the sofa, the high back of which concealed her from the writing-table, regarded him intently through half-shut eyes. How tall he was; how perfectly ripping! How she adored the crispness of his fair hair, and his general just-had-a-bath-and-a-shave appearance. Sybil wished vehemently that she was thirty-seven—instead of seventeen years of age—and married to a perfect brute, instead of being merely Sybil . . . just think then, what exciting possibilities! . . . Why didn't he look up and see her? She was getting fearfully stiff from lying still so long. He must've seen her.

"Is it asleep, or only being funny?" said a quiet voice. Sybil's heavy white lids dropped closer over the green eyes. "I think it's asleep. Let's wake it up according to the best traditions, and then pretend we're a bad dream."

Allan stood looking down on her for a moment; on the perfect oval of her white face, the delicious sweep of those dark lashes, the original way in which her black bobbed hair—delightfully innocent of permanent waves—went out in a peak against her cheek; realizing, almost for the first time, what an exquisite manner of child this was. Then, in the best manner of a flirtatious uncle, he bent low over the gracefully twisted form on the sofa, and kissed the red mouth very gently.

Sybil's eyelids folded suddenly back. Allan was looking down—straight into those generally half-shut and very secretive green eyes; being twenty-seven, a great and wonderful age as compared with seventeen, he realized pretty plainly what he saw in them.

Sybil was aware, in a flash of annoyance, amusement, and—could it be?—contempt, in the wide blue eyes that looked back into hers. In an instant she was on her feet, a furious, palpitating, and for once genuine, Sybil.

"How dare you? I hate you! You beast, you—you loathsome cad! I hate you!" and she flamed from the room. He heard her light feet running with extraordinary rapidity across the hall and up the stairs to her room, heard her door bang.

Allan seated himself heavily upon the sofa so recently vacated, and leaned his head in his hands. He had had a heavy day, a day of many developments—this last surprise being by no means the least of them.

CHAPTER XII
Dennys and his Sister

ELIZABETH banged heavily upon the door of the
bath-room.

"Dennys!" she called. "Hurry up, for goodness' sake, I
want to get in."

Her brother ceased splashing for a moment.

"Why, I thought you had washed. Haven't you, Elizabeth?" A long pause. "Haven't you, Elizabeth?" repeated
Dennys sternly.

"I had a bath last night," replied the lady in the voice of
one announcing something of an achievement. Then,
pathetically, she added: "*Must* I wash my neck?"

"If you want to come out schooling with me this
morning, you'll jolly well scrub not only your neck, but
your ears, and have your nails decent too," commanded
an awful voice from within.

"Well, all I can say is I think you must be beastly
dirty—you're never done having baths," retorted Elizabeth shrilly, "and you can go out schooling by yourself. I
can go with father, or Johnny Brien, without having to
skin myself with a loofah first. So squash!" Having thus
relieved her feelings, Miss St Lawrence retreated in good
order to her own apartment, where—despite her late
diatribe against over-cleanliness—she proceeded to wield
her loofah, and to ply orange stick and nail-brush with
vigour.

She then struggled a while with intricate buttonings,
finally clothing her nether limbs in a pair of riding
breeches. After a prolonged survey of the effect, she

supplemented the inadequacies of her attire with boots, leggings, and a flannel shirt and taking from a drawer a hunting stock of immense length, she pounded down the passage to Dennys's bedroom—knocked, and was admitted.

"Oh, Dennys, will you tie this for me the way it won't come off," she implored breathlessly.

Her brother led her to the light.

"Your hair's very wet, old thing," he said. "Did you wash your neck?"

"Yes."

"Good for you! Buzz me over that towel and I'll dry your head."

From the depths of the bath-towel came a small voice:

"I washed me neck, *and* me ears, *and* me nails. Dennys, can I ride Aurora this morning?"

Dennys ceased his activities with the towel, and proceeded to wind the stock round his sister's neck.

"Can I?" she asked again.

"You know you can't, Elizabeth. What's the matter with Biddelia? You used to be fond enough of her?"

"I am. I love her! But she's got so blooming old lately. She's not up to her work and she's not half up to my weight," announced Miss St Lawrence aggrievedly.

"Well, look here, old girl—tell you what. You ride Biddy to-day, because I want something steady to give me leads over the leps, and later on, we'll see—you might have the bay pony, perhaps." Dennys's tone was most conciliatory; it entirely failed, however, to soothe his small sister.

"Devil take the bay pony! It's Aurora I want to ride," she replied with some acerbity.

Her brother turned his back upon her.

"If you use beastly language, you'll just have to ride Biddelia till she goes into the hounds' trough," he announced sternly. "Now cut along down to breakfast—and put a coat on," he called after her; "you're too old to sky around in breeches." Dennys sighed heavily as he buckled on his wrist-watch—a young sister was such an awful responsibility, if one took her seriously.

Below stairs, Elizabeth saluted her father and seated herself at the breakfast table.

"Isn't Dennys very late?" observed that gentleman in tones of jovial censure. "If I were you, I'd go up to his room and empty the jug on him. I'll bet he's snoring asleep this minute!"

"Well, he's not," returned Elizabeth coldly, as she helped herself to the smaller of the two fried eggs, and the paler of the two rashers in the breakfast dish, carefully covering up the remainder for her brother. He's only after tying my stock for me, and that's what kept him, if you want to know."

"Well, well." Mr St Lawrence surveyed his adored daughter indulgently. "Don't you think you're the lucky little girl to get off from school in the middle of term? I tell you, when I was a kid, we didn't get off home if there was scarlatina in the school."

"Perhaps you would have, father, if the girl who got it was sleeping in your room," suggested his daughter incontestably.

"Oh, well, I don't know—perhaps I would," agreed Mr St Lawrence with some haste. "But anyway, you must remember—and you're to remember too, Dennys"—he turned to his son, who had at that moment entered the room—"that Elizabeth's in quarantine, and she can't be going into people's houses, or shops either, and no more should you, my boy—except when you can't help it."

"I suppose not," agreed Dennys.

"I don't care a twopenny da——" Elizabeth here caught her brother's eye, and refrained. "I don't care a tinker's curse," she amended hastily. "The only place I'd want to go is Ballinrath, and Rick isn't at home anyway. So it doesn't matter; I'll see Ann hunting."

"Well, you will not," replied her parent pleasantly. "Do you want to give scarlatina to all the boys that'd be picking you up when you fell off? No, I couldn't have you hunting at all."

Elizabeth's face fell ominously. "For how long?" she asked desperately.

"Oh, a long time. It might be months and it might be years," replied Mr St Lawrence, with mistimed joviality. His daughter ignored the sally freezingly.

"For how long, Dennys?" she asked, her underlip trembling.

"It's not very long, dear," Dennys assured her cheeringly. "We'll look it up in one of father's old medical books after breakfast. And, anyway, you and I and Johnny'll have a couple of byes on the quiet. So cheer up, old girl."

"What a silly fool you are!" observed Elizabeth witheringly to her parent. "Didn't I just know that you were talking through your hat? And don't start making faces at me. You're not a bit funny—all right——"

"Elizabeth!" remonstrated her brother a moment later. "It was perfectly rotten of you to throw that bun at father, and to put marmalade on it too! You're just a spoilt baby.

Go and pick up the pieces now before Driscoll makes himself sick eating them."

Elizabeth complied willingly. Then, returning to her place, she finished an excellent repast, after which she and Dennys collected their crops and hats, and Driscoll, and repaired to the stable yard.

Dennys saddled and led forth Biddelia—a gaunt grey mare with a lean, clever head, her legs thick with the honourable scars of many winters. Elizabeth climbed into the pad saddle and kicked her mount cheerfully round the yard till Dennys and Aurora were ready to start; her hands were quiet and perfect, but those drumming heels were never still.

"Come on!" Dennys rode out of the yard and jogged off down the avenue—Aurora sidling and hanging on her bit. Elizabeth following, tried hard to convince herself that Biddelia was full of buck and needed riding. Biddelia, however, jolted complacently along, even passing a traction engine without the least trouble; whilst Aurora, snorting with horror at the loathsome monster, reared round, and made a good attempt to jump the hedge. Dennys dealt with her heavily for a moment, then turned, laughing, to his sister.

"Isn't it a good job you weren't riding her then? She'd have been clean over the fence with you."

"Rot!" replied Elizabeth, unconvinced. "I'd be just as well able to ride her as what you are. Johnny Brien says so."

"Oh, well, if you mind all Johnny Brien says——"

Dennys dismounted in order to open a ramshackle gate, and together they cantered across a wide green field; Aurora catching hold, and treating her rider to a series of dislocating buck-jumps as she got going. Dennys steadied her down as they drew near the first obstacle—a gap, filled in with furze bushes and a wooden pole.

"Go on now, Elizabeth," he called; "give us a lead!"

Elizabeth smote Biddelia heavily upon her fat side; they sailed on ahead, charged down at the gap, and were over with a hoist and a heave.

"Dashed good!" commented Dennys when he joined her. "You sat her well."

Elizabeth's cheeks glowed and her eyes shone with pleasure and exercise combined. How she did love schooling with Dennys!

On they rode for many miles, skirting fields of wheat and winter oats, galloping on sound grass land, stumbling and jig-jogging where turnips grew, and jumping all sorts and conditions of fences; stone-faced banks, narrow, only room for a kick-back here, furze-grown banks, over which Aurora arched out in best style, big doubles with November rain filling the dykes on either side, and treacherous, slippery banks—not two foot high. It was in crossing one of these latter that Biddelia put her foot in a rabbit-hole, and came down heavily on the point of her shoulder. Elizabeth was thrown clear, and arose dizzy, coughing, but unhurt.

A rather white-faced Dennys felt his small sister all over, and resettled her carefully in the saddle. Soon afterwards they scrambled down a bank into a muddy lane, which finally debouched upon the high road near Ballinrath. Dennys rode fast past the old house, just visible through its well-planted groups of beech and fir. But Elizabeth lingered; she did so want some one to see her and ask the reason of her muddy condition. Then she could explain just the horrific manner of fall Biddelia had given her.

Thus it was she who saw Sybil, accompanied by the pack—two gallumphing hound puppies, the little white West Highlanders, and Benbow, slobbering majestically—walking towards them across the field. She waved a stick in cheerful greeting, whereupon Elizabeth shouted to her brother to stop, and immediately enmeshed herself in cheerful conversation.

"What's it doing away from school?" Sybil asked, as soon as Dennys appeared.

"Scarlatina," was the reply. "We're all in quarantine for the present."

"Oh! that's rotten luck. What d'you think of Ann's puppies?"

"Coming on well. Yeu-Leu Ravager—Boy! Good bone there."

Sybil seated herself on the wall, leaning her back against Benbow's mighty frame, and prepared to be conversational.

"How long since you've been over here, Dennys?" she asked.

"The hounds keep one pretty busy, you see. Now we're in quarantine, otherwise I'd love to——"

"Oh, well," Sybil laughed, and conversation languished. Presently the pair rode away down the long grey road. Sybil shrugged shapely shoulders.

"These devoted men," she murmured, "how they do hash things up. Can he've done that about the cheque? Anyway, Ann's a little fool. Come on, Benny! Rachel! Ravager! Co-oop," and she departed.

As Dennys soothed Aurora into a frame of mind

sufficiently calm to allow of his opening the avenue gate, he was shyly accosted by two little girls, whose violet eyes were fixed in terror upon his mare's heels.

"Ask 'em what they want, Elizabeth," he said. "Stand, mare!"

"A letter for you about a horse," Elizabeth told him later, as they stood together in Aurora's box.

"For father, probably."

"No, it's addressed to you, Dennys."

"Right. Thanks. Buzz on into the house and tell Lizzie we're ready for lunch."

Elizabeth departed, and Dennys, left to himself, tore open the flap of the flimsy envelope and read the letter contained therein. An illiterate scrawl, but it set forth pretty plainly the miserable story of Mary Dempsey. When he had mastered its contents, Dennys felt over Aurora's legs with minute exactness, straightened her sheet, and leaving the stable, walked slowly up to the house.

Elizabeth and her father were already at lunch when he entered the dining-room—impossible then to discuss this matter immediately. All through that endless meal Dennys studied his father curiously, a tall, lean-faced man with a benevolent expression. Candid blue-grey eyes allied to a thatch of iron-grey hair lent an expression of benevolence to a face otherwise hard and determined; determination was in the rather under-shot jaw, while the lines of the mouth were as though cut in steel; a thick neck, and those thick, fat hands plying knife and fork in a slightly studied manner—was that really all he knew about his father? Dennys asked himself curiously. About all, except that he had never liked him much, but then on the other hand he had always rather admired him. His consummate horse-manship, his gifts as a huntsman, and his cleverness where sick hounds and horses were concerned—all these things had formed a bond stronger than might be imagined between this father and his son.

On the whole, St Lawrence liked Dennys a good deal less than Dennys liked him. The boy had been born at one of those times—frequent in his married life—when Joan had been in what her husband considered a damned mawkish frame of mind. He felt that his small son, even at an early age, disapproved—as he thought his father—a dam' blackguard, a low-down cheat, *not straight*. . . . God! he hadn't thought of that—*not straight* . . . whereas he was merely a fool, the silly tool used by a knave. Dennys knew deep bitterness of spirit. He could never explain; for how was it possible for him to go bleating to her that his father, and not he himself, had done this thing?

"I thought I couldn't ask her to marry me when I was father's partner," he reflected; "now I couldn't ask her to marry his son. Ann, my dear, I care for you more than that. Really, Ann, really."

He dug into the innermost parts of his writing-table, producing therefrom three short notes written to him by Ann during the last eighteen months. One contained an invitation to a tennis party, another proposed a badger dig, the third dealt chiefly with some knotty point connected with the feeding of hound puppies. Dennys tore them into tiny bits and dropped them into his waste-paper basket. Better so!

Then there were those snapshots. They were really awfully bad, no one but himself could possibly recognize them as likenesses of Ann. Surely he might keep these. He would, anyway! That one was so like her seat on a horse; she was holding Driscoll in this one—yes, certainly he would keep the snapshots.

Now to write that cheque for Mary Dempsey. Forty pounds gone at one fell swoop reduced his bank balance to a ridiculously low figure. Never mind; enough to take him to Canada anyway. No more Africa for him ... Australia perhaps ... his thoughts roamed far afield.

A knock upon the door startled him from his reverie. By Jove! Elizabeth. How could he have forgotten Elizabeth? How was he to face leaving her behind, as he would have to do if he set his face once more for the Colonies? What a dear funny kid she was, with her thin, eager little face, and untidy streaks of hair! He watched her covertly as she pursued her aimless wanderings around the room.

"Are you nearly done writing your letters, Dennys?" she asked at last. It was tactful, for she could see him sitting staring at the litter on his table, but writing—no. He felt touched by the mite's consideration, which forbade her to pry when she saw there was trouble.

"Yes, old thing. Shall we go and see if Johnny Brien has sulphured Romeo and Regent yet? Or we might clip the new filly."

Elizabeth assented joyfully. Seizing her brother by the hand, she tore madly downstairs and out of the house.

Ensued an afternoon of pure joy for Elizabeth. She covered herself with sulphur and train-oil in the kennels, succeeded in cracking Johnny Brien's crop three times, only catching herself on the nose once in the process, and held gamely on to the woolly filly, till—over-wrought by the unaccustomed clipping machine—the mare struck out dangerously with her forefeet, missing Elizabeth by inches.

"Ahaa! That one's the right pill!" observed a stable underling, as he fixed the touch on the filly's poor soft nose; but whether he referred to his employer's daughter or to his mare was not very clear.

Then, as they walked up to the house for tea, a few words from her adored Dennys scattered all her happiness like chaff to the winds.

"What'd you do," he asked casually, "if I had to go away?" He felt her hand in his (Elizabeth invariably dragged her walking companions along by the hand) grow hot and moist, then cold and clammy as a little frog.

"Dennys!" It was like the cry of a little animal, badly hurt. "You aren't going away, Dennys? Never? Promise! Oh, do say you won't go away!" She hopped from one foot to another in a very frenzy of despair.

"I must, Elizabeth." It was better for her to know now.

"Oh, Dennys, then you must take me! Dennys *please*. You *must*! I must go wiv you!" He shook his head slowly.

"I can't, dear. Not now——"

She dropped his hand then, and fled from him, her long brown-stockinged legs streaking through the dusk.

Half an hour later Dennys found her, lying abandoned to despair, on a heap of turnips in an out-house. She refused comfort, only sobbing to him—Elizabeth who never cried—to take her, take her too. . . . Surely the way which he had chosen was hard.

CHAPTER XIII

The Way of a Maid and the Wiles
of a Minx

THE short November days slipped by, unmarked by any exciting event. Rickey's holidays came within measurable distance, and still Allan stayed on—a very welcome guest beneath his cousin's roof.

Ann went cheerlessly through the days, her white face pathetic witness of the dull ache of misery within her. Major Hillingdon—seriously occupied with the planting of a new orchard—perceived nothing amiss. True, he noticed with some surprise that Ann did not seem as keen as usual on the hunting. Often enough she would lend her precious Garry Owen that Allan or her sister might fit a second, or even a third day's hunting into a week, when she, perhaps, had not been out at all. However, she seemed as interested as ever in the horses, and would go by herself for long lonely rides around the country.

Oh, those long rides in the short November afternoons! Ann soaked herself in misery as she rode along the narrow muddy lanes, and looked out over the bramble-filled fences and sodden green fields to the distant line of grey, stark mountains. She wondered futilely then why she had ever been born, why she had ever met Dennys—why everything was so impossible and so lonely. She never wondered now about the affair of the cheque. That was over—finished. She had accepted the facts as she saw them. Dennys had let her down all round—badly! Well she could do without him and never show a sore heart.

Her father was right enough; Dennys *was* tarred with the same brush as that old reprobate St Lawrence. Ann flushed hotly at the thought; could it be—her Dennys?

"But he's not mine, and I don't care—I won't!" And pushing her horse into a canter she would strive desperately to leave the tumult of her thoughts behind. But always the dull cloud settled down on her mind again, always the persistent echo of the dear fun of past days came back to mock her. Ann had not strength utterly to forget or utterly to remember. She was just acutely, persistently miserable.

Her spasmodic efforts to appear cheerful before Sybil and Allan were ably seconded by her cousin, who sought to alleviate her unhappiness in diverse ways. He bought an immense case of bath-salts, which he placed unostentatiously in the bath-room—Sybil used most of it, and mocked him for his pains. He imported a choice make of cigarette—not procurable at Lalors of Nassau Street—from a London tobacconist; only at great expense and after the weary writing of many letters could he get them through the Customs. No good! Ann was off smoking for the moment.

He endeavoured to vary Sybil's present after-dinner programme—Kriesler records, mounting in poignancy from his accompaniment of John McCormick's 'Barcarolle' to the 'Caprice Viennois'—by teaching his cousins to play bridge. Sybil grasped the essentials in three nights, and loudly announced her preference for 'Old Maid.' It took many nights and much weary explanation to get the rudiments into Ann's head. Although she tried her best to be intelligent about it, the mysteries of the game were too baffling, its intricacies bewildered her. By the end of a rubber, her fair curls stood on end from perpetual ruffling, her mouth drooped pathetically at Sybil's exasperated censure of her methods, and a puzzled frown puckered her forehead, while Allan's laborious explanations fell on uncomprehending ears.

The three were playing cut-throat. Major Hillingdon, looking on cards not so much as the devil's books as a rank waste of time, repaired to his study of an evening—there to sleep, enshrouded in the *Morning Post*.

"Don't go black in the face, old thing," observed Sybil anxiously to her cousin, during a pause in the harangue, "most unbecoming. Very! Loosen your collar, then you'll feel better. And you'll never make her see she shouldn't 've played that king, 'cause she can't see why she should. See?"

Allan put the cards together despairingly.

"When Sybil starts getting complicated, I give it up. Don't you?"

Ann nodded; she felt too over-wrought to speak after the recent mental strain. Sybil reached for the cards which Allan was shuffling absent-mindedly.

"Cut left and cut right," she commanded. Allan obeyed and she gathered up the three heaps of cards. "And now," she announced, "*now* I am going to tell you your fortune."

Allan groaned and hid his face. Ann gathered up Jibber and rose to her feet. "All women and children will now leave the court," she murmured as she left the room.

Sybil continued for some time to scrutinize the cards which she had laid out in mystic patterns on the table, her black brows drawn together, an expression of the utmost concern upon her face.

"Well, out with it," implored her cousin. "Can't you see the hideous suspense has me all of a dither?"

Suddenly shuffling all the cards together, Sybil put her elbows on the table and hid her face in her hands.

"What's the matter, Sybil?" he asked. "Is it very lurid?"

Her shoulders shook, but she made no answer.

"Sybil, dear, what *is* it? Anything I've done? No? What is it, then? Can't you tell me?"

She shook her head, fishing desperately for her hand-kerchief; then slipping from her chair, she seated herself upon the hearth-rug, and held her poor quivering face close to Benbow's. Benbow, extremely bored, possessed his soul with what patience he could compass. After a while Allan joined the group. Seating himself upon the fender, he picked up one of Sybil's hands for a moment; a moment only, for Sybil pulled it away, gently yet firmly.

"What is it, Sybil?" he asked, leaning forward as he spoke. He could see a large tear gather upon her eyelashes and roll sadly, forlornly, unheeded, into her lap. The poor little thing!

"I can't tell you," said Sybil at last, in her clear, firm voice; "I never could tell anybody my—my troubles, and it wouldn't be fair to worry you about them, Allan dear, I'd only bore you."

What a plucky kid!

"Of course you wouldn't bore me," he assured her stoutly.

"Shouldn't I?" Sybil looked up, a pathetic expression of pleasure on her sad face. "Sure? Quite, quite sure?"

Moving nearer to the fire, she laid her arm along the leather fender and gazed reflectively into the smouldering turf. She knelt there in silence for some minutes—very sweet, very young, every line of her drooping; very close to Allan.

"I love some one," she said at last, "desperately." She lifted a strained white face to his, and the firelight made great shadows round her eyes, her mouth was tragic.

"Oh, Sybil!" said Allan uncertainly; and, he felt, very inadequately. An appalling spasm of fear smote through him, but he stilled it instantly—ashamed. He thought of the day on the bogs when Ann had told him about Dennys, and gulped down an insane desire to laugh ... instead, he fiddled soothingly with Sybil's hair; she quivered under his touch, and instantly he removed his fingers, the awful fear coming over him again.

"I met him," continued Sybil in the same brave voice, "when I was staying with Cousin Agatha in London last spring. He was wonderful. His name is Ian Lubrenski. Yes, a Russian, of course. Ian Lubrenski. . . ." She lingered over the name. "We loved each other. . . . Allan, can you understand? Loved each other. Oh!" she spread out her hands in a supreme gesture, "it was mad, and bad, but while it lasted, very sweet."

Her face fell among her fingers, the bowed shoulders quivered.

Allan, feeling as though he had listened to some one reading aloud a peculiarly hectic passage from a contribution to *Nash's Magazine*, cleared his throat uncomfortably.

"Not, not *bad*, Sybil," he protested gently. "You really mustn't say things like that, dear."

"Yes, very bad." The dark head was still bowed. "Cousin Agatha wouldn't let me see anything of him— anything. So we took the law into our own hands. We

went to theatres and dances. You wonder how I dance so
well, Allan. Ian taught me—he does everything well——
Oh, my sweet!"

Again the narrative broke down, while Sybil lost herself
for a while in that flowing irridescent past where she had
loved greatly. . . . And again the brave voice continued—
albeit brokenly:

"It's over. Done with! He has forgotten, utterly. But I
can never forget. He has killed something in me—just
snapped it right off . . . dead."

Her voice trailed off.

Allan was moved, and also strangely exasperated. Why
should Ann, and now Sybil, have seen fit to treat him as a
sort of privileged uncle? He adored Ann, and Sybil had
been his to flirt with up till quite recently. Indeed, he had
thought . . . but it would seem that the Czech or Pole, or
whatever the fellow called himself, had all the time been
occupying her thoughts to the exclusion of aught else.
Why then had she——

"And I try," went on Sybil, "to forget. You know! Men
like me, and flirt with me. One can't be an utter stick, one
must be sporting; but it's very hard sometimes—very.
You wouldn't understand, but it's *because* of Ian I am—
like I am. People say I'm a shocking little flirt—lots of
girls dislike me on account of it. Is it my fault that men
want to dance with me and be nice to me? And all the
time my soul is drowned"—Sybil drew a deep breath—
"in Ian's," she added, as her cousin looked mystified.
"Yes, it was because of Ian, I was so angry the other
evening when you kissed me—when I was asleep." Her
voice was gently reproachful. "I thought it was Ian. I

opened my eyes, and it was you—— Oh, Allan, the horror of the moment!"

Allan swallowed uncomfortably. Confound it all, she needn't have put it quite so bluntly.

There was silence for a brief space. Sybil smiled—a cheerless mockery of a smile, and rose to her feet.

"You understand," she murmured, "there are two Sybils. Good night." Her cool fingers fluttered a moment in his, and she was gone.

Allan felt strangely moved. More, he was puzzled. The thing sounded so—so overdone, somehow. Yet why should she have pitched him such a yarn? What possible motive could it serve?

"I suppose I shall have to start in comforting her, too," Allan addressed the supine Benbow. "Nice prospect, I must say."

Benbow arose, placed his large feet upon his master's knees, and gazed into his face: "My advice to you," he said plainly, "is don't."

Allan's days became—if possible—more full than before. "Being nice" to Sybil took up, he found, not a little time. He rode with her a great deal, and as they jogged their horses quietly home after a long day's hunting, he discovered this new sad Sybil to be possessed of some likeable qualities which he had up to now failed to realize, Of course she was prettier far than paint; undeniably witty, and equally undeniably a shocking little flirt. But Allan understood now why she flirted. He would amusedly smoke many cigarettes, while the lady deftly handled some smitten youth of her train, who, perchance, dangled along beside them for the first few miles of their homeward way.

How perfect those long rides were upon the days when Ann also took horse and rode to hounds; the misty November days when the very coverts seemed to steam, and hounds ran hard on a breast-high scent. Then the return home across newly broken ploughland, up and down wandering and muddy bhoireens, by many a short cut till they reached the high road that wound its way along a shining river, under the dim beeches of Ballinrath, and away on again. Passing pleasant days, indeed! And, as they rode along, the three of them—Ann, Sybil and Allan—would discuss the day's sport with passionate intensity, jump all their fences o'er again, and cheerfully compare the rival merits of their precious hunters.

And so home! Back to the ecstatic welcome of the little white dogs, to Fox's curt questionings on the day's sport, to tea, to a fight for the first hot bath, and to a long evening with one's feet on the fender—a dog reposing upon one's chest—to ruminations, in Allan's case, on Ann's hair, and the softness of her voice, and altogether on why she was such an eminently desirable small person.

Sybil, curled up in an arm-chair, knitting a shapeless mass—some day to become a silk jumper—would curl up a little closer, and smile secretively to herself, remembering how excellently she had sat Pet Girl's eel-like bucks when hounds had first got going. And Ann? Ann would think thoughts into Jibber's rough little head—thoughts she would scarcely have owned as her own, and gaze with smiling eyes into the heart of the turf fire, till some one shifted position, or addressed a question to somebody else; then, her brain spinning back to realities, she knew again with a curious sickness the rotteness of all things; how Dennys had let her down, how lonely and much to be pitied she was, how nobody seemed to care—except perhaps Allan, and even he had been more than a little taken up with Sybil lately, or so thought Ann, with an utterly unreasonable stab of jealousy.

It was on such a night that—as she ran along the corridor from the bath-room to her bedroom, clad in her blue kimono, her curls wet with steam, and her absurd satin mules flapping off pink heels—that she came upon her cousin. He was endeavouring, by the light of the passage lamp, to examine one of Benbow's paws. Benbow was protesting, so naturally Ann dropped soap, sponge, and towel, and stayed to assist.

"Ann," said Allan, as she exhibited a large thorn which had up to the moment, been causing Benbow acute discomfort, "we're properly grateful. Do you think," he went on, "that there is the least chance of you ever marrying me? I'd like it awfully. You see, I love you—as it were." Ann's head, still bent over Benbow's prostrate form, was shaken vigorously. "Can't be done? Absolutely not?"

Ann picked up her sponge and prepared to depart to her room. "I can't," she answered in a low voice. "I like you better than anyone—except Dennys—but, you see, I like him best."

"Then for Heaven's sake," said her cousin, "don't biff round any more in that blue dressing gown—unless you want to drive me mad, that is."

"I'm very sorry," sighed Ann. Gathering the folds of the offending garment closely about her, she fled down the passage to her own room—her slippers still flapping on the dark boards, her heels twinkling rosily.

Allan stared at nothing in particular for a moment, then slowly descended the stairs. In the billiard-room he took Benbow's head between his hands.

"You're quite right, old son," he observed wearily; "we'll have to 'op it—you and I. This thing is a size too large for us, if you know what I mean."

Benbow thumped the floor with his tail and looked enthusiastic—it was the best he could do.

The following week, however, found him still at Ballinrath, and contemplating a few more days' hunting before his departure to England.

Ann had been adorable to him since his announcement of his impending departure.

"Must you go, Allan?" she had asked wistfully, at which his heart leapt within him.

"'Fraid I must, old thing," he had answered, and proceeded to stay on for another week or so; during which time the lady, though proud, proved also passing sweet. Together they shot the bogs and devoted much time to the schooling of a filly called Mary Ann. He was also allowed to accompany her on some of her long lonely rides; and once, despite her protests, he had sacrificed a hunt, in order to stay behind and flog her refusing filly over a steep place. In such ways did the bond between them grow and strengthen; thus it fell out that a week after his decision to leave Ballinrath, Allan spent an enjoyable day shooting the bogs—with Sybil this time, returning late for tea and more than a little wet.

"I must apologize for my cousin," announced the lady, after greeting some neighbours assembled for tea and gossip in the billiard-room. "He is at the moment engaged upon the difficult task of fitting a fifteen-and-a-half neck into a fourteen-and-a-half inch collar. I've had a bath and done my hair since he started wrestling with it. Thank you, Jimmy—cherry jam, *please*."

Muriel Dane came round with her teacup, and seated herself beside her hostess.

"You all hunting day after to-morrow?" she asked.

"Yes, rather. Ballindrum's a sure find. D'you remember the finish of last season—what a topping run we had out of it?" They reminisced pleasantly about the run.

"By the way; Ann, I suppose you've heard about Dennys St Lawrence?" observed Lady Muriel casually.

"No. What? Come here to mother, Jibber." Ann felt that she must have something to grip if she was to hear things about Dennys.

"Oh, just that he's going away. I'm awfully sorry—we all liked him rather, and he's shown us the best of sport these last two seasons, hasn't he?" Muriel's voice rambled on. She did not want anyone else to notice how white Ann had suddenly become.

"Where's he going?" inquired a very small voice at last.

"The Colonies, somewhere. Canada, or Australia. I rather think Canada."

"Oh, why's he going, d'you know?" Ann, seated behind the enormous old silver teapot, looked small and shaken.

"Running away from all this gossip about his shady methods of horse-coping, *I* should think. Anyway, he's off next week, or so Johnny Brien told our man. I'm sorry; he was a useful person for tennis, or bridge, or anything. I think he's wise, though, to cut adrift from that appalling Papa—don't you? I bet half of the beastly stories every one's telling about him now are really the old man's lurid past. Well, cheerio! We'll have to beat it now. See you to-morrow."

Muriel collected a younger sister and departed in a breeze of chaff and good-byes.

"Ann looks a trifle washed out," she said in a low voice, as Allan helped her into her coat.

"Yes, you're right. She does," replied Ann's cousin.

"She'll get over it." Muriel stood pulling on her gloves.

"I hope she won't get it at all."

"Why, what *are* you talking about?"

"All this 'flu there is blowing around. Weren't you?"

"No, I wasn't," said Muriel, "but I see you know what I mean. Take care of her, won't you? Good night! Come on, Dorris! This mare won't stand for ever."

Allan, left alone in the dim hall, seated himself upon a sofa, an affair of pale green damask, upon which was hung a moth-eaten skin—a relic of the Major's Indian days. He gave himself up to meditations on the ways of women and the wiles of horse dealing. As he aimed the butt of his second cigarette at the coal-scuttle, he was aware of a small presence which sniffed searchingly round the dimly lit hall. A moment later, Jibber pushed an interrogative cold nose into his hand, then padded away into the darkness of the outer passages, wearing an apologetic, Sorry I can't stay—looking for my Mummy expression.

Allan rose and followed. Now he thought of it, Ann had looked rather rotten at tea. He pursued Jibber's swiftly retreating white body down the dark and tortuous passages to the gun-room, at the door of which she paused and snuffled loudly.

"Hullo, Ann! May I come in and hold your hand, as it were?"

Ann was sitting on the window-sill, her profile dimly outlined against the cold green of the evening sky. She moved to one side to make room for her cousin. All the chairs in the gun-room were either broken or—owing to the frequent families of kittens reared in their depths—uninhabitable.

"Now tell me all about it?" he invited, as he seated himself beside her.

"Why should you imagine there's anything the matter?" inquired Ann coldly.

"Don't be a small juggins. Why, it's as obvious as daylight."

"What is?" she flashed at him aggressively.

"Well, aren't you off your feed, off smoking, dancing, backing winners, playing the gramophone, hunting—what not? Every imaginable old thing! And you tell me there's nothing up—well, you know. . . ."

"Suppose I consider it strictly as my own affair?" Ann's tone was dangerously honeyed.

"Oh, in that case, of course——" Allan lit a cigarette with studied calm. "Nice weather we're having isn't it? Not a sign of frost to-night. Scent ought to be pretty good if it keeps like this."

"Hope so! It'll probably be Dennys's last day, Thursday. I—I hope it'll be a good one."

Despite her air of indifference, there was a quaver in Ann's voice.

"Not off already, is he?" Allan seemed only slightly surprised at what Ann regarded as a most portentous announcement—a matter to shake earth and heaven.

"You knew he was going?" she queried, wide-eyed, "and you never told me. Oh, Allan!"

"Well, I didn't exactly know for certain. That is, I didn't know he'd actually accepted old Bill's billet. I——-" Allan floundered hopelessly. He had not meant that Ann should realize that he had borne any hand in this matter; now, of course, with his usual tact, he had told her nearly everything. Cursing himself for a clumsy fool, he smoked on in a silence grown slightly stormy.

"Who's Bill?" inquired a cold voice; "and as you seem to know such a lot about it, perhaps you can tell me where—where Dennys is going?"

Allan pulled desperately at his cigarette. It proved, however, singularly devoid of inspiration.

"Well, I rather gathered he was going as a sort of foreman to old Bill Lammingham," he admitted at length, with immense caution. "Texas, y'know. Chicken farm, or horses, or something. Might be both! I'm sorry for the chap if it's chickens. They have an extraordinarily depressing effect on people who have a lot to do with them. Did you know that? Fact! Why, I knew a bloke once—used to be in the regiment—went out with the axe. Oh, a topping chap. Dashed amusing, frightfully funny fellow! Well, as I was saying, he took up hens on a large scale, and it absolutely blighted the unfortunate beggar. He got so as he would chatter openly about things like egg-yields, and dead-in-shells, and he'd hurl statistics from *Eggs* at you. That's the hen fanciers' pet journal. I forget what breed it was he went in for —Gaverolles, or Wyandottes, I think. Or was it Rhode Island Reds? Anyway——"

"You're sure it wasn't red herrings?" interrupted Ann suddenly. "I want to know how your friend Bill heard about Dennys, and why he offered him the billet on his ranch?"

"Well, if you must have it, old thing,"—Allan was fairly cornered at last—"I wrote to him about a month ago putting friend Dennys's case. And he's evidently jumped at the chance of getting a dam' good man for his job."

"A month ago," repeated Ann. "Why, he'd've had oceans of time to tell me about it. Is it a good job, Allan?"

"Oh, fair to middling. About four hundred a year, I should imagine."

"Four hundred? Why, it's riches! Think of it, and the horses and things. What a topping life! Tell me, Allan"—she laid a small pink forefinger on her cousin's wrist—"why did you do it, old boy?"

"Do what?" asked her cousin comfortably.

"Wangle this job for Dennys?"

"Well, dash it, you know, my dear old thing, I couldn't possibly tell you. As a matter of fact, I had nothing whatever to do with it—beyond telling old Bill about the fellow. Bill ran the show himself. Yes, that was it—ran it entirely solo, Bill did."

"Do you want to know what I think?" Ann's voice was dreadfully solemn.

"Oh no, Ann. I mean to say yes, rather, old soul. Rather!"

"Well, what I think is that you wrote and told your friend all about Dennys, just so as Dennys could marry me if he wanted to, and that explains why he never comes here now. But it doesn't matter, for I don't care a *damn* about him; not one single damn! I think he's behaved rottenly. I think he's a perfect cad—and I've got the most appalling headache, but it doesn't matter, for nobody minds about me, and no one cares. Oh, Allan, life's too rotten. It's rotten. . . . Beastly!"

Ann paused, breathless and hysterical, a white and shaken child, her mouth trembling piteously. She put out vague hands to her cousin. Promptly he gathered them both to his heart, and picking her up, threaded his way through the room's debris to the most stable of the arm-chairs; there he seated himself, and holding her close against him, whispered ridiculous, precious words of love and comfort.

Ann, poor girl, lay in his arms, yielding, every inch of her; glad only that some one needed her—cared for her. Relaxed, she lay against him; she felt herself gripped and held, and kissed, as in a dream—from which all ecstasy was strangely absent. . . . *Il y a toujours un qui baise.* . . . Why should the tag come unbidden to her mind? Because it was true, true! She didn't care—she *didn't!* "I love you, really, Allan—really. Keep me! You're the only person that minds. . . ." Her voice sounded odd and stifled in her own ears.

Hours seemed to have passed before the dressing gong sounded. Ann was scarcely conscious of changing her frock for dinner. All through the meal, her thoughts were in a mist—a warm golden mist, beyond which were shadows—shadows where she would not probe. Enough that she was needed, enough that she was loved; and supremely enough was the thought that she could now show Dennys how little she cared.

How little she cared! She learned to a fraction how

much that meant the same evening, when, dinner over, Sybil, according to custom, turned on the gramophone in the hall and invited her cousin to dance.

Ann, pensive over a cigarette, leant against the high carved mantelpiece, watching them. How awfully well they danced together, and what an attractive darling Sybil was! Her laugh, her expressive gestures of eyebrows, and quick white hands, all her intricate charms—how extraordinarily apparent they were this evening! Allan's fair head was bent over his partner's dark one. He was telling her "about it," Ann conjectured, a thought forlornly. She caught the words, "A secret? Yes, rather," in Sybil's voice, as they drifted past her. Sybil was excited. Did the girl realize what she was doing? Her very dancing was a caress. The truth leapt before Ann's mind in an instant. Sybil cared for Allan; cared as she herself did for Dennys, needing desperately to be close, close . . . to lose her soul in the ecstasy of his nearness . . . as she cared for Dennys— as she could only care for Dennys.

In the semi-darkness of the far end of the hall, she saw Sybil lose step, stumble against her partner. Dear heavens—surely the girl was not going to give herself away in any greater degree? But no! The next moment Sybil sped alone down the length of the room, lifted the gramophone needle, and faced her sister—smiling and jaunty.

"I say, I do congratulate you, old bird," she cooed. "Allan's just been telling me how he—er—er— looked on the lip-stick when it was red, this evening. Good work! Good work! An aunt's blessing, *mes enfants*. And now, shall we play bridge or break it to Pop? I'm all for bridge. Ann can be dummy and hold your hand, Allan." She fled to the billiard-room, pursued by an avenging Fate in the shape of her prospective brother-in-law.

Ann stayed behind and put away the gramophone. The custom of months is not lightly broken.

Ann's play that evening was erratic in the extreme; the thought occupying her mind to the exclusion of aught else being the hope that Allan would not see fit to kiss her good night. Like a little coward, she slipped up to bed when he left the room to let the dogs out for their evening run.

Half an hour later, heavy breathing outside her door announced the presence of Benbow. There was a knock, and Jibber entered discreetly, eyed her basket with manifest disfavour, and leapt neatly upon the bed.

Then came Allan's voice: "Good night, Ann."

"Good night, Allan." She knew that he expected her to come out into the passage and say "good night"—properly! But she couldn't—she *couldn't*.

A pause.

"Good-night, you darling . . . my sweet . . . Ann . . ."

Ann buried herself beneath the bed-clothes and held her breath till she heard his step retreating down the passage. Then she came up to breathe and take counsel with the darkness.

What had she done? Why had she done it? She was mad, mad! For the moment she had lost her head. It was so dear of Allan to care, to comfort her, to wrap her about with his love when she stood stripped of the last shred of what she imagined to have been Dennys's love for her. And she had taken this love of Allan's; surrendered herself passively to his kisses—passively, why, she had returned them. Her whole body scorched at the memory.

Yet that hour of madness had brought with it enlightenment. She was desperately aware now that she could never marry Allan. The warm sense of safety that had wrapped her round earlier in the evening was a mist, the substance of a dream, part of the semi-conscious state of mind in which she had suffered and returned his kisses. She had hungered, poor Ann—and a stone had been given her instead of the bread she craved.

At the end of an hour, during which she lay writhing in an agony of self-abasement, two ideas only remained clear before her mind. The first: "I can't let Allan down—I can't let him down." The second an unspeakable urgency of longing for Dennys—his dear presence, his hands to touch her, to lift her up, to hold her . . . sobs tearing her throat, Ann groped in the darkness for Jibber. She must have something, some one.

Much later she fell asleep, with the best little pal close against her, blowing warm breaths down the back of her neck.

CHAPTER XIV

Rabbits and Bathroom Windows

SYBIL yawned immensely and sat up in bed. Then, shivering, buried herself once more among the blankets. Her dreams had been adorable, she would not let them escape her yet awhile. So, dragging her bed-clothes closely around her, she strove to recapture the elusive glamour of her first waking moments.

Her dreams had been amber-coloured. Amber with flecks of jade—warm happy dreams; yet she could not remember at all what they had been about.

Come, was it not passing strange that she should have dreamed happily on a night when even a new pair of crêpe-de-chine pyjamas had failed as a solace for the acute heartache which had been her bed-fellow?

How was it that she could have forgotten—even for a moment—the events of the previous evening? Sybil drew a breath through closed teeth, and curled and uncurled her toes and fingers, in very real agony of mind, as the cruel relentless facts marshalled themselves once more before her mind.

She saw again the almost dazed look of happiness she had seen in Allan's eyes during dinner the previous night. A look which mellowed into adoration—blind, dumb, ecstatic, when his eyes and Ann's met. Ann's she had noticed, fell away each time; quickly, almost nervously.

A very fury at her sister's idiocy swept anew through Sybil. The fool would spoil her own life, Dennys's, Allan's and hers—*hers*—Sybil's. And why? For what reason? Because of her innate incapacity in the management of her affairs? Because of the sickly sentimentality which was her guiding star through life? Yes, for both these reasons; but, moreover, and above all, because she was a fool, a *fool*. First and last, Ann was such a hopeless fool.

Had the idiot cared about Allan, Sybil felt she would not have minded half so much. But Ann didn't care—at least, not in the marvellous, flaming way in which she, Sybil, cared. Ann belonged utterly to Dennys. She was his perfect mate, he was hers. It was so obvious; and so easy—now that he had got this job—for them to get married, tell Daddy off properly, and then dash happily away to South America (or wherever it was the ranch was situated) and then settle down among the cactus and bring up a family.

That is what Sybil would have done, given the circumstances. And very nice, too. Very simple and expedient. But, unfortunately, not very much in Ann's line. Sybil realized this, so casting the obvious and simple solution from her mind, she grappled afresh with the vexing problem.

She thought till her brain reeled, but no coherent plan of action suggested itself to her.

The beat of the tune to which she had danced with Allan the night before threaded itself maddeningly through her meditations, recalling ever to her mind some would-be forgotten incident of that hideous evening.

The early morning tea came as a heaven-sent interruption. She stretched forth a thin brown arm to pour it out, and drank thirstily.

Her black hair stood out like feathers round her head, instead of being sleeked close as usual. Her skin was soft and damp like that of a newly wakened child . . . the new pyjamas were very jaunty. She looked, in fact, not unlike a puckish boy of thirteen or so.

With her cigarette came inspiration.

Rising swiftly, she thrust her feet into slippers, donned the shot-silk man's dressing-gown which she had filched from the wardrobe of a long-suffering uncle, and hastened along the corridor to Ann's room.

Ann was sitting up in bed reading a Bible. This was vaguely disconcerting. She would not be able to start matters quite according to programme . . . however . . .

"Hullo, bird!"

Ann smiled and put the Bible away. "Hullo! Mind Jib. She's under the eider-down."

Sybil pulled out a warm, protesting Jibber, and settled herself upon the edge of the bed.

"Dear old thing," she murmured, ruffling the ash of her cigarette into Jibber's coat as she spoke. "I just wanted to look at you—make sure it was still *my* little Ann. You know."

"Oh, dry up, Sybil. Stop being funny and tell me what you've come to borrow. If it's tooth-paste, you may; but if it's a clean camisole, you can't."

"Oo, I didn't want to borrow anything, Ann—why should I? I just felt I'd like a few words with you about the bridesmaids' dresses, and what not. You see, we must fix things up before the aunts come, or they'll bully poor Pa into saying yes to all their sticky ideas."

Ann lit a cigarette feverishly. This was awful.

"Well, but, Sybil——" she hesitated, allowed her cigarette to go out, and fumbled for the matches.

"Take mine," Sybil handed her stump over. "You see," she continued, "we haven't really so very long, y'know.

When is Allan's leave up? March, isn't it? Ann, who'll you have for bridesmaids? Me—of course, an' I suppose Muriel. Oh, d'you remember you once promised that Elizabeth child you'd have her? You can't though. She's too big for a train-bearer; and 'sides . . . er . . . oh, well, I suppose it's out of the question, anyway."

"Course I'll have Elizabeth," declared Ann hotly. "I promised the kid."

"Oh, Ann! Will you? Would you? *Do* you think—I mean, to me it seems rather, well, rather the edge. But of course it'll be your funeral—I mean your weddin'." Sybil sat twisting the cord of her dressing gown in her hands, regarding her sister with earnest, troubled eyes.

"Perhaps you're right," agreed Ann slowly. "But, anyway, there's no earthly hurry about the blessed thing. We haven't told Daddy yet. He mayn't like it." Despite herself there was a tremor of hope in her voice.

"That's right." Sybil nodded sapiently. "But you know he never likes any of our young men. Don't you remember how beastly he was to Dennys? Oh, I'm *sorry*, Ann, I *am* a fool." She paused to bite her lips in sorrowful amazement at her own unpardonable stupidity. Then: "My dear, if I was you, I'd let it dawn on him gradually. Give him a week or so. He may find it out for himself, and then he'll think he worked it all and be quite pleased. Oh, Ann, I think that's a lovely plan!" Sybil finished on her most ingenuous note.

"Yes, I think I'll tell Allan that—it's quite a scheme." Ann ruffled her curls and corrugated her brow in deep thought.

"Well, if you do, remember, it's your idea—not mine. I wouldn't interfere with love's young dream for all the world." Sybil stretched out a very long leg, and kicked off her shoe. "I say, don't you love these pyjams? I think they're simply wonderful. Will you have pyjamas or nighties in your trousseau? Well, so long, bird. I *must* have a bath of sorts."

She slipped off the bed, retrieved her shoes, and wandered vaguely round the room. With her hand upon the door-knob she hesitated.

"I say, Ann——" She paused in delightfully simulated constraint.

"Well, what is it?" Ann prompted, not because she wanted to know, but because she was well aware that Sybil would not leave the room until she had unburdened herself of whatever unpleasant tidings she wished to impart.

"Well, Ann—I don't know if you know, but I think I ought to tell you. It's about Dennys." She paused again.

"Yes, what about him?" inquired Ann at last.

"You know all the scandal that's been about him. I didn't believe a word of it myself. You know how I hate scandal——"

"I know you're the biggest little gossip in the place," interrupted Ann. She spoke in a small, flat voice. "What *did* you hear this time?"

"Well, I thought I ought to tell you. I think you should know, that is—that there's not a word of truth in the story about the cheque. At least so far as he's concerned."

"How d'you know?" Ann still spoke in a flat, tired voice. She felt like that. As if nothing was worth while any more, or ever would be again. "How d'you know?" she repeated dully.

"I met Mary Dempsey yesterday when I was out

shooting. She told me. She sent you a sort of message about it. But I didn't quite *understand*. I thought——"

"Did Allan know?"

Sybil thought swiftly. Then: "Oh, no, he didn't. He'd gone on. I only saw her for a couple of minutes. You see, I felt I *ought* to tell you, Ann."

She opened and softly closed the door, and slipped down the passage to her own room—a slim, swiftly moving shadow.

Rather an evil-looking little shadow? Perhaps.

She would have preferred the adjective "puckish."

Ann was late for breakfast, of course. It was a bad attempt at evasion of Allan's matutinal salute, because she met him on the stairs. He caught her up just before the wide turn in the flight which led into the hall.

"Hullo, Ann darling!" His smile was as wide as that of any dental-paste poster. "Mayn't I? Oh, *Ann*!" He caught her as she dived aside, kissed the soft parting in the top of her hair, and let her go again.

"You horrible boy!" Ann went headlong down the last eight steps.

Allan, following unabashed, slipped his arm through hers as they crossed the hall, and kept it there until the dining-room door was reached. Then:

"Allan, *don't*! I don't want Daddy to know yet. Tell you why later."

He dropped her arm at once and picked up Jibber.

"All right, my blessed. D'you call this a sound enough—er—alibi?"

"What d'you mean?"

"Oh, Jib, isn't mother dense this morning? Why, who'd want to kiss her with you around?" Allan stooped down to the little white head. That he did not hear Ann fervently murmur, "My precious!" was perhaps as well, since her eyes were all for Jibber.

Within, Sybil, seated behind the coffee pots, was all demure. She greeted them sweetly, thought the sight of Allan, attired in that brown tweed coat which so perfectly matched Ann's gracefully aged suitings, gave her a most unreasonably acute heart stab.

"You're devilish late," the Major's greeting was, to say the least, curt.

"Sorry, Dad." Ann kissed her father and put Jibber out of the window before she sat down.

Ten minutes later, a crash of music from the pack—Jibber, Twink, Benbow, the two hound puppies, and a lean setter bitch, all of whom had, up to the moment, been seated on the hall door steps impatiently awaiting their breakfasts—announced the arrival of the postman.

The Major went to the window to call them off. "Here, Jibber! Twink, come here, sir! Benbow! Curse the dog! *Benbow*! That's a most disobedient brute of yours, Allan. B'gad, Tom, they damn nearly made a chop at you!"

Tom proffered the letters through the open window. "Ah, them's very gamey dogs. They have great heart. Down now, poor fellas! Go off!" He placed his bicycle between himself and the hound puppies, who, after the idiotic manner of their kind, still kept up the affectation of treating him as a stranger.

Rachel and Ravager regarded his legs in awed silence through the spokes of the wheels, before retreating to a safe distance from which to bay their surprise at the phenomena.

"There's a shilling porterage to pay on a telegram, sir."

"Right." The Major produced it, and Tom departed amidst renewed vociferations from the pack.

"Here, Sybil——" The Major was sorting out the mail. "Catalogues. More catalogues. Patterns. Miss S. Hillingdon—Miss S.—— Oh, take the lot."

"Who's the wire for, Daddy? Me, too?" She tore it open and read the message aloud. "All Goods meet Temple Danis 11.30. One and a half couples required.— DANE."

"Yes," Ann stretched out an arm for the honey. "Muriel said she or John'd wire if they got the stopping finished in time. A rabbit hunt," she explained to her mystified cousin. "We'll go, of course. Jibber adores them. The All Goods? Oh, a pretty mixed lot. We bring our terriers. Six and a half couple we had last time—wasn't it, Sybil? It was quite good fun."

Sybil looked up from her letters. "M'm, yes. Nothing to the day we laid the drag, though. D'you remember? Ferrets' bed soaked in aniseed, wasn't it?"

"No." Ann gravely contradicted her sister. "Some one had cleaned out the ferrets' box by mistake, hadn't they? We had to use a skinned rabbit smeared with anchovy in the end. It was quite all right, thought."

"Screaming scent," Sybil endorsed her sister's statement. "We got together most of the puppies out at walk," she explained to Allan. "Had a grand hunt. John laid the drag. Awful line of country he took us, too."

"Shocking business!" the Major snorted and left the room.

Sybil looked after him, her eyes gleaming with devilment. Even Ann giggled.

"He doesn't know yet what really happened," Sybil took up the tale. "You see, John's line happened to lie through the hounds' exercising field. Well, Baines (the kennel huntsman) and one of the boys had sixteen and a half couples out for exercise, and old Daphne started feathering along the line, and 'fore Baines could think, the whole pack broke and simply romped away on a screaming scent—— Oh, the anchovy tickled them to death! A grand hunt, wasn't it, Ann?"

Ann nodded. "What I like to remember," she said, "is the way those blessed puppies cast themselves, with no one near 'em, when John lifted the line for a check. Weren't they splendid? And it was my little Why Not hit it off again. She was a topper." Ann sighed and proceeded to bestir herself over the dogs' breakfasts.

Later in the morning, Sybil drove the car to Temple Danis. Allan sat beside her; Ann, upon the pretext of mothering the dogs, having early taken her place in the back seat.

During the short journey Allan several times had occasion to dig his teeth into his lower lip, and fight hard for self-control. For self-control, that is, sufficient to enable him to refrain from snatching the steering wheel from Sybil's careless grasp, setting his foot upon the brake, and requesting her instant removal from the driver's seat.

Ann from her place in the rear, viewed without concern the perils through which they passed—unscathed, it is true, since an undeserved share of luck attended each circumstance.

Allan drew a deep breath of relief as they neared the end of Temple Danis's long avenue.

"Sybil, my child," he observed, "I've suffered horribly—horribly. How she missed the old lady in the ass-cart——" He turned to Ann, "I say, do we apologize to Lady Glencurry for the shattered gate-post and battered minorea, or does she? I think she should."

"Idiots!" Sybil drew up with a flourish at the hall door, and proceeded to divest herself of her coat, revealing an attractive leather garment of jerkin persuasion, a short skirt, and palely clad understandings terminating in weather-beaten brogues. She stepped out of the car and disappeared into the house, leaving Ann and her cousin to wrestle unaided with the activities of three nearly demented terriers.

Within, Sybil was deep in converse with John Dane.

"Five couple, John—that's good," Ann heard, as Twink and Jibber towed her past the pair. "I've brought our three. Who else is here? When do we move off? What's your first draw?"

At eleven-thirty of the clock the pack were romping through heavy covert with every sign of exhilaration.

At eleven-thirty-eight was heard a crash of music from the heart of a bramble patch.

"Only old Wendy—awful babbler." John Dane damped the newly aroused ardour of his field.

"No, John. There's Jibber giving tongue now—don't you hear?" Ann caught at his sleeve.

"Jove, yes! Stay where you are every one. Don't head, for God's sake!" John moved away to cheer on his hounds.

A moment later an enormous Persian cat broke covert,

and with two and a half couple within two and a half inches of her plumed brush, sprinted wildly for a group of Scotch firs about two hundred yards distant from the bramble patch.

"John! That's Aunt Aggie's Sultan—it's *Sultan*!" Muriel Dane's agonized shriek rose above the hysterical yelpings of the dogs.

Even as she shrieked, two and a half couple rolled over their quarry in the open, and even as Sultan's ear-splitting cry rent the air, a tall old lady, grasping in either hand her flowing black skirts, launched herself into the fray.

Needless to describe the ensuing moments. Suffice it to say that from Pandemonium's depths a draggled Sultan was rescued by his intrepid mistress.

Grasping her cat firmly by the scruff of the neck (the animal seemed equally disposed to bite his mistress and his late pursuers) Lady Agatha Dane let loose—for five all too short minutes—the flood-gates of her wrath upon her nephew and her niece, their friends, their dogs, and all their works.

"It's not invective—it's oratory," murmured Allan with heart-felt admiration, as the old lady, turning upon her heel, strode away in the direction of the house.

"She could give points and a beating to any MFH in the country," supplemented her nephew. "My greatest regret in life is that I was no more than a four-year-old when she gave up a pack of harriers she used to hunt here."

A voice uplifted itself from the background. It was that of the lodge-keeper's son and earth-stopper. "Didn't her ladyship prove very good?" it inquired. "Sure she had to shoke Vixy out o' the cat, and that Vixy the real cute little lady, and she fasht in the cat. Ah, she was surely courageous!"

A half-eaten rabbit—evidently Sultan had been disturbed during the consumption of a meal—kept the remnant of the pack occupied in covert for some further time. Finally, however, each All Good answered the call-over, and hounds and hunt moved off to the next draw.

"The snuggest bit o'covert in the place," according to John Dane, held a brace. The pack divided, and two several and notable hunts took place.

Naturally, where Twink and Jibber went, Ann went too. After a hunt of quite eight minutes, which included a lot of work in covert as well as a two hundred yard point, they marked to ground in a hole in the open which had been overlooked during the previous evening's stoppings.

"Never mind, precious," Ann comforted her sweet, and pulled some one else's Sealyham out of the open earth by a stubby tail.

"Nice little burst"—Allan was there too, of course. He had not at any time during the morning been very far distant from the small lady of his affections. Now, he grasped her by the arm as she stooped above the rabbit-hole. "Sssh! Quiet! There's their rabbit trying to break."

Indeed, at the edge of a patch of briars, Ann viewed the hunted rabbit. It hesitated for a moment, a still brown form, immobile, yet alert. Then, with the chorus of the main body of the pack growing ever louder and clearer behind him, as they conscientiously hunted the line through covert, Peter Bun—a stout-hearted and straight-necked fellow—broke covert, made a gallant sprint for safety, and was rolled over after three and a half minutes' fast in the open.

"Sorry we didn't get you the scut, Sybil," John Dane apologized to her as (all appropriate and orthodox rites concluded) terriers broke up their rabbit. "But there *were* reasons. You see?"

"*Dear* John, I see. I'd've loved it, though, after a hunt like that. Twelve minutes, with two fast bursts in the open. They deserved their rabbit—bless them!"

The huntsman wiped his heated brow. "I think I deserve *my* lunch . . . Y'know, no one's said anything about the way I lifted 'em to your holloa, Allan. . . . a pretty enough performance, too. I say, every one'd better sort out their own dog, or they'll start scrapping over the fragments. An' then come on up to the house for lunch."

He picked up two little white ladies as he spoke, tucked one beneath either arm, and set off across the field.

Sybil kept pace with him, stride for stride. Her talent for capturing the undivided attentions of the most eligible male member of any party in which she found herself was only equalled by her genius in making it appear to the rest of the party as though the eligible male was well-nigh forcing such attentions upon her small shy self. A pretty talent enough, and one of which the lady availed herself with adorable dexterity. If she was not one to hide her light under a bushel, much less would she give to a useful talent decent burial.

To-day the marvellously complex machinery of her fertile brain was working, not so much overtime, as against time. Still, she bestowed undivided attention upon John's absurdities as they walked towards the house together.

Lunch over, the party settled themselves in diverse attitudes of repose round the well-furnished hall.

One elbow propped against the heavily-carved mantel-piece, a coffee-cup within reach, and a cigarette in the corner of her mouth, Sybil held converse with one of the few and favoured females who delighted to number her amongst their friends. She waved John Dane away as he approached. "Sorry, old dear, we're busy, Beppy and I. Yes, Bep, what else was she wearing?"

Beppy, a lady of slow soft speech and assured manners, threw her cigarette into the fire before replying. "Oh, that was all. A cyclamen-coloured nightie, an' a pair of silver *mules*. She always rather liked herself in her undies, but I call that over-doing it . . . You know, Sybil . . ." She spoke quickly in her delicious soft voice, inaudible to all save her chosen audience. Sybil laughed delightedly.

"Puppy—how perfect! You *have* got a low mind."

Beppy lit another cigarette, and waved out the flame of her match with exquisite unconcern.

"*My* mind? Oh, yes, I've got a mind like a sewer . . . D'you know I rather like that jumper you're wearing. What'll you swop for it? I'll let you have rather a nice silk petticoat. That's too good, though. How about a pair of crêpe-de-chine things like these?" She pulled aside her short wrap-over skirt with enviable dexterity. Half an instant, and Sybil had taken in the possibilities of the garment in question.

"M'm, yes—might do it. If you throw in that red silk hankie, I will." She yawned and let her eyes wander round the room till they met John Dane's. Then she smiled. He came up at once.

"I say, how about moving off? What d'you think?"

"Me? Oh, I don't think at all, John—not in my line. But it's started to rain. Shall we have a look-see round the stables? I'd like a look at that young one of yours. How d'you say she's bred? Sungirth? Oh, come on."

A few minutes later John Dane stripped a rather leggy chestnut mare, and standing back, surveyed her with that air of challenging criticizm which youthful owners of horses of doubtful value never quite know how to discard.

The mare was of that class of three-year-old thorough-bred which may or may not turn out well—probably the latter. Not up to any weight, yet not a weed—more of an extravagance than a sound investment for her owner.

"There you are," said John crossly. "I admit she's a trifle poor behind," (no one had said so) "But when she feeds up a bit ... and she gives you a grand feeling galloping. She——'

"Call her 'Bath Salts'," interrupted Sybil irreverently.

"Bath Salts. What do you mean?"

"I'm sorry, John, I thought you said she gave you a nice feeling."

"Unfortunately she's entered as Sunny Jane in the Book," replied John stiffly.

Ann advanced, carefully noted the point to which her chin reached on the mare's wither, and turned to John.

"What does she stand, John? Sixteen three about, I should say. Sixteen two—oh, near enough. You've got nice flat bone there ... a grand sloping shoulder too. Her front piece is topping, and, as you say, she'll be putting up condition every day. I'm sure she can gallop." Ann stepped up again, and gravely and gently patted the neck and felt the legs of the much-criticized animal.

John was smiling and feeling greatly cheered about his purchase when he replaced the clothing.

In such small matters did Ann's unique gift of selflessness find expression. Now, the same quality of selflessness prompted her to linger behind with Allan, as the rest of the party passed from loose-box to loose-box.

He was so happy, and such a dear, that she could not bear to spoil his day by avoiding him. After all, she couldn't marry Dennys, so why not marry Allan?

As they passed out of a dark loose-box his hand touched hers. For a moment he seemed to bend over her. To own her. To claim her. A perfect agony of sickened revulsion swept through Ann. She couldn't bear it, couldn't bear—

"I say, precious, there's half a cobweb *and* a spider in your hat. Steady a moment." Allan's voice was perfectly calm and ordinary. Yet, as a pink-cheeked and tumultuous-hearted Ann scurried up the passage to join the others, a very unhappy boy shot the bolt home in the door of the loose-box. "I can't understand her. I *can't* understand her," he thought despairingly. "She *said* she would, and I mayn't even kiss her. Oh, hell!" He lit a cigarette and proceeded on his way round the stables shrouded in unutterable and impenetrable gloom.

The rain, which had begun to fall after lunch, continued implacably. However, shrouded in burberries, the party made its way to the woods to dig a badger which was fabled to have its stronghold in an old artificial earth. An easy place to block him in—said John Dane optimistically.

Sybil, seated upon a wall, smoked the cigarette which she had discovered in the pocket of a burberry some one had lent her. She also gave valuable advice to those who delved in the earth, and also to those whose office it was to stand and get wet, holding straining terriers on nearly breaking leashes.

Every one's dog had to have its turn at going to ground. Some were good, some brought dire shame upon their owners.

"Oh, that's a devil to go—take care of him, Puppy, he'll get himself killed some day." John thrust a reluctant Sealyham (winner of more than one championship) into the mouth of the earth. The Sealyham advanced unhappily for a few yards, then beat a hasty and undignified retreat.

John returned the dog to his mistress, and with the remark that there must have been something dangerous there to scare the poor fellow, thrust a long briar and the full length of his arm down the earth.

An instant later he withdrew the briar hastily.

"Block up that far place, quick!" he called. "The fella caughta-holda the briar in his mouth. He's there right enough. Let's have Jibber, Ann, she's the best of the lot."

In a scurry of excitement Jibber was put in. She disappeared from sight in an instant, and smothered growls and yelps of excitement were heard from the farthest end of the passage.

For some eight minutes this continued; then John Dane's voice—muffled, since his head was buried like an ostrich's in the sand—"He's coming out! 'God's sake gi' me the tongs some one. Got a bit of rope, Allan?"

"Masther John, sure he'll eat the face off you," warned the earth-stopper as he proffered the tongs.

John withdrew his head from the earth for a moment. "Wait a minute, I'll put Whiskey down too." He stooped to slip the strap of the neck off a small working terrier. Even as he did so there was a tremendous upheaval in the earth, and a small vixen fox bolted clear between his wide-straddling legs, to disappear into the woods amidst the

222

furious tow-rowing of the captive terriers, and the horrified yelps of their owners.

John pulled a filthy Jibber out of the ground and handed
her over to Ann. "Well, that's pretty average awful," he
observed.

Muriel Dane lit a cigarette philosophically. "Thank God
Dennys wasn't here," she said. "You know, John, there's
never been a fox in this artificial earth since me father
made it fifteen years ago. You know that."

"Well, they certainly won't breed in it *this* year." John
surveyed the ruins unhappily. "As you say, thank God
Dennys wasn't here."

Sybil slipped from her place upon the wall. "Cheer up,
John, old pal," she soothed. "None of us'll talk about it.
An' if Micky does—well, we'll know who it was."

The earth-stopper grinned sheepishly, and rubbed one
clay-encrusted boot against the other. "It must be 'twas in
the shore in the far wood Johnny Berney seen the badger,"
he volunteered. "Sure I sees this fella sneakin' up here
every night, from the back of our house, an' he going very
wary."

"Then why the——" John swallowed. "Why didn't you
say so?" he demanded with impotent fury.

Micky removed a flag which was blocking a corner of
the made earth, before replying. "Well now, I thought yez
wanted a bit o' sport."

"*Sport!*" John turned from him choking. "Well, come
on. Let's have a drink on something an' try to forget . . ."
He led the way towards the house.

The terriers were dried—a couple at a time—in the hot-
air cupboards of the several bathrooms, the while owners
either danced upon a quite exceptional floor, to the strains

of an equally exceptional gramophone, or played bridge, according to their several moods and likings.

Ann played bridge. Deeply as she detested the game, anything was preferable to dancing. At the first sound of the gramophone she had scurried wildly for the bridge table, and now sat wondering despairingly what it was Allan had told her to call when she had six of a suit to three honours in her hand.

Sybil noted her sister's disappearance with a narrowing of green eyes and a puckering of one corner of her red mouth. During her dance with John Dane she was *distraite*, and remained passionless and preoccupied when— alone with her in his own private den—he kissed the back of her neck and told her how much he loved her.

"May I kiss you, Sybil?"

"Oh, yes, if it amuses you. Of course."

She stared out of his arms at the prints of Armour's sporting pictures, the Kirschner girls, and photographs of horses and dogs which hung on his walls, noted the dilapidated, comfortable furniture, the confusion of gun-cases and wrecks of fishing-rods. . . .After all, John *was* rather a dear. She turned in his arms to look wonderingly into his eyes. Touched his chin with a quite impersonally caressing forefinger, and slipped from him unobtrusively. Other matters claimed her attention.

She found Allan conversing animatedly with the dullest girl of the party; a girl with pale eyes, who wore black cashmere stockings. His apparent disinclination for being rescued was most characteristic.

"Miss Elton was telling me she taught in a school," he informed Sybil as they danced their way round the big, nearly empty room. "Fancy that now, Sybil—such a nice girl too. Who'd 've thought it?"

"'My children.' 'Our system.' 'The PNEU,'" mimicked Sybil mercilessly. "My poor Allan, I do pity you."

"Not t'all. Devilish interesting." Allan steered his partner with much success through an extravagant intricacy of his own devising. Their dancing was very nearly perfect. Then some one changed the record—a favourite—they frowned and ceased at once by mutual consent.

Sybil led the way to John's den. She deemed it unlikely that he would bring his present partner there. That would have spoilt a memory. And a pretty memory too.

She helped herself abstractedly to a cigarette and forgot to light it as she watched Allan unhappily coasting round the small room upon the pretext of examining prints and photographs.

"Dear, can't you tell me what's the matter?" She was kneeling upright in her chair; her small troubled face turned to him, the unlighted cigarette twisted and broken in her long, dark fingers. "Please tell me, Allan. You know I'd love to be any help."

"Rot, Sybil. There's nothing the matter." He stooped to look closely into a picture which hung low down on the wall. "I say, you know Armour isn't often wrong, but I don't *think* that horse'll get over. . . .Oh, well, funny world, isn't it?"

He sat down on the sofa opposite, produced his pipe and tobacco-pouch, and smiled at her thoughtfully. It nearly broke Sybil's heart—that smile. At least, she hoped so.

Stretching out a foot, shod in a shoe which had been first pick from the lot of dry footwear Muriel Dane had placed at her guests' disposal, she touched her cousin on the knee.

"You'd better tell me, old man," she counselled. "I know, anyway, that Ann's in one of her silly moods. Is that all?"

"She's not silly," Allan defended his lady hastily. "She has a right to any mood she likes, I suppose. But, but, my God, Sybil—what's the *matter* with her? I can't make her out, I swear I can't. What did she mean last night——"

"Or did she mean anything?" Sybil interrupted softly.

The next instant Allan was on his feet, his back turned to her. He was staring out of the window into the rain. Staring, staring. Seeing nothing, hearing nothing.

After a measureless time, however, an insistently unhappy little sound came to his ears, something between a gulp and a whine, a sound of claws scratching, a futile little sound.

A dog probably, demanding shelter from the rain.

Allan flung open the window and leaned out. Immediately below nothing was to be seen. To the left lay a large zinc tank for rain water. Six feet above it, a window, propped open by a brush, proclaimed a bathroom.

At Allan's whistle the yelping and whining redoubled with pathetic intensity. Leaning far out of the window, he caught a glimpse of a little white dog, a dog who beat the dark waters of the tank only very feebly, whose efforts to scramble up the perpendicular walls had nearly ceased.

A minute later an utterly collapsed Jibber was laid before the fire. An incoherent Sybil was demanding brandy from the butler, and Allan was working very tenderly over the poor white scrap.

"Ann, Ann——" Sybil sped to the library. "Jibber—Ann! We've got her—she's alive. But do come before—I mean, she was nearly drowned."

Dismayed, and in the grip of a terrible fear, Ann faced her sister calmly. "Where? John's room? Brandy, Sybil. Hot-water bags—I'm going to her."

For nearly two hours Ann and Allan worked unceasingly over the patient. Brandy was applied, both outside and in. Hot-water bags, hot flannels, and ceaseless, tireless rubbing prevailed.

At the end of the two hours Jibber coughed and rose to her feet. It was then that Ann broke down and wept. And Allan, when he had warmed John Dane's pyjamas thoroughly before the fire, wrapped Jibber in them and put her in a basket, turned and kissed away Ann's tears. She let him.

And he was so happy.

Later, Sybil entered, Twink in her arms. He struggled down, and carefully licked as much of the invalid as the pyjamas permitted.

"That's a quare smell off your mouth," he observed when he reached it. Jibber bit him. One had to keep one's life partner in order. And, anyway, that stuff they'd given her made her feel so decent and warm . . . and . . . so . . . safe. . . .

She sighed and slept.

Sybil stepped up. "You know we've got to meet Rick at the station," she said gently. "John's going to drive you and Jib back in the closed car when you think she's fit for it." She bent over the thing wrapped so warmly in mauve-striped pyjamas, and smelling so strongly of brandy.

"Y'know, old lady, bathroom windows are rotten things to jump out of——"

Jibber opened one dark eye. "A lot *you* know about it," she protested, before once more resuming her drunken slumbers.

CHAPTER XV

"D'Ye Ken John Peel?"

"It's a fine hunting day, and as balmy as May,
When the parson unites the fond pair;
But he hears the glad sound
Of the horn and the hound——
And he knows it is time to be there!"

trolled Dennys incorrectly; as, together with Elizabeth, he rode at the head of his hounds from Clonbeg to Ballindrum—the scene of the meet.

His last day's hunting for some time, he reflected unhappily. Breaking off his song, he turned in his saddle to run a proud possessive eye over sixteen and a half couple of the best—the very best. Ravager and Daphne (the old rip, but a good hound too), Dainty and Dauntless, the young entry of which he was so proud. Hadn't Dauntless taken a first among un-entered's at Clonmel?

He was to leave them all, and his hunting that he loved if ever a man did. His horses too; Aurora who would be a first-class hunter by the end of the season, the Sweep, and that bay pony-mare—a useful hack; leave them to go seeking his living, a stranger in a strange land. Not such a friendless stranger, though, for was there not that chap Lammingham—how the deuce had he heard Dennys's name or hearing remembered, and having remembered, why come forward with his offer of this wonderful billet precisely at the psychological moment? Just a streak of wonderful luck, of course. But God knew it was hard to go! He glanced at Elizabeth, silently kicking Biddelia along beside him. Her silence and her small white face smote him afresh, raising a dull ache of pity in his breast.

Who would have thought a kid like that could care so awfully? Her first day's hunting since the quarantine, and she gave no sign of pleasure or excitement. Since that terrible evening, when he had first told her of his intended departure, she had importuned him no more to take her with him. When he had told her of the ranch in Texas, she remained coldly silent. His invitation to her to come out and keep house for him when she should have attained the woman's estate of sixteen years had been greeted with contempt.

"Five years! You'll be old by then. You'll have stacks of children prob'ly. What's the good of saying five years? You'll take Driscoll?" she had queried with sudden energy.

Dennys, swallowing something enormous in his throat, replied that he had thought of leaving Driscoll with her. Elizabeth shook her head vigorously.

"No. You know, well, I'll be away at school all the time. How could I mind him? He'd only get mange off Tatters"—Tatters was a peculiarly hairless kennel terrier—"or Johnny Brien would get mad with him for going to the hounds' larder—or something. You take him, anyway; I know well you want him, far more'n you want me."

To his protestations to the contrary, she turned a deaf ear, merely repeating monotonously: "I know well you don't want me——" and retired to the turnip-house or nettle-grown haggard to sob herself sick, when her young over-laden soul could bear no more.

This was the last day that she would ride at the head

of the hounds with Dennys; the last day she could watch and imitate the way he held his reins and crop, the last——

Hullo! who were those people riding on ahead of them? A boy and a girl—why, it was Rick—*Rick* and Sybil. In her unhappiness she had almost forgotten Rick. She greeted him rapturously and together they fell in behind the hounds, leaving Dennys and Sybil alone.

The lady conducted the conversation somewhat deftly. A word of inquiry as to a hound, a side-long glance at Aurora, coupled with the remark that she seemed hardly up to his weight, and Dennys unbent to explain how much weight exactly (in excess of his own) the mare was up to.

"I see," she said, at the close of a lengthy explanation, to which she had listened in becoming silence. "Y'know I'm an ignorant little thing about horses really. I'm not like Ann; she just sizes them up with one look. I've heard Charlie Jeeves say she's nearly as good a judge as himself."

Dennys assented in an expressionless manner, and the pair rode on in silence for some minutes—a silence broken at last by Sybil.

"Canada's a nice place," she observed conversationally, "not but that I've heard Texas is better. What do you think, anyway, Dennys?"

Dennys laughed, and flicked an amused eye at the girl riding beside him.

"Yes, thank you, Sybil; I'm sailing for America just three days from to-day. It's worth just four hundred a year to me. I couldn't say for certain whether there's a bath in the house or not, but you can never tell. Now, is there any other little point on which I can enlighten you . . . as the bridge experts say."

"Yes, just one little thing. Have you asked Ann to go with you, or are you waiting till you find out about the bath? One never can tell with girls any more than baths, you know. I mean—the hottest bath water gets chilly if the kitchen fire goes out. You get me?"

"I don't, I'm afraid." Dennys's tone was distant, even a trifle haughty. Within, his heart was in a wild tumult of amazed hope, of unbelievable ecstasy, tempered by misgiving.

"You don't?" Sybil laughed. The look she shot at him was composed and a trifle incredulous. "But—you funny man—must I explain to you that Ann adores you and that you adore Ann, can't you *see* it?"

Dennys grew crimson. The eyes he turned to Sybil were for the moment those of a boy of sixteen—shining, hopeful eyes.

"She can't," he stumbled over his words. "Gad, Sybil, she can't . . . not after . . . Tell me, Sybil, she didn't believe—*she* didn't believe all that talk there's been about me?"

"Not for one moment," lied Sybil carelessly. "The only thing that worried her was your not turning up; you were an ass not to, Dennys, because she and Allan——"

"Yes, what about them?" inquired Dennys, as Sybil hesitated. All the fears and jealousies of the last months came crowding back to his mind, and the horizon of his hopes, so suddenly and wonderfully cleared, shrouded itself once more in gloom. "Tell me what about them, Sybil?" he repeated dully, flicking as he spoke at a straying hound. "Damsel! *Damsel*!" The lean bitch yelped and shuddered back to the main body of the pack. Dennys turned troubled grey eyes upon his companion. "I must ask you, Sybil, if it's true what they're all saying—that Ann and Allan are as good as engaged."

Sybil thought swiftly.

"Yes, it's a true bill," she admitted. "But"—she raised her hand in a gesture supremely reminiscent of her father, to check Dennys's attempted interruption— "that, my sweet young thing, is absobloominlutely your own dam' silly fault. Listen to me now, and I'll tell you exactly what you've done. First of all, you and Ann were awfully smitten with each other last summer—yes, you were, even a senile baby could've seen that at once. But I don't think you were engaged—were you? No! Why? 'Cause you knew there'd be the devil of a rumpus and Daddy would turn you down?"

"It wasn't that at all," protested Dennys in a low voice.

"I know it wasn't," said Sybil swiftly. "The real reason wasn't my Papa at all—but yours, and it does you great credit—not your Papa, of course, but the reason. Dash it! I'm tying myself up in the most awful knots. You might help me, Dennys!" she laughed.

But Dennys had turned a dusky red at the mention of his father, and now preserved an angry silence. Sybil continued in her most silky tones:

"Then Allan came along, didn't he? You got a slight attack of green-eye, which developed something amazing, didn't it? Yes, I know—it always does! And then everything that happened made you perfectly sure you were Allan's inferior in every way, and that Ann couldn't help liking him best. Then—forgive me, Dennys—came the Dempsey affair, after which you behaved like the perfect little gent of fiction. No explanations; renunciation, and all the rest of it; while Ann, poor little devil . . . Oh damn! here we are in the middle of the meet——" She broke off, surveying the assembled crowd at the cross-road with huge disfavour. "Well, ponder my words, old thing, and don't go on making such an ass of yourself. You're still young enough to know better. Cheerio, James!"

She greeted and plunged into conversation with one of her train of perennial danglers, just as Dennys opened his mouth to deliver himself of the acid and biting remark which he had been pondering in his mind during the latter part of her homily.

Ann and Allan did not put in an appearance at the meet until some five minutes before hounds moved off to their first draw. Dennys watched their approach in sullen aloofness, from his place amongst his hounds. It might be true, as Sybil had said, that Ann still cared for him. Why then, if such was the case, did she appear so radiant after a four-mile hack in the sole society of that fatuous ass Hillingdon? And how dear she looked this morning; how unutterably small, yet somehow conveying the impression of extreme competence, perched as she was atop of seventeen hands of a strong-backed, hard-conditioned five-year-old. Garry Owen had certainly come on well since the beginning of the season. Fox had a great way of putting condition on a horse, Dennys reflected; and Ann the best way of getting them across country.

As the couple—giving a wide berth to hounds—rode past him, Dennys received a fleeting impression of a very perfectly cut iron-grey habit, an exceedingly white stock, and carefully repressed hair—more brown than gold to-day. He was also aware of a low and honeyed laugh,

which hung in the air a moment before she broke it off to
bid him a cool "Good morning," and passing on, continued—in as far as Garry Owen's delinquencies would
permit—the intimate and amusing conversation with her
second cousin which was not, evidently, to terminate in
the honeyed laugh—so often the death-knell of such *tête-
à-têtes*.

The sight of Allan, his tall hat pushed to the back of his
head, cigarette case open in his hand, a large grin of
supreme content splitting his hatchet-like profile, conveyed to Dennys an impression of careless ease and easy
opulence—very remote from the state of life unto which
it had pleased God to call him—Dennys St Lawrence.
Sourly he contrasted Allan's faultless kit—the magic
touch of Reynard & Co. stamped on every line of it—
with his own stained and battered pink, bought second-
hand from those purveyors for the poorer sportsman—
Moss Bros!

The thought of Ann and Allan riding forth to the
chase—"the sport of kings, the image of war"—in Allan's
own county, Warwickshire, came to his mind. He saw
them going as well as anybody, and better than most, in
the country of men and women who "mean it." And at
the vision his spirit fainted, growing hard and bitter within
him. What had he to offer Ann, worthy to be accepted in
comparison with such a life; what, indeed?

Johnny Brien's harsh admonishment of a hound recalled
his thoughts to their proper channel, and the dear familiar
feel of the small battered horn in his hand did much to lift
his heart. Nodding to Johnny, he moved off, the hounds
surging round his horse in the narrow bhoireen which led
to Ballindrum gorse.

"A sure find," Ann had said, when speaking of Ballin-drum, the evening before; nor did she put the case too high. Five minutes after Dennys put his hounds into covert, they were out of it like a shot from a gun, and away with a scream on the line of the little red rover—now more than two fields in front of them and heading determinedly for the woods of Ballinrath, to make which point he must cross the finest bit of going in a very variegated country.

"Thank God, we stopped the main drain," called Sybil to her cousin, above the thunder of first enthusiasm. They had not yet met a fence of sufficient dimensions to quench the ardour of all but the elect whose hearts are with hounds, and who fain would have their horses there too.

Allan only grinned in response, and edging away from the crowd drove Sailor at a great solid green double. From its summit he was aware of a precipice which yawned below, a precipice terminating in a wide and sticky ditch.

"Can you do it, old man?" he asked. "Rather!" replied Sailor—or words to that effect. "Hold tight." And with a mighty bound, he landed cleanly somewhere near the middle of the next field. Cramming down his hat, Allan caught hold of his horse's head, and rode hard to make the best of a good start. Hounds were running fast on a breast-high scent, and it required a man with his heart in the proper place, and a big-jumping, galloping horse, to live with them at all. Happily Allan was possessed of both these requisites, and added thereto a certain measure of judgment and perception acquired only during the last couple of months.

Ann felt a queer motherly pride in his progress. She had taught him a lot, certainly, but the essentials had always

been there. She galloped beside him through the well-
stopped woods of Ballinrath.

"Forty minutes of the best!" she shouted; "good job
you stopped that drain."

Allan only grinned again.

Charles Fox was very nearly beat. His brush was full of
mud and hung heavily. The jaunty grin he had worn when
he slipped out of covert, such a short while before, was
now set and desperate on his mask. As he whisked away
from the furze-filled entrance to the dry drain, where last
summer he had reared a young and promising family, he
realized that his only hope of saving his brush lay in
reaching the demesne wall before his pursuers, running
mute for blood not eight hundred yards behind him. Once
there, he knew of a tough ivy root—many a time he had
slid down it, carrying the warm body of a newly slain
fowl for the aforesaid family—by which he might attain
the summit of the wall, and thence, two fields further on,
a certain dry forsaken earth, concealed by a stubble of
whin bushes.

As he slid through the fast binding undergrowth of
hazel saplings and bramble wreaths, Charles thought with
poignant longing of the sharp worn rock at the mouth of
the haven where he would be.

With a backward eye on that awful throng behind him,
he broke once more into the open. Racing with the
swiftness of despair across two wide fields and a third, he
reached the demesne wall with the leading hounds not a
hundred yards off his brush.

But the stout ivy root, his path to safety, to that dry

deserted earth lipped by sharp slaty rocks—where was it? He had misjudged his point, the stout ivy root was sixty yards to his left, and death was very, very close behind him.

He sprang at the bare face of the wall like a cat, and hung, clawing futilely for a moment, before dropping back into the dry ditch. Then turning, he faced his pursuers with a snarl—of hatred, not of fear.

Allan and Dennys dismounted together and flogged off the hounds, while Ann—radiant and breathless—climbed down to see the kill and help keep back the baying half-circle. Johnny cut off pads, mask and brush; then the huntsman, sounding heart-stirring music on his battered little horn, trailed the red corpse along the ground before flinging it into the air with a whoop, to fall among a pack grown suddenly silent.

"Well," Allan was examining Sailor's legs for cuts, "that was as nice a gallop as ever I saw. Fifty minutes of the best. Finest fox wot ever was seen—wot!"

Dennys was not attending to him in the least. He and Ann, standing side by side, their arms through their horses' reins, their eyes upon the red muzzled hounds, were raptly discussing every aspect of the run; agreeing, contradicting, arguing, enthusiastic. . . . Allan watched them a thought sourly. Surely Ann realized that everything in that line was over and done with. A horrible fear smote Allan; a cold, sinking feeling attacked him in the region of his waist-coat. Some words he seemed to have heard very often stood out, spelled in black letters across his brain. A ghoulish little voice whispered the same words to him over and over again: "Took you on the rebound," said the fiendish little voice. . . "on the rebound . . . on the rebound . . . didn't care a damn about you really. Quite a different fella in the case."

Allan had known this all along; it was no new aspect of the affair which faced him. Had he not been in Ann's confidence, comforted her as best he could, done all he knew to make the path straight for her small feet, and incidentally for Dennys's large ones. Was it his fault that those large feet had blundered elsewhere?

Now, when the wonderful, fairy-story reward of virtue—the Princess—was his, come to him of her own free will, was he with misplaced chivalry to permit the fool who had so lately, through short-sighted folly, bruised the princess's heart, to wear that heart again? Certainly not! He precipitated himself cheerfully into their conversation.

"Pretty good going that, Ann. Warwickshire won't show us anything better."

"N—no," agreed Ann. Her eyes, like a scared rabbit's, avoided his; Allan, hoping she was not going to cry, felt every sort of beast and found nothing more to say.

"We'll be getting on now, Johnny," said Dennys some minutes later, breaking a silence grown somewhat stormy. "Co-oop hounds! Dauntless—Dalesman—*Leave* it, Dalesman! Come into whip, hounds—come in t' whip!" They moved off.

Allan, when he had mounted Ann, turned to find Sybil behind him, smiling one of her snake-eyed smiles.

"You use the possessive case too much, me lad," she observed, laying a deft hand on his horse's rein while he mounted. "*I* heard you. Put both feet in the trough with a nasty splash—didn't you?"

"You go to hell," replied her second cousin at white heat.

"Ah, not yet, laddie, not yet!" returned the lady soothingly. "My ultimate end, no doubt, but I'm still young in years though old in spirit, and my advice to *you* is——"

But Allan, with a rudeness of which he was not often guilty rode away and left her there.

Instantly Sybil called a halt until the unmistakable figure of Tessie Jeeves loomed upon the horizon.

"Hullo, Tessie!" she called, as soon as the lady came within speaking distance. "Heard the big news?"

"No, what is it? Sybil, you're a holy terror for scandal."

Tessie fell in beside the holy terror, and together they rode along, chaffing and laughing, Tessie's broad sallies parried by Sybil's barbed shafts of wit.

"Well now," inquired Tessie at length, "what's this you were going to tell me? I knew *all* about that baby months ago; and as for Muriel Dane and that Jameson boy—it's as stale as the monkeys."

Sybil stared demurely between her horse's ears.

"Ann's engaged," she announced at last, with befitting solemnity. "I should go and congratulate her if I were you—only for God's sake don't say I told you."

"Engaged?" repeated Tessie on her highest note of interrogation and amazement. "Who to?"

"For heaven's sake, Tessie, shut up! Eat a sandwich, or do something to muffle your voice. The whole hunt knows by now that *some one's* engaged. Think it's me prob'ly."

"Ah, go on, Sybil! Sure there's no one within half a mile of us. Is it Allan she's engaged to?"

"It is," replied Sybil unemotionally, "since yesterday evening."

"Well, I suppose you're all delighted." Tessie being a lady of some insight, gave her companion a keen and searching look; but Sybil, trim and spruce on her cobby mare, gave no sign of any emotion other than satisfaction.

"I am," she admitted. "It hasn't been broken to Daddy yet, but I'm sure he'll be pleased. I don't mind telling you that I've had some anxious moments over this affair. An elder sister is a great responsibility."

Tessie shouted her appreciation of the jest; then she became suddenly serious.

"Ye know, Sybil, we're miles behind every one. They'll be through Ballybreen by now. Holy Smoke! is that the horn I hear?" Raising herself in her stirrups, she turned to stare towards the gorse knock a quarter of a mile distant, Ballybreen covert. "They're away!" she exclaimed excitedly. "Come on! We've just a chance to hit them off if we hurry."

With a hoist and a heave, Tessie's big chustnut was over the briar-masked, razor-topped bank by the roadside. Sybil following blindly, thanked her God when Pet Girl landed with a scramble, not to say a flounder, but still landed safely, on the far side. She had occasion to render thanks not once but many times in the course of the next few minutes; for Tessie's short cut provided—after the manner of short cuts—many a precarious, not to say awe-inspiring "lep," before it finally brought them to a little bhoireen, winding its forlorn way up a lean hillside. Down this they clattered, only halting when their way was barred by a formidable iron gate, behind which pranced a small, but very fierce old woman. She was waving a broomstick and yelling furiously.

"They shwept me little finces," she screamed. Tears of rage were in her eyes, but no sobs impeded her shrill utterance. "A hellish posse o' thim went through my poor little place, and devil a sod they left afther! An' a man in a caroline hat at the top o' thim—Aha! I'll sweep the heads off the lot o' yez!"

She advanced to fulfil her threat, but Tessie, judging the case to be one in which discretion was certainly the more expedient part of valour, whirled her horse about and followed Sybil through an open gate leading left-handed out of the lane. Many deep hoof-marks showed where the hunt, headed no doubt by the man in the caroline hat (could that mean Allan's tall silk?) had already passed.

"If there's anything more deadly than banging along on the tail of the hunt, with hounds six fields ahead of you, I don't know it," observed Sybil, whirling Pet Girl round again at a stone-faced bank that the mare had flatly refused to have, save only in the place which the "posse," jumping as one man, had already shaken to its rotten core. "Come *up*, mare!"

But Pet Girl, making a determined sideways dive, jumped crooked at the hoof-broken, crumbling spot where so many had crossed before her, failed to change on the treacherous foothold, and subsided gracefully into the wide and muddy ditch on the far side.

"Oh God!" exclaimed Tessie, with some emotion, when Sybil—wet, muddy, and in a devilish temper, but quite unhurt—had picked herself out of the mud and rushes into which she had fallen.

"What an *awful* place! Here, Sybil, look out for a better one for me. Oh, never mind the mare, she'll lie there soaking herself till Christmas."

Sybil obediently vetted the landings of the three places selected by Tessie. The third was situated some twenty yards from where Pet Girl lay in the muddy water, and it was to this that Tessie finally squared up her weight-carrying hunter, hit him a whack and let him have it.

As Nimrod—jumping with the best will in the world and no little skill—landed safely on the far side, there was a splurge, a sound as of a mighty cork being drawn, and Pet Girl, rising as swiftly and suddenly as a partridge from the lee of her sheltering bank, was up and away, galloping with hanging reins and much determination, straight and wicked as a bee, towards the wire which fenced the field on three sides.

"Now she's done for," observed Sybil, with the calm of utter hopelessness.

"Now you may say your prayers," added Tessie. "Oh! Oh! What will your Daddy say?"

Even as she spoke, two figures appeared atop the wire-enforced bank, two pairs of arms waved semaphore-like together, and two voices shrilled horrid imprecations at the swiftly advancing Pet Girl. Pausing horror-struck, she swerved aside and dashed head-long through an open gate in the corner of the field, to find herself bogging to the fetlocks in wet and heavy plough.

Sybil's feelings, when she recognized in the saviours of her mare the identical old woman who had reviled the hunt and all its works not ten short minutes past, aided by a minute grandchild, and still wielding the broom which was to have swept the heads off the members of the hunt, were chaotic. Alone and unsupported, she approached the beldame, Tessie being occupied with the recapture of Pet Girl—and proffered fervent thanks, coupled with promises of redress for her shattered fences.

"Never mind them, asthore!" Mrs Tierney balanced on top of the fence, her grey hair floating in the breeze (she looked very like one of her own ancient goats), held high and lofty converse with Sybil, pending the arrival of Tessie and Pet Girl.

"It's what I was a little annoyed," she explained as one lady to another, "what with that devil's trash having me little garden pocked to ruin on me. But sure yourself knows, and the world knows, Miss Hillingdon me dear, that anyone out o' your mother's family might ride through the thatch itself and I'd say no word til' yez. Aha! that's the sort of you! 'Tis over the house ye'd lep. Ye have great courage." They parted with expressions of the greatest amity on both sides.

"Not that I'll ever be able to get her fences mended," said Sybil, recounting the interview to Mrs Jeeves, "but she's as pleased as if I'd sent two men and a boy to do it for her on the minute."

"She may be," returned the lady. "I must say I'd be better pleased if I knew where the hounds are now, or where they're likely to be."

Directed by a series of more or less misinformed country boys, they finally fell in with hounds and hunt jogging along a by-way to their next draw. The two coffee-housers were greeted with laughter and loud commiseration; also with soul-shaking accounts of a topping nice bit of hunting, and a fox marked to ground under Brien's Rocks.

"Well, well," Tessie lit a cigarette philosophically, "there's no use cyring over spilt milk."

"Or a spilt Sybil," chipped in Allan. "Where did you get all the mud, baby? Out of the sky as you came through? Don't say this perfect lady gave you a toss."

"Of course not," returned Sybil. "I was jumped off—silly fool!"

"And the mare lay down in the ditch to cool herself—I *don't* think."

Sybil had forgotten Pet Girl's coating of mud. "A horse must fall sometimes," she admitted. "Yes, James it *was* bad luck——" She turned to recount the events of the last half-hour to one of her faithful train.

Allan and Tessie rode on together in silence, for a while. They had grown to be very good friends, these two; the gentlemanly youth (no word other than gentlemanly quite describes Allan) and the vulgar, good-hearted, remarkably clever woman.

"Well, Allan," she broke the silence at last, speaking in a lower key than usual, "so I hear you're a very much to be congratulated young man."

"Thanks awfully." Allan coloured up pleasingly beneath his tan. "But—er—it's not official yet, you understand. What I mean is—Ann doesn't want it blasted abroad, if you get me."

"Oh, I do, of course. No, I won't," responded Tessie. "Well, good bye now: I must go and talk to Ann."

"Don't tell her *I* told you about it," interpolated Allan swiftly.

"Right-o, I won't. Oh, look—will you *look* at that big brute of hers? Wouldn't you think those two hunts might have cooled him?" Tessie indicated Garry Owen, sidling, fighting for his head, and plunging riotously as he felt turf beneath his feet again. They had turned off the road to cross a series of fields *en route* for the covert. "As good as Ann is, I think she's hardly able to hold him. *Look* at that now!" she added, as Garry Owen gave vent to his feelings in a couple of shattering buck-jumps.

"Oh, she's all right," Allan laughed easily; "the only time that horse is dangerous is at his fences, and then it's not her, it's the fella in front who takes risks."

"Ah, go on! I never saw Ann jump on top of anyone yet," scoffed Tessie. "Did you?"

Allan stooped in his saddle to light a cigarette, laughed pleasantly, and rode away.

He had by this time quite laid the unpleasant little ghoul which had mocked and taunted him earlier in the day. A smile from Ann had laid it. A smile none the less swift and sweet in that it was prompted by her pricking conscience. No matter; Allan—caught in its rays—basked and rejoiced.

He was thinking about it now as he stood by the covert side; and a host of other dear, warm thoughts merged pleasantly and hazily with the memory. "Ann," cried a voice in his heart, "my funny sweet, my darling Ann!"... Then, "She's little but she's wise, she's a—oh dammit, no, that won't do!" ... And again, "Ann, my darling Ann ... mine—mine. ... Mine for ever, God of Love ... and she's so little, so awfully small. ..." It was at this point that his formless maunderings were interrupted by the lady in question herself. She rode up to him—a bright spot burning in either cheek, and a light of anger in her eyes. Her hands were low down on either side of Garry's withers—a wild-eyed Garry who simply wouldn't stand still.

"I thought I asked you, Allan—stand, boy, can't you *stand*?—I thought I'd made it quite clear that I didn't want you to say anything to anybody about our——" She paused, confused. "About last night," she finished lamely.

"But *I* didn't, me dear," he told her; "the cat was thoroughly out when Tessie's felicitations started. . . . I thought you must have told some one."

"But I didn't. I didn't tell anyone! And now everybody knows!" Ann's eyes were swimming; her voice shook.

"Ann, didn't you mean them to—some time? Don't you want it? What do you want, Ann?" There was some sternness in Allan's young eyes and in the set of his mouth as he questioned her. Ann, realizing it, liked him better than she had done all day; and with those whom she liked, or even approved, Ann could not be firm.

"No, of course not. Oh, Allan—how can you? You know I can't . . . I mean I won't—oh, you'd never understand."

Allan put a gentle hand over hers for a moment. "I think I do, old lady. Don't you worry," he murmured.

Ann's soul was in a tumult. Marry Allan? She couldn't do it. To tell him so, was equally impossible to her. When she remembered all he had done for her, and been to her, during the past months, she could not summon courage to take from him his present great gladness. Ann, who would not have hurt the slug or earwig in her path had not the resolution of spirit to prevent the shipwreck of two lives—her own and Dennys's. There was very little of the egoist about her; just too silly—she was—and too lovable, for words. As Garry bucked large over a loose stone wall, the wish uppermost in his rider's mind was that she might take a toss before the day's end, which would finish her troubles once and for all.

Through the grey hours of early afternoon, hounds and hunt jogged from covert to rain-soaked covert. One short spin—sorry going round a wet bog—alone relieved the monotony. At three o'clock the rain began to fall, but three-thirty found the hounds on their way to one more "sure find."

"I like this—do you?" Elizabeth turned a wet and shining face to Rickard.

"Yes," he agreed, "only my reins are so dam' slippery. Wish I hadn't borrowed Sybil's shammy gloves. They're no use."

She nodded silently. "Dennys says string ones are the only kind," she observed some minutes later; a "lep" of fair proportions had interrupted their conversation. "How's that setter pup you're rearing?" she inquired.

"It's getting on well now. We have it in the chickens' foster mother at night; and in the day it's shut up in a box with a kitten to keep it warm."

"That's a right place," approved Elizabeth. "And are you still keeping it on Mellins?"

"No; Ann thought Glaxo. It takes it better too. The keeper gives his one twelve drops of castor oil a day, but I give mine magnesia. . . ." They drifted into intricacies of diet and dosings.

"You'd wonder anyone'd be bothered rearing babies when they might be rearing pups," observed Rickard, à propos of a squalling family through whose farmyard they had just passed.

"Yes, and Johnny Brien had a baby two nights ago.

You'd think he'd have more sense." Elizabeth's tone was damnatory.

"Boy or girl?" inquired Rickard.

"Oh, I dunno. Didn't ask; more or less, I suppose." And having thus satisfactorily settled the question of the infant's sex, they passed on to other and more engrossing subjects.

Through the rain, Ann rode with Allan. He did not speak to her often, but occasionally his eyes smiled into hers, and when that happened, a cold pain ran over her heart. How could she tell him? How could she! Dimly through the rain she saw Dennys—separated from her by many people on jostling horses, by his hounds, and above all by the news which must surely have reached him by now, of her engagement to Allan. Almost she hated the dear, nice boy who rode beside her and smiled into her eyes.

Her reins, like Rickard's, were wet and greasy, they slipped maddeningly through her fingers as Garry snatched and pulled. She searched under her saddle flap for the woolly pair of gloves she generally put there, but of course she had forgotten to bring them to-day. Ann felt sick and tired—she had not touched her sandwiches; almost for the first time in her life she wished her horse at the devil, and herself at home.

"That's a big place coming, Ann," Allan's gentle voice broke into her reverie.

"You go on," she replied dully, holding Garry in as well as she could.

It certainly was a big place. A tall stone-faced bank, jumpable only in one spot, with a bad take off, and what looked like a worse landing. Sailor was up, and—heavens! he was down. Left his legs behind him—or was it wire? But Ann had no time for further cogitations on the matter. The slippery reins were wrenched through her fingers, Garry's neck turned to iron. Quicker than thought, he was on top of the bank . . . a plunge . . . a confused vision of a white face below her—Allan's; Sailor beside her, struggling to get his hind legs clear—that was all Ann realized before Garry jumped. Jumped—but not big enough; he was into the wide boggy gripe right on top of the man with the white face. . . .

With a gasp, Ann—thrown clear—jerked herself to her feet. Her mouth was dry; she was winded, but not badly. A moment of exquisite pain enabled her to regain her breath, and showed her the confused medley of horse and man in the deep ditch.

"A saddle!" she screamed. "Quick! Oh God—some one——" She tried to reach Sailor's girths; tried and failed. Another minute—or was it a year?—and the members of the hunt were all about her—doing everything efficiently. She saw Charlie Jeeves putting his saddle over her cousin's head, others holding the plunging Garry as quiet as might be, saw Allan pulled out from under him and laid on the grass, flasks produced, and coats taken off. . . . Ann covered her face with her hands and moaned.

"Sure he's all right!" It was Tessie's voice full of reassurance that Ann heard. She opened her eyes to see Allan standing on his feet, looking somewhat pale and dazed, certainly—but seemingly unhurt.

"It's quite all right, thanks. Stunned for a minute, was I? Oh, no. Head hit something hard, perhaps. No, thanks—really!" Declining several proffered flasks, he made his way through the circle which surrounded him to Ann, who raised a strained white face to him.

"Allan—*are* you hurt?"

"Dammit, no! Right as rain." He said nothing of an old wound in the back with which Garry's hoofs had played the very deuce. Taking Garry from the farmer who had finally picked him out of the ditch, he mounted Ann with extra care.

"Don't be a little idiot," he whispered once, noticing her pathetically working mouth; "not a feather out of either of the horses—so what the dickens does it matter?"

Ann stooped to adjust her stirrup. "I might've killed you, dear," she whispered very low.

Turning from her, Allan hid the gladness of his eyes beneath Sailor's saddle flap—his girths needed a great deal of tightening.

Ann's cup was full—full, moreover, of bitterness. A lonesome helplessness surged through and over her. There was no light in all the world. She had been a fool—a fool! A mischievous fool too. That no great harm had come of her folly was scarcely comforting to her in her present sorry state of mind. The last touch was put to her misery when Garry began to go lame. She reflected bitterly on the ten weary miles of wet grey road which lay between them and home. Allan, after a lengthy examination, reported no cut and suggested a strain.

"I wish I could open my mouth and howl," said Ann, upon receipt of this statement.

"It might be a relief," Allan grinned, adding hastily: "Please don't, old thing, my hanky's filthy. Try a few of the worst words you know instead."

She turned her horse round and made for the road—a

dreary little figure enough. Allan, following through the grey, falling rain, found all his protective instincts surging to the surface; the first two miles of their homeward way gave them, however, very little scope. Ann was fully occupied with Garry, who—well aware that he was on his way to stable and feed—seemed to forget his lameness, and acted more like a two-year-old than he had done at any other period of the day. Allan's attempts at conversation were conspicuous failures.

"Dear, you're awfully tired," he observed twice in the first half-mile; and Ann replied twice: "It's not that I'm tired—only that I've been *such* a fool." He spoke of the morning's run; Ann said "Yes" or "No" at intervals, but without enthusiasm.

They rode a mile or more in silence, unbroken save for their horses' uneven footfalls. Allan found himself almost longing for Sybil's enlivening presence. In Ann's mind was a picture of endless years, cheerless and grey as this ride of theirs together. She dug her teeth into her lip, moaning little futile "damns" below her breath.

At a cross road, four miles from home, Allan pulled up Sailor. "Blest if I don't hear the hounds!" He turned to Ann. "Shall we wait?"

A wild, choking gladness came over her as she too heard the unmistakable sounds of hounds' progress along one of the converging roads, heard Dennys's voice . . . the crack of a whip . . . a moment before she had been deadened by misery. Now she was alive—glowingly alive. Her heart within her was radiant.

"Shall we wait, dear?" repeated Allan; and at the sound of his voice, the sick misery of indecision descended on her once more like a pall.

"No. . . .Oh, I don't know—no, let's go on."

But it was too late. Following on Dennys's "Hounds! Hounds, please!" the little pack surged down the road— no one with them save huntsman and whip. Allan turned his horse perfunctorily, not to face them, called a greeting to Dennys, and the three rode on together, Allan in the middle, Ann on his near side.

Ann, after she had said: "Hullo, Dennys! A great day"—in what she felt to be an obviously unnatural manner—lapsed into silence. The absence of his greeting to her had not hurt her so much as his unskilful manoeuvre to ride on Allan's off-side.

Tears pricked at her eyelids as she rode along in the gathering dusk, listening to her companions' tireless, technical discussion of the day's sport. Another time, and she would have joined as warmly as any, and with much more knowledge than most, in such a discussion. Now, the bruised, tired thing that was her heart bade her be silent—not open her lips in speech, lest she break down and sob openly before them all.

Noticing Damsel—a pup she had walked the previous year—Ann called her out. Damsel came up, but gave no sign of pleasure or recognition. Somehow the trivial circumstance put the finishing touch to her misery. The memory of Damsel suffering from yellows rushed to her mind. . . .Dennys pushing pills down a pup's reluctant throat; Dennys sitting on the straw-filled kennel bench, gravely commending her treament of the patient; Dennys stooping in the low doorway—Dennys's eyes in the sunlight. And now—she jerked her mind back to realities as she heard Allan's clear-cut, gentlemanly voice bidding Dennys "Good-bye."

Of course, their roads parted here. More than their roads! Here ended for her, love, fellowship, all gladness.

Could the trite voice she heard speaking to him be her own?

"You'll come over before you leave, won't you? . . . the day after to-morrow? Oh, as soon as that? Well, good-bye then; and—and the very best of luck."

"Thank you." Dennys's unemotional voice was as even as ever. "The same to you, Ann. The very best! Sound banks and straight foxes—all the rest of it. Well, good-bye." He touched the peak of his blue velvet cap and rode into the dusk—his hounds jostling around and behind his horse.

Garry, impatient at having his head turned from the hounds, plunged and reared. "*Look out!*" came Allan's horrified yell. "WORHOUNDS!"

The warning came too late. Garry came down, plunging, and Dauntless, best hound in the pack, straggling unmarked in the dusk, was somewhere among those plunging hoofs.

Allan's call brought Dennys to the spot. He found a white-faced Ann kneeling in the mud, where Dauntless—by Warwickshire Dalesman, out of his own Restless, and winner among the unentereds at Clonmel—lay dying; his head on her knees, his blood stains on her hands.

"I'm afraid it's no use," she whispered hoarsely, as Dennys knelt beside her, feeling the smashed ribs with gentle hands. "I rode—simply all over him . . . he must be . . . pulp. *Ah!*" The hurt hound opened his eyes an instant, moaned once, and lay—his flanks fallen in—still and quiet in the mud.

Dennys silently helped Ann to her feet. The weight of

her sodden habit dragged at her; her feet inside her waterlogged boots were numb—numb as her blood-stained hands, numb as her heart. For the first time in all the weary day, she felt that tears were indeed idle—could bring her no relief.

Haltingly, she approached Garry, whom Allan held as quiet as might be alongside a heap of stones. Ann put her foot in the stirrup, was half-way up, when Garry plunged away—snorting meaninglessly.

"Dennys, would you mind? I can't get up, I'm so stiff. I'm—I'm awfully sorry to bother you."

He picked her up and would have mounted her as easily as a child, but seeing her trembling mouth and nervous awkwardness, he set her on her feet again.

"Don't ride Garry," he urged. "You're not fit for him. Don't do it, Ann."

"No, Ann, don't. Ride Sailor home. You'd much better, dear," interpolated Allan.

Ann, facing the pair of them in the road, laughed nervously—hysterically.

"If I don't, it's because I'm afraid. I'm in a beastly funk. I've only missed killing Allan—I've ridden over your best hound—and now I—I think my nerve's gone. Oh, Dennys, my dear—I'm broken up now. What'll I do? I don't know what I'll do, at all. . . ." Overwrought, she sank, a shuddering mass of wet humanity, upon the stones by the wayside.

Allan regarded her fixedly for a moment before he turned to Dennys.

"You'll get her back, and all that," he said. "I'll take your horse and help Johnny get the hounds into kennels. Best of luck—er—you understand? Er—good night."

THE KNIGHT OF CHEERFUL COUNTENANCE

The Knight of Cheerful Countenance raised his hat to the drooping figure upon the heap of stones, mounted and passed whistling down the road.

CHAPTER XVI
The Deuce of a Gallop

ALLAN returned to Ballinrath in the first week of a wintry April. The hunting season was over, point-to-points were the excitement of the moment. In two of these Major Hillingdon's br. g. Sailor 6 yrs.—and far too fit a horse for Fox to exercise with any degree of comfort or confidence—was entered in the Open Heavy-Weight Race. Allan, very properly was to be his jockey.

The morning of his return was wintry in the extreme, very different from that soft September evening of his first coming to Bungarvin. This time no smiling-eyed Ann met him at the station gates. Ann was very far away now, and walled all about from him by the exquisite selfishness of her love. A love which had at last proved strong enough to enable her—with judicious backing from Allan and Sybil—to defy her aged parent even to the extent of a London wedding. This ceremony over, she had departed with Dennys and Driscoll, all the stars of El Dorado alight and burning wonderfully in her eyes; and the brown beaver coat, which had been a wedding present, hugged close about her as Dennys put her carefully into the car piled high with their suit-cases. . . .Allan remembered with gratitude what a marvellous pal Sybil had been to him that evening. Her liquid wit had made more than a success of his dinner party. Her unspoiled and perfect enjoyment of dance and cabaret show, her thrill which charged the taxi with electricity at the magic word "Night Club," had been several inspirations: had made him forget—almost.

And now—now, he was back at Ballinrath; due to ride a bucking fit horse over Irish country again. Not an altogether unpleasing prospect even after his two months at Melton. . . . Well—hullo! Sybil. Always as smart as be damned, that kid. He liked her slim, brown-checked back, also her earnest manner of conversing with the station-master. Money passed between the two. "My book-maker" —Sybil explained, as, her impersonally cheerful greeting to her cousin finished, she and Benbow enthused over each other for a space. "Yes, he has given me four winners in the last ten days."

"An adorable bookie," was Allan's comment. "How do you *do* these things, Sybil?"

"Me? Oh, you know me, Allan. I don't. I just get them done. Would you swing the car now, like a dear? Your train was so beastly late, I'm afraid she's too cold for the self-starter."

As the Ford spluttered and back-fired, Sybil ground down her clutch, releasing it with a devastating jerk, and when the faint throbbing engine finally gathered power, settled her down into her usual snatching, tireless 35 m.p.h. gallop, and proceeded for the remainder of the way to discuss whole-heartedly Sailor's prospects of winning either or both of the races in which he was entered.

Certainly the big horse looked fit and ready to run for his life, when Fox led him out of his box and held him for Allan to mount on the afternoon of the same day. Every muscle in his frame showed like steel wire under his clean, well-strapped skin; in his usually mild eye a certain fire had been kindled by much sound corn. He humped his strong back unkindly beneath Allan's small Whippy saddle. Sybil on Pet Girl laughed wickedly. "Doesn't look a joy-ride, does he? I'm glad I'm not sending him into his fences to-day."

"God then, ye have as much Schools ridden on him as'd sicken an ass," Fox put in, as he manoeuvred Sailor up to the block, "and in regard o' that this fella was as simple and kindly as a Crisken till you gave him his fashion of going the devil's own belt into all that'd be before him. A pairson would never get to ride a hunt in comfort on him again," Fox prophesied dourly, while he evaded with undignified agility the kick which the simple and kindly Christian launched in his direction.

"Well, Fox"—as she spoke Sybil noted with approval Allan's subtly effective way with Sailor, who was all on edge to buck—"that big mare of Mr St Lawrence's is the only thing I'm afraid of in to-morrow's race. She takes her fences faster than we do, an' you couldn't put her down."

"Sha! Is it that one?" Fox's contempt was great. "Sure she have a neck on her like a short-horn bullock, and I declare to God ye could hang yer coat up on her hips."

Sybil laughed and led the way out of the yard. They rode together down the long lane to the schooling ground, where the crooked fences had had their proportions altered to conform to the usual "made-up" bank of the natural course. Here they took walking exercise for the space of one hour, during which time Sybil proved herself—as she so well knew how to do—the most amusing and joyous of companions. The thorny side of her wit she casually suppressed for the moment, nor did she directly speak of Ann. The wedding they discussed devastatingly. Allan roared over Sybil's strictures on her Saxon relatives. She had the quaintest way of putting things—the most ordinary things—a way which moved one to chuckles of complete mirth.

The hour's walking over, Sybil held the dancing three-legged Pet Girl quiet in the middle of the field, and kept time with a stop-watch while Sailor galloped the mile, and subsequently giving her unreserved approval of the form he showed over his fences. Allan approved of it too. "Jove, it's a future National horse!"

He pulled up beside Sybil, a hand on the big horse's hard neck, soothing him with that unconcern which alone quietens the obstreperousness evoked by sound corn and plenty of it.

"Let's have the hurdles together," was Sybil's suggestion. They galloped down at the dark furze just as fast as the Lord would let them go; and their horses, sailing over side by side, snatched at their bits and raced for the next in a manner that filled their riders' souls with seething exaltation. They walked again after that, talking earnestly in the gathering gloom of the late afternoon. "Eight o'clock every morning for the last month I've been at this game," Sybil told him, as, with the deftness of long practice, she closed the rickety gate of the training paddock, and their horses pricked eager ears towards their stables.

"You've done wonders," Allan's voice was warm in commendation of her efforts.

"Oh, I dunno. Just a little bit of time and trouble——" She slapped Pet Girl rhythmically behind the saddle and laughed up into Allan's face. "After all, one does a lot for one's own horse—it's fun."

"Yours?"

"Yes. Daddy gave him to me, you know. I felt nothing

else would really be a comfort to me after poor Ann's disastrous marriage." The old devilment was back in Sybil's smile and screwed-up eyes.

"Good Lord! Why don't you ride him yourself to-morrow?"

"Me? Oh, well, I'd have to make up the dickens of a lot of weight for one thing and for another I rather wanted you to have the ride. You know the horse, he'll do best for you." Her tone implied implicit confidence in Allan's jockeyship. She slipped off Pet Girl, and stood leaning confidentially against the mare's warm shoulder while Allan led the brown in, and Fox toddled across the yard towards her.

A minute later Pet Girl stuck her cheerful cob's face out over the half-door of her box, and Sailor put his long, lean hunter's head out over the neighbouring door. Sybil and Allan stood together regarding the pair thoughtfully. "Our two hunters, side by side," Sybil murmured, "don't they look decent?"

"Whopping!" Allan agreed, "only Sailor isn't mine any more now—unless you'd sell, Sybil?" he paused tentatively.

She laughed and moved away towards the house. "No, I'm not selling, Allan." He laughed too, and caught up with her. He had nearly forgotten how Sybil could make one feel that one minute not spent in her society went down to eternity a wasted sixty seconds—or was it just that he had never fully realized the fact until to-day?

The thought that Sybil was grown-up, as fully developed in mind and body as she would ever be, struck him forcibly this evening; *and* she was such a lovely thing. He lay back in his leather chair watching her covertly as, tea over, she stood with her back to the glowing turf fire feeding the little dogs. Her legs, unlike those of her many less fortunate sisters, appeared to distinct advantage in a misused, but well cut, pair of breeches which had once belonged to her father, as had also her canvas leggings. The long jumper she wore was her own. The red silk handkerchief knotted round her throat, having once pleased her as the property of another, had promptly been annexed. Her short, straight back was delightful, so was the carriage of her small dark head. One could not tell whether her eyes mocked and glinted, cold as a kitten's, or whether they held in their slow depths soft fires of enchantment—Allan shook himself upright in his chair, and lit a pipe feverishly. Good Lord! Not three months— No. The thing was not possible.

Sybil was talking to Jibber. "*No*, darling, *not* good. Spit it out! Did you ever see the like? *Never* was, and never shall be again such a little dog—a little white girl, wiv *such* a tum—most beautiful tummy in all the big wide. *Best* little girl . . . did you see her spit out that cake when I told her to, Allan?"

"Doesn't she miss Ann frightfully?" Allan asked. "I should have thought she'd have taken her along."

"Well, you see Jib is really Daddy's, and he wants her to have some more puppies before she goes, an' so we're just considering the matter for the moment, *and* taking care of our Auntie Sybil."

"As opposed to which the cares of a family would be a heaven-sent rest-cure," Allan put in sourly. The remark moved Sybil to some show of indignation. "You're becoming embittered," she warned him. "Now look at me, and just—er—take a lesson. I'm not the same Sybil I was three months ago. I've had a frightful time battling with Mrs Burke, feeding *all* the dogs, trying to cheer Daddy when he insists that Dennys will be just like his father—morals and all—in twenty years' time. I haven't had one moment to get into mischief."

The regret in her voice was so manifest that Allan laughed aloud. "I wonder what'd steady you up, Sybil; the cares of a household don't seem to."

"A baby—of course." Sybil, looking peculiarly slim and elfin, clung with both hands to the edge of the mantelshelf, and smiled a Madonna smile. "Think how sweet it would be," she murmured. "Can't you see me punching round a large navy-blue perambulator——"

"One moment, my dear," Allan broke in. "I'd so much rather have dark claret body-work."

Sybil shrieked with delight. "Well, anyway, to look a little further ahead, I insist on Harrow for the boy."

"Good God!" Allan became quite heated. "Why, my dear girl, you must be mad; if you say much more I'll put his name down for Eton immediately, if not sooner."

"Oh, all right; anything to please you, dear, so long as he plays cricket——"

"I rowed——"

Sybil gave it up with a squeal of pure joy.

Later they retired to the gun-room, where George the pantry boy had lighted an enormous fire, as Mr Fox had told him there wasn't as much heat in the harness-room fire as would dry a hankercher, let alone Mr Allan's breeches he was after whitening for the race.

They removed the breeches from the forefront of the blaze, and ensconcing themselves comfortably in two battered basket chairs, they spent an amiable half-hour hunting for fleas on two little dogs. After which—a dog reposing in well-earned slumber upon each of their chests—the pair conversed, amicably, tirelessly, and endlessly, on the morrow's prospects.

With his boots upon the mantelshelf, and Jibber stretched prone upon his person, Allan felt more delightfully at peace in mind and body than he had done for many a long day. It was extraordinary the power Ballinrath had of making one its own, so that one returned thither conscious that in so much as the ways of other houses differed from the ways of Ballinrath, in so much also did they greatly lack. The warm comfort of the house, the friendly little dogs, the manner in which even the cook's tantrums were made subservient to the sport of the moment; the great and unaffected welcome extended to all who came within its doors, affected this English boy, who had hardly known a home of his own, to a strange point of warm delight.

His English cousins made him welcome in their beautiful homes, and showed him their large hospitality chiefly because blood is, after all, thicker than water, and he was, of course, "poor Mary's son," and such a *nice* boy, they were always glad to see him. But the serene surety of his welcome at Ballinrath was such that no one was "glad to see him back"; they took him as much for granted as they did Rick when he returned from school. Fox had said by way of greeting, "Miss Sybil is knocking Puck out o' me young horses; I hope in God, Master Allan, you'll regulate her better than meself."

George had asked for his breeches as though he had the day before worn them in a run through the bogs of Breen, instead of which it had been a fast thing with the Pytchley ladies. Major Hillingdon had muttered hastily, "Me dear boy—that's right, that's right! We haven't seen you since that shockin' affair in January. Too long! Too long!"

But it was Sybil's attitude that pleased him more than all. The Sybil whose critical eye and blistering tongue had so marred the peace of his former visit—this Sybil was merged in one whose green eyes said: "I may have been a fool about you once, but I've got over it. Now, I'm just the best pal God ever made—the most amusing, the prettiest, the most capable. Just play with me, we'll have the devil of a lot of fun together——"

And for this Sybil his heart held an almost shy tenderness while some exultant spirit within him cried: "Hang it! She's a proper bit o' blood, that child. With her one could have the hell of a gallop, and with her the Long Hack Home would prove itself a good way, yes, very good."

He pulled her out of her chair when the dressing gong sounded, and with an arm thrust through hers, propelled her upstairs to change; past the familiar, dusky turns on stairway and landing, to the open door of her room. A room that seemed strangely full of jade and amber colours, with some sweet smell; a warm glow hung on the air; the window was a purple square for the light of the wood fire to play upon. And on all this, warm, scented contrast to her gaitered, outdoor self Sybil closed the door, leaving Allan outside, with her old cry, "I simply *must* have a bath," ringing in his ears; and in his heart a deep, sweet consciousness—a breathless sense of urgency.

And within, Sybil, when she had pulled off her jumper, smiled engagingly at the image in her glass.

II

A bare hill-side, where lean furze bushes were whipped by a devastating dry wind; at its base a straight run-in between two flags; and from its summit a good view of the point-to-point course over which Sailor and Allan were to distinguish themselves, or otherwise, this windy afternoon.

Sybil, Allan's weight-cloth over her arm, surveyed the scene around her dispassionately. The place was thronged with people—a motley crowd indeed. The cars drawn up on the hill-side were numerous, but they were far out-numbered by the donkey-carts and bicycles which nestled in their scores behind the hedges. The raucous voices of the bookmakers dominated every other sound: "Two to one the Fi-eld—*two* to one—*bar* one! *Two* to one, BAR one! I'll lay even money *Little Daughter!* Two-to-one-bar-one!" Sybil smiled as she listened to the betting, comfortably conscious of a tenner carefully distributed at 10s and 8s.

She smiled again when Allan came up and touched her on the shoulder. His saddle was over his arm, he took his weight-cloth from her with a "You got the extra lead?" and strode off to the weighing tent. Sybil slipped beneath the ropes and went across the ring to speak to Fox, who was holding Sailor. Sailor, who—with his saddle off, and the single rein of his plain snaffle turned over his head— was looking full of quality, and bad to beat. The favourite stood near him, Mr St Lawrence's Little Daughter; a strong, big-boned mare, rather low, and with a distinctly too lengthy back, she looked as though she could not gallop, but was in reality the fastest thing in the field.

"Hullo, Fox! What about it?" Sybil greeted him. "I got 6 to 1, and I got 4 to 1," answered the single-minded Fox, "didn't he sink very fast? Sure he's even money now only, and odds on Mr St Lawrence's mare."

"Ah, you're no good, Fox. Didn't I get 10s and 8s."

"Well, well, isn't it well to be you!" was Fox's only comment. "Here's Mr Allan now—lay a hand on this fella for me, Miss Sybil; thank you."

Allan, burdened with saddle and weight cloth, came across the ring to supervise the fastening of every buckle as Fox saddled the big horse. Then he turned to Sybil: "Will you fasten this for me like a good girl?" He bent down so that she could fasten the ribbons of his cap. And Sybil, remembering another occasion when she had helped him on with his boots while all the devils of jealousy raged in her heart, was filled with a surging gladness. She could have kissed the sleeve of his pink coat when she tied his number on his arm. It was all so divine. She knew.

After that she saw him mount and ride out of the ring, almost as though she were in a dream. It could not be true; what had he to do with her—that big, dark-faced man who held his horse so quietly in hand as he rode down to the start. And then she looked down at the rather battered box of cigarettes in her hands, which he had given her to keep for him when he got up to ride his race; and as she did so she suffered an intensely awful spasm of fear. Suppose—suppose Allan was hurt—killed, even. People were killed, quite often; well, not often, perhaps, but at any rate frequently enough to be unpleasant. If anything happened to Allan she felt she would die—would go mad. And, quite illogically, she knew she hated Ann because Ann had not married Allan, who loved her then, and taken him away on a nice, safe honeymoon, far removed from the dangers of this horrible game of cross-country racing.

All these thoughts chased each other through Sybil's brain as she crossed two fields and their high fences on her way down to the start. At the second fence someone stretched down a shooting stick and the full length of his arm to pull her up. She transferred her own stick and glasses to her left hand, and giving him her right, swung up. It was John Dane. "Hello! Pensive Peggie—complete with bevelled edges," he greeted her, "how can you look so sad and wear such a good coat all at the same time. I like your checks."

"I've got a horse running," Sybil explained in sepulchral tones.

"Oh, I see. I mean, so I see—I mean, I saw it on the card. But what I mean to say is—if it's so hopeless, why is it running?"

"Hopeless! Who said he was hopeless? We're going to win to-day—Allan's riding him for me. It's the brown Daddy bought from him last Christmas."

"Oh, sorry! You sounded as though the third fence was about their limit."

Sybil, her eyes on the medley of horses in the field below, said nothing. There was Sailor, fighting his bit, and plunging away. False start! And all to do over again. Quietly, Allan. Be very quiet with him. *Now*, old fellow! The flag was down now, and the field, led by Little Daughter, whirled down at the first fence. It was a tall bank, indecently close to the start; hardly room to steady a horse, and Little Daughter's jockey did not even try to do so. The big mare flipped on and off the bank, clean and clever. Allan steadied Sailor down a trifle, then sent him along into it. Sybil gulped, for very little she would have shut her eyes; but they were up—were over. Yes, the big mare certainly beat them over her fences.

For the next three fields she could see Allan and Sailor going along collectedly, lying back about fourth. Then a strip of plantation interrupted her view. She put down her glasses and turned to John, to whose remarks she had, up to the moment, lent an indifferent ear. "We're doing nicely," she said, "aren't we?"

"Young Hillingdon's down"—it was the excited voice of a young farmer in the field below her. "Almighty Lord God! Should the horse have fallen with him?" queried an emotional lady friend.

"No, but he fell from the horse the fence beyond the wood."

"Oh! Oh! Is he hurted?"

"Hurt! He's killed surely. Isn't the head burst!"

Sybil, whose glasses could not hope to equal the hawk-like vision of her informant, said nothing. She focussed them on a point beyond the plantation, and waited for the horses to appear. When they did Allan and Sailor were, as she had indeed supposed, still among them. "Come on, John," she said, "let's go down to the water and then leg it back for the finish." They jumped down from the fence and joined the crowd which was hurrying across the field. "Come on, chaps!" she heard one youth cry excitedly to his fellows. "We'll likely see death here." "I seen a great fall last time the races was in it," replied a friend. "Michael Leary was cot under his horse in the water, and I declare to God ye'd hear the ribs cracking the very same as rotten sticks. 'Twas hardly we got him drew out of it."

"Sha! It never done him a taste o'harm, then—" a less picturesque narrator concluded the story, "didn't he win a race in it, the same day, after!"

"Ah, what matter!" "Here they come, boys!" "Go back out o' that!" "Give the horses room to lep——" "Ah! what matter the horse—let the best man win!"

An intense excitement surged through the knot of men and boys as the thunder of the horses' hoofs drew near them. Sybil felt it going through her, jarring waves of it, as she strained her eyes down the course. Ah, here they were! Six of them in it still; racing now, as they came down the straight for the water jump. Little Daughter still in the lead, a rag of a chestnut mare second, and Sailor third. Behind them—but Sybil did not trouble to look behind them. Little Daughter was over. The chestnut mare jumped short and was into the water right in front of Sailor. With a little piece of really consummate horsemanship, Allan swung the big horse, without putting him out of his stride, and nicked him over at the corner of the fence.

Sybil let all her breath go in one big gulp of relief. Turning her slim, checked back upon her companion, she ran back up the hill, at a pace which left John quite in the ruck amongst their fellow-spectators.

"Ah-haa, that's the right girl!" he heard one remark approvingly, "I declare ye'd say she was that sort she wouldn't think she'd see a race without she'd got the horse's breath on her face."

"Look! Oh, that for a lep!" another exclaimed, as Sybil came off a not inconsiderable fence in a manner which was neat, almost showy.

The crowd was already thick round the two flags at the

finish when she arrived. Somehow, she snaked her way through to the front ranks, where she waited an interminable eight minutes while the two whips in their pink coats accomplished their almost superhuman task of clearing the course. Another minute, and they had cantered their horses out; another—and Sailor, quietly over the last fence, galloped into the straight. Then Little Daughter, never dwelling an instant, was on and off the bank, was up with him—drew away from him, led now, by nearly a length. "*Come* on, *Little Daughter*!" The roar of the crowd was fraught with enthusiasm, as they saw their money coming home so comfortably.

And Sybil, her forehead wet with excitement, and hands and teeth clenched, said in her heart: "Allan, Allan! *Sailor*, old man! *And* again! We must, we must——"

Little Daughter's jockey got out his whip, but Allan sat down, and sat still, and Sailor drew level again. They were neck and neck in the last stride. But the judges gave it to Sailor—a short head on the post. Eight lengths dividing second and third.

Sybil, as she led in the winner, was her old jaunty self once more; only, as Fox unsaddled, she laid her cheek on Sailor's wet shoulder, and raised to Allan's, eyes that were shining. He went off to weigh out carrying with him the memory of that look. And a very pleasing memory, too.

Later, when they had started Sailor, sheeted and hooded, on his homeward way, the pair spent a pleasurable enough twenty minutes collecting some not inconsiderable winnings. But that by the way. The priceless glow of achievement was on them both. The joy of it all went a little to Sybil's very level head. She forgot her staid pose of an unemotional race-goer (and owner). She laughed, she thrilled; she chattered joyously and aimlessly. She forgot to listen to John's felicitations because Allan was telling her at the moment how Sailor had pecked coming off one fence in such a manner that he (Allan) could have touched the ground with his hand—of his marvellous recovery. Yes, she ignored John Dane—that most useful second string to her bow—ignored him completely and utterly.

The day ended, as point-to-pointing days so often do end—in rain. Allan huddled Sybil into his old Burberry for their homeward drive. It was a good Burberry, an old Burberry, and it was Allan's Burberry. Sybil, with Allan's wet tweed arm beside her, sent the old Ford up into her collar with joy singing loud at her heart.

And when, the long drive over, and the car safely housed, they twain stood together in the deep straw of Sailor's box, and Allan said, "Do you think Sailor would quite like it?"—Sybil answered, as she ran her hand under the sheet to get the comfortable feel of Sailor's warm shoulder, "I don't now what he thinks about it, but *I* should say he'd look very nice in print as 'the gift of the bride'—don't you?"

Allan thought so, too.